ALL OR NOTHING SERIES

ALL *your* FIRSTS

AMARIE COLLINS

Editing: Editing4indies

Proofread and formatting: Nicole Kincaid at Naughty Nook PR

Paperback ISBN: 979-8-9929896-2-5

Ebook ISBN: 979-8-9929896-1-8

To the ones who never thought they could, you can.

Content Warning

Dear reader,

This book contains dark themes that may be triggering. Abusive parent, general violence, kidnapping, torture, murder, death, juvenile prison, past food insecurity, organized crime, drug/gun trafficking, exploitation of a minor in committing criminal acts, past child neglect, parent death (off-page).

Playlist

"No One's Gonna Love You" – Band of Horses
"American Money" – BORNS
"Wild Child" – The Black Keys
"Coffee" – Miguel
"Counting Stars" – OneRepublic
"Electric (Feat. Khalid)" – Alina Baraz
"Hope (feat. BRAVE)" – Tim Legend
"Almost Lover" – A Fine Frenzy
"Can't Help Falling in Love" – Haley Reinhart
"Cherry Hill" – Russ
"Lonely Day" – System of a Down
"Cosmic Love" – Florence + The Machine
"Past lives" – BORNS

One

Rosie

An overwhelming sense of dread courses through my veins as I silently implore the universe to spare me from a tragic demise that ends with me plummeting to my death.

The lattice covered in vines on the side of the house makes it hard for my feet to find stability in my Docs. This was a whole hell of a lot easier when I was younger and twenty pounds lighter. Trembling with anxiety, I stare down at the ground from the window of my childhood bedroom on the second floor.

Just as I think I'm nearing the end of the descent and about to touch the velvety grass, I lose my balance and crash down; the impact sends a sharp jolt of pain through my ass, which quickly numbs. That will hurt like hell later. Pushing myself up from the ground, I dust off the blades of grass and release a frustrated sigh while looking around.

After retrieving my phone from my back pocket, its screen illuminates my face with dim light, exposing a glaring crack across the front.

Lovely. This trip home has turned into a nightmare.

Glancing at the clock, I'm hit with the realization that I've let valuable time slip away. With the guard's rotation ending in approximately seven minutes, this is my only opportunity to escape undetected.

If Papa learns our home is left unguarded and unprotected for even fifteen minutes during the late hours of the night, his reaction will be swift and severe. I've seen people lose their head for far less at his command.

I carefully navigate the house's exterior, using the cover of nightfall and the occasional shrubbery to conceal my movements. As I make my way past the kitchen, my steps falter at the sight of my mama sitting with a glass of wine in her hand and a book resting on her lap. Waves of emotion rise in my chest, making it hard to breathe, and tears threaten to spill from my eyes.

My leaving will upset her, but deep down, I believe she'll understand. She always has. I press my hand against the cold glass. *I love you, and I'm sorry.* With one last glance, I continue my trek around the house, leaving her behind.

In my haste, I almost overlook the next window, its soft light creating what would be an ethereal glow on the grass if I didn't know the darkness that lurked in this room.

I pause, pressing my back against the cold brick wall of the house. I cover my erratic, beating heart with my hand and inhale deeply. This is the last room I must pass without being detected, inching me closer to my long-awaited freedom.

Peeking through the window, I see my father sitting behind his desk. His back is turned toward me as he holds a glass of his ever-present golden-amber liquid. With his intense stare fixed on the wall, it's clear he's engrossed in deep reflection, likely conjuring up new schemes to make my life miserable.

As he rises from his chair, I quickly crouch low under the window, hidden from his view.

My throat feels parched and scratchy as if it's filled with coarse sand, while my hands are clammy and soaked with sweat. What an odd combination. I take a moment to count to three, hoping it will help me gather enough courage to continue.

It's now or never, Rosie.

Don't be a coward.

As I crawl past his window, I can't bring myself to glance back inside, fearing what I might see.

I stand and sprint away as fast as I can, feeling as if the devil himself chases me.

As I run across the cold, wet grass, my gaze keeps trailing over my shoulder. The mere thought of my father finding me with a getaway bag in my hand sends shivers down my spine. I can't give a sorry-ass excuse like 'I'm going for a night run,' like I did last time they caught me. I received the most severe beating I've ever experienced, and now I dread what an even harsher punishment would be.

While consumed with fear of the monster behind me, I fail to notice the brick wall until I collide with it.

I shriek as my ass and back hit the ground for the second time tonight.

With utter disappointment and a crushed soul, I acknowledge the truth. The exhilarating sensation of freedom's breeze against my face will be a distant longing once they escort me back to the house.

My gaze lifts, and I'm startled to find myself locking eyes with someone I haven't seen in years.

"Gage?" I say in confusion as I rub my eyes. Maybe the two falls so close together are messing with my eyesight. "What the hell are you doing here?"

He reaches his hand out to me. "Here."

Slapping it away, I hoist myself up from the ground, a bit more leisurely this time since there's no longer any urgency now that I've been caught.

"I see your stubbornness hasn't changed."

"I'm amazed you remember after disregarding me for years as if I didn't exist."

Gage scans the yard. "How about we talk about this somewhere else?"

"I'm not going back in there." I point at our family home behind me with a hitch of my thumb. He will have to sedate me with a horse tranquilizer before I willingly walk back into the house.

"Neither am I. Let's go, Ro," Gage says, his voice carrying through the air as he turns toward the towering trees that line our tall wrought-iron fence without looking back.

I bite my lip and watch him as he continues to saunter away from me.

I don't know if I trust him. There was a time when my trust in him surpassed the trust I had in myself. However, that was years in the past. He's been gone for a long time, and I can see his changes from just a glance—he's not the same brother I once adored.

His dark aura has nothing to do with his midnight-black hair or his deep ocean-blue eyes. He's packed on muscle, has a hardness to his eyes, and lacks a smile that once shined brightly. Then there are the tattoos peeking out of his suit jacket that wind up his neck. He looks like trouble and destruction.

He halts and turns, his gaze piercing into me as I grapple with my conflicting emotions.

Can I trust him? My other brother–Gage's twin, Marco–has been no help to me. So why would he be different?

"Time's ticking. Alfonso will be awake soon."

I stride toward him and murmur, "Why would he be sleeping?"

Gage just smiles, and it's not the cheerful type of smile. It's a malicious but satisfied smile.

"Are you done asking me questions, or do you plan on getting caught?"

"I already did." I look at him with narrowed eyes. "By you."

"I'm here to help you make your great escape. But we need to go now."

"Why would you want to do that? Why now?"

"I was trapped, just as you are now. I'm here to right the wrongs of not getting you out sooner."

Okay, not what I expected him to say.

He could be telling the truth because that sounds more like him from before. But still. "I don't know if I can trust you."

"There's only one way to find out. Come on," he says as he extends his hand out to me once more.

I have no other choice but to trust him. This is better than the alternative of walking back into that house and dealing with my father.

I take his hand, and together, we walk through the dense canopy of trees. He pulls me to the right, and I stop dead in my tracks.

"Is that...? Is he dead?" I whisper as the toe of my boot nudges the limp body of my father's guard, Alfonso, his gun still holstered to his chest.

"He's just taking a nice little nap."

Red crimson trickles from his scalp. "Is that blood? Why's his head bleeding?"

"How else was I going to put him to sleep?"

I look up into Gage's soulless eyes. "Who the hell are you?"

"Your savior, but if you don't hurry, I'll end up being your cellmate in the basement. Let's go."

"Peace out, Fons," I say as I wave, giving the incapacitated guard my middle finger. He's the one who caught me the last time I tried to escape a year ago from one of my father's arrangement attempts.

Alfonso's joy was evident as he brought me back and watched with a gleam in his eye as my father repeatedly struck me with his belt. The only thing that kept me from screaming was the chant I repeated in my head, hoping for them both to die a slow, painful death. History will not be repeating itself tonight.

My foot rears back and connects with his ribs with a delightful thump, but unfortunately, he doesn't make a sound since he lies limp and unconscious.

Two

Rosie

The landscape outside Gage's car window transforms from the bustling city of Chicago to the vast expanse of Illinois, disappearing before I can fully take it in. I've been so wrapped up in my head—between the worry my father was following us and what leaving with Gage could mean.

I glance upward as we pass a sign, and I see the words 'Welcome to Indiana' against a backdrop of black night.

I whip my head toward Gage. "What are we doing here?"

"Where were you planning to run off to before I stopped you?"

I bite the inside of my cheek as I contemplate my answer. He doesn't need to know I had planned on just winging it.

My plan was not to have a plan at all. My whole life has been planned out. I wanted to embrace the freedom, feel it sweep me away and shape my authentic identity.

Everyone has always known me as Rosie, the straight-A student. The goal-oriented good girl, as praised by my teachers. Rosie, the well-mannered and obedient daughter. My peers have labeled me a prude on multiple occasions, albeit not to my face, as nobody would dare disrespect a Mafia princess. But I've heard the whispers.

I don't want to be confined to a box of labels that I never chose. Mafia Princess being at the top of the list of labels.

I desire freedom.

To embrace mistakes, forge cherished memories, and assertively reject what doesn't benefit me.

I reject the notion of being a passive vessel for my future husband's desires with no sense of my own identity.

"Just to a friend's house," I say with a shrug.

"Alexa?"

"No."

He must consider me stupid. Running to my best friend is the first place everyone would look.

"Then where?"

"I-I don't know."

"It's not safe for you to just leave without saying a word. Our family has enemies everywhere. You should know this better than anyone after you almost got kidnapped."

My head snaps toward Gage, my eyes widening in disbelief as he resurrects one of my deepest buried emotional scars.

"Don't you ever bring that shit up to me."

The thought of the day I was almost kidnapped from my art class at nine years old makes me want to throw up or have a panic attack, maybe both. I've prayed to forget that day, and his mention of it pisses me off. From time to time, I'm reminded of that day through unsettling nightmares that continue to haunt me.

Guards are part of our everyday life, and I didn't think twice as I walked out of my afternoon class and trailed a man in a black suit. The moment he directed me toward the rear of the building, I could sense something was off. I looked up, but the guy staring back at me was a stranger, and before I knew it, it was too late. As his massive hand closed around my arm with a death grip, I couldn't help but scream in pain.

The bullet fired and struck the back of the target's head silently, but its impact echoed through the man's body. He let me go and collapsed to the ground with a resounding thud, taking my canvas painting with him.

That was the day I witnessed the grim spectacle of a life being snuffed out before my very eyes.

The day I realized our life, our family, was devoid of happy colors. It was filled with tragic blacks and ugly reds, just like the man's blood that stained my canvas painting as he bled out onto it.

From that day on, I felt the suffocating grip of my freedom being reined in. I wasn't able to join art class, ballet class, or any other class I had been looking forward to.

Two teachers, one specializing in art and the other in dance, came to my house for private lessons. The only time I could escape the confines of the property was during school hours, but always with strict supervision. This lasted until I went to college, and even then, I had constant surveillance. What twenty-one-year-old wants their every move to be monitored?

"It's the truth, Ro. You shouldn't have just left without saying a word."

"What? You think I'd have been able to just leave? You haven't been around in almost seven years, Gage. News flash, I'm no longer the naive fourteen-year-old girl you remember, and you sure as hell don't look like the sixteen-year-old I remember. So let's cut the bullshit. You have no idea what our father has been like. What he's capable of."

I can feel the inside of the car reach subzero temperatures the second the words leave my lips.

My attention shifts to Gage, who has a white-knuckle grip on the steering wheel, his narrowed eyes fixating on me.

"Where the hell do you think I've been all these years? Vacation? Our father is the one who practically locked me up."

I tear my gaze away from him and shift my focus to the dark view outside the window. I can be upset all I want about how our father has treated me, but when I think about what Gage has faced, my grievances seem insignificant.

I remember him and Marco going into my father's office. Their sobs echoed through the halls when they emerged, sometimes with visible bloody wounds. It makes me feel petulant and childish compared to that.

"I'm sorry."

Gage sighs heavily. "Me too, Ro."

The longer we sit in silence, the more the anxiety builds within me, like a volcano ready to erupt.

"Are we almost there?" I murmur as I look out the window. "Wherever there is."

"Almost," Gage says as we pass a welcome sign that looks straight out of a Hallmark movie where small-town girls return home for the holidays and reunite with their long-lost loves. *Experience Wilding. Population of forty-five hundred.* What the hell are we doing here?

"I have a friend who lives here and will watch over you for a while," Gage says as if reading my mind.

"So, I won't be free. I'll just be handed off to another. Forever a prisoner."

"It's the safer alternative to your half-assed plan."

"How did you know I was planning on running tonight, anyway? You practically showed up out of thin air."

"I have my ways."

"How unbelievably vague."

As we pull into the driveway of the large two-story home, the sight of the rich red and brown brick, black shutters, and two towering columns at the entry catches my attention. This is the type of home you'd read about in a book with a happy family, complete with a white picket fence, nightly family dinners where everyone talks about their day, and a cute little dog.

"This is your friend's house?"

"Yeah, his name's Vic. He has a guesthouse you can stay in."

"Why aren't I going with you?"

"I'm in Chicago. It won't be safe."

"And what if I don't want to do this?"

"I take you home. I don't want you somewhere unknown for anyone to just take advantage of you."

"Even if I have to marry a psycho against my will? Do you know who they planned to marry me to? Manuel. He used to pluck the wings off the butterflies in our mother's garden. A true fucking psychopath hurts harmless beings. I'd be whacked before we hit our first anniversary."

Gage remains silent, much to my dismay. The sweet older brother who used to take me to get ice cream when I was upset is no longer here. Like everyone else in the family, he grew into a hardened Mafia man with little to no feelings. He cares for nothing but his own personal agenda and rules. If I didn't feel so disgusted by the revelation, I'd be disappointed and heartbroken.

Gage blows out a breath. "I won't take you back home. Just—"

The shrill ringtone of his phone pierces the silence, prompting him to swiftly answer, listen with a couple of grunts, check the time on his watch, then hang up.

"Listen, I have to go. I wanted to introduce you to Vic, but he's taking longer than I thought. Will you be okay?"

"Yep."

"You'll be safe here. Vic will watch over you. Don't run. Enjoy your freedom," he says with a smile.

"That's quite contradicting, don't you think?"

Frustration bubbles inside me as he remains silent again, his gaze distant and uninterested. "How long will I be stuck in this place?"

"I haven't decided yet."

"What will happen after here?"

"Haven't decided that either. We need to wait for the dust to settle. I'm sure Alfonso has woken up by now and alerted our father to what happened, which means they probably know you're gone and will be scouring all of Chicago for you. Take this." He reaches into the pocket of his suit and pulls out a card.

As he hands me the card, I can feel its weight in my hand, a tangible symbol of limitless possibilities and funds. I stuff it in my pocket, knowing my dear brother, who has returned out of nowhere, will pay heavily for interfering with my plans of freedom. The credit card in my pocket feels scorching hot as I turn around and flash him a smile.

"Anything else?" I say with a sneer.

I'm so over everyone dictating my life.

"Give me your phone so I can program my number in."

I reach into my bag and hand it to him.

"Shit, I'll send you one. It's probably for the best, anyway."

"What?"

Gage turns the phone over, and the whole screen is cracked beyond repair. Alexa instructed me to use a burner phone and leave mine behind, so I don't have much on it, but still.

Not having a phone is like losing a limb. Dramatic but accurate.

"Lovely. This night keeps getting better and fucking better. Anything else before I get in my cell?"

"I missed you, Ro, and I'm sorry for not coming back sooner."

"Everything's been fine," I say, my words laced with bitterness at how not fine things have been over the years since he's been gone.

There were small slices of happiness, such as college with Alexa and my pen pal, Rush, and I lost both. Out of survival, we've kept our circle small, so when you start losing loved ones, it affects you more than one would think. It leaves you with a sense of desolation as if you're the only one left in the world.

Abandoned. Empty. Forgotten.

I reluctantly fix my eyes on the house that will become my captivity under Gage's rule. Even as I'm cursing Gage's horrible timing and the demise of my freedom and plans, my heart aches to wrap my arms around his waist like I used to do when I was younger.

I want him to tell me everything will be okay, but I'm too upset to have this heart-to-heart now. He's different, and he screwed up my plans. Now, depending on how tightly the reins are drawn here, I am barely freer than I was at home.

"I only ask one thing of you besides staying here and not running."

I direct my gaze toward him but opt to remain silent.

"Don't tell anyone I'm back yet. I'm not ready."

"Whatever you say, brother dearest." With a swift motion, I slam the door shut, its force causing a slight tremor as his irritated grunt barely registers in my mind while I walk around the house to the back.

I'm greeted by the shimmering pool just before the small guesthouse. With a sigh of relief, I slip off my shoes and socks, eagerly dipping my feet into the glistening water. It's deliciously warm and calms some of my nerves.

I love to swim, or rather, peacefully float in the calm waters. Experiencing the feeling of weightlessness, with half your body gliding on the water's surface and the other half submerged, is pure bliss. It feels as if you're simultaneously existing in two separate realms.

I walk toward the adorable bungalow-style guesthouse, with oversized windows and cascading plants adorning the front. I can already imagine drinking tea while sitting on the small porch. Maybe this won't be so bad after all.

The unlocked door protests with a loud creak as I enter the small living room and kitchen, only to find a surprisingly nice and impeccably clean space. The idea of sharing a house with a stranger fills me with a sense of unease, but being back here, I doubt I'll cross paths with this Vic guy.

The echoing sound of my steps fills the room as I investigate the rest of the small guesthouse. The remaining stop on this tour is a cozy bedroom with a convenient en suite bathroom.

After shimmying out of my grass-stained jeans, I climb onto the bed, savoring its delightful warmth and cozy embrace.

I have just drifted off to sleep when a sudden, ear-piercing noise startles me awake. I remain frozen in place, debating whether it's an intruder or simply a product of my own vivid imagination.

With narrowed eyes, I lean in closer to the door, my ears tuned in for any faint sounds. The room echoes with the chaotic clatter of objects being flung about, intensifying my feeling of being trapped without a way to escape.

I reach for my phone and remember how useless it is unless my aim and force can incapacitate someone, which isn't likely. Shit.

Out of options, I resort to the most childish and stupid action possible. I place the blanket over my head and hold my breath.

The door slams open against the wall with a deafening crash, causing me to startle as something lands on the bed beside me. My scream is so piercing I'm convinced it carries all the way back to my parents in Chicago.

With a burst of energy and my fight-or-flight engaged, I tear the blankets from my body and leap out of bed. I make a beeline for the door, only to be halted in my tracks by a blinding light that engulfs the room, making me narrowly avoid a collision with a towering man.

Despite being of average height, I still have to crane my neck upward to meet his confused gaze.

Three

Rosie

"Fuck... what day is it?"

He looks down at me with a regretful expression on his face. This is weird because I should be the one regretting my choices right now.

I'm uncertain if the question is rhetorical or if he genuinely expects an answer.

"W-Wednesday or Thursday," I stutter.

I don't know this man, and from what I can see, I have no desire to get to know him. As he stands half naked, his body becomes a living art gallery, showcasing a myriad of tattoos that cover most of his skin.

Normally, I wouldn't back down from any man, but in my half-asleep state, I can't shake the feeling of vulnerability in this unfamiliar but supposedly safe place.

I'm going to murder Gage.

He looks me up and down with his bottom lip between his teeth, and that's when I feel it.

The air hits my legs and exposed ass.

Shit.

I hurriedly yank down my short shirt, which barely extends an inch farther. I can't help but feel both embarrassed and confused as I lock eyes with the man standing in front of me.

"What the hell, Vic!" A shrill shriek pierces through the air, prompting me to swiftly turn around. There, in the bed, I see a naked woman who doesn't even bother to hide under the blankets I'm supposed to sleep in. "Who is she?"

He ignores her question and looks back at me. "Rosalinda?"

"Yeah," I say, wondering why it's a question. Is it common for him to have unfamiliar women sleeping in his bed without his knowledge? "And I go by Rosie." I hate my full name. The only time it's ever used is when my father yells at me about some invisible line I've crossed.

"You're supposed to be in the main house, Rosie."

"You'll be sleeping in here, then?" I ask with a tight smile. If the guy wants to give me access to a full house while he sleeps here, who am I to argue with such a generous offer?

"Absolutely not. I'll have the room next to yours."

My smile vanishes.

"Are you serious?" the naked woman shrieks. Despite the squeaking, high-pitched tone coming from behind us, neither of us acknowledges the other person in the room. I'm not sure why he doesn't, but I happen to be mortified by all of this.

"Lovely," I say as I spin around to pick up my bag and jeans from where I left them on the floor by the bed, purposely avoiding eye contact with the woman on the bed.

"Yeah, lovely," he whispers as he gazes into my eyes.

My face contorts with disgust, and my cheeks burn with humiliation as he gawks at me while a naked woman lounges on his bed. Men can be such pigs.

Once I make it out to the living room, I hastily pull on my jeans. Enough people have seen my exposed skin tonight. I don't want to give the neighbors a show.

Sensing a burning sensation at my back, I spin around.

My green eyes collide with his caramel-colored ones as he leans against the doorframe. His relaxed posture is evident as he leisurely slides his inked hands into the pockets of his faded jeans. Yet his underlying tension is apparent in the sharp definition of his clenched jawline that's covered by a touch of dark stubble.

He smirks at me as he senses me appraising him.

I feel a prickling sensation against my skin, causing goose bumps to rise along my spine as we have a stare down. What the hell is happening to me?

I angrily extend my middle finger toward him, slam the front door, and head to the main house.

As I wander around the house the following morning, I can't help but stifle a yawn. Judging by the enormous bags under my eyes, it's clear I barely slept for maybe two hours after the bizarre encounter with Vic and the naked woman.

My frazzled nerves had me on edge.

I recall seeing a gym on my quest to find my room last night, but now I can't remember where it is.

Faint music drifts from an open door down the hall, so I follow it.

The sight of exercise equipment neatly arranged in the room catches my eye. The room is spacious, with a large mirror that spans the entire wall and even a sauna off to one corner.

I was excited to come in and take advantage of the space. During my time at college, the girls' dorm housed a small and overcrowded gym where camera shutters clicking was more common than weights clinking.

My joy is momentarily suspended as I watch the devil from last night effortlessly doing pull-ups.

He should be proud of his impressive physique. I'll give him that.

His back muscles flex and undulate as he moves up and down effortlessly. A prominent gray and black skull tattoo adorns his back, spanning from one shoulder to the other. It looks ominous, with demons swirling in the midnight orbs of the skull's eye sockets. The blood-orange ember eyes practically glow. What would make someone want to get something so dark and disturbing?

My eyes continue to explore the plethora of tattoos that cover his body. On the back of his right calf, an eagle with its talons ready to strike perches, while on the other calf, an angel and devil appear to be engaged in a lively dance. I strain my eyes to absorb every intricate detail of the stunning artwork.

"You're more than welcome to come in and work out something more than just your eyes," Vic says as he jumps down and faces me with a smirk.

He caught me looking at him. How unfortunate and embarrassing.

"Funny," I say with a sarcastic tone, rolling my eyes to emphasize my indifference, even though I'm mortified.

As I stretch on the black mat, my stiff muscles protest with every movement, screaming at me in discomfort. The pool would have been a better choice overall, especially once Vic works out on the bench press.

I find it impossible to tear my gaze away from him as he firmly grips the bar, his back arched with a noticeable bulge outlined on the crotch of his dark gray gym shorts.

I look down at the mat quickly. What in the hell am I doing?

I'm going to chalk my fascination with him this morning up to lack of sleep, never being around a man by myself, and a nonexistent sex life. At some point, I'm bound to cave when I see a fine man in front of me, right? It doesn't mean I like him. I just enjoy the view.

He seems to be a mess. Well, at least last night, from his disoriented state of me being in his house. Surely, Gage told him. Then there's the girl he threw on the bed. I assume his guesthouse is for hookups, which makes me want to jump in a pool of bleach. The bed I slept in is probably an STD cesspool.

The question is, why have a beautiful family home if you don't have a family?

"Well, who do we have here?"

I glance up at a man grinning down at me who would be attractive if not for the visible hickeys dotting his neck and the overpowering smell of alcohol emanating from his pores. Gross.

With his dirty-blond hair casually tied up in a messy man bun and sporting sunglasses inside, he looks like he had a really tough night.

"Gage's sister. Hands off." Vic's gruff voice fills the room as he speaks between reps.

I notice the new guy wince and give me a wide berth as he makes his way into the room.

Ugh.

This repetitive cycle has been the soundtrack of my life for as long as I can remember. I attract attention solely from men who belong to powerful families and possess a deranged mindset. The guys I've liked lose interest as soon as they uncover my true identity and my family's notorious reputation. Needless to say, dating has been filled with disappointment and frustration.

I've had one boyfriend who lasted five seconds, and that was in middle school. Poor Cody only got half a dance in at the winter formal before my brother, Marco, punched him in the face for touching me. Blood sprayed everywhere. Both my pretty pink dress and my social life were ruined. It was awful. Since then, I've decided to save future Codys from my family's wrath.

In my countless daydreams about running away, I often envisioned becoming a ghost, stumbling upon a charming, remote town where I'd escape the demands of my current life. I'd open an art studio, a place where I could share my passion for art through teaching and hosting exhibits. Maybe even find a tall, dark, and handsome type of guy who makes me laugh and takes me out on epic dates. It seems that won't be happening here, or anytime soon. *Thanks, Gage.*

Midway through my downward dog stretch, a sudden weighty presence hovers above me. I move into a triangle pose like I don't feel shit and tilt my head upward to make eye contact with Vic.

"Can I help you?"

"We have work in an hour."

Sweat glistens on his abs in the light, captivating my attention and causing me to lose focus.

Did he say we have work?

"We?" I say, pointing between us.

"Be ready in forty minutes."

"What will we be doing? I've never worked before."

The thought of a job makes me giddy. Under my father's roof, getting a job was out of the question, and it's one of the many things I'm eager to cross off my list while I'm here.

He brushes past me without acknowledging my question, his footsteps echoing down the empty hallway.

"What a dick."

"Don't let him hear you say that." The mystery guy chuckles from the treadmill as he runs.

Did I just say that out loud?

"I'm Axl, by the way," he says as he pulls off his sunglasses and squints.

"Rosie," I say with a small smile. "Electrolytes and toast." Those seemed to be the go-to for everyone at my college.

"What?"

"For that gnarly hangover. Maybe a shower, too."

"Thanks... I think."

"Anytime."

What world did I wake up in?

Vic drives us to work, the only sound being the hum of the engine. I'm completely unfazed by his lack of communication and brooding presence. It's better than the piercing gaze he gave me last night or his playful comment this morning.

I plan on treating this as a business transaction, determined to convince him to release the reins and let me roam freely. Maybe I'll even take over his guesthouse—after I disinfect it, of course.

The road during last night's drive with Gage was shrouded in darkness, with only the faint glow of the moon illuminating it. In the daylight, I can admire the picturesque view of Lake Michigan on our right as we head down Main Street.

Vic takes a left, and we end up in the town square, as the sign says.

This downtown area is adorable, with cobblestone walkways and sugar maple trees showcasing a breathtaking display of neon red, orange, and yellow leaves. Cozy seating areas are scattered throughout, and a stunning fountain stands at its heart.

I imagined ending up in this type of town, with colorful storefronts lining the streets around the square, each offering a unique small-business experience. Above each door, business signs with store names sway on chains, dancing in the gentle morning breeze.

We pass a restaurant, coffee shop, flower shop, clothing boutique, dog groomers, used bookstore, salon and spa, and a tattoo parlor, among others that line the square.

I wonder if there's an art studio with classes available?

Vic parks his truck in front of the tattoo shop with a sage-green sign that reads *Alchemy Ink* in an Old English font.

"We need to lay out a couple of ground rules," he says as I reach for the door handle.

I sigh. "Gage already talked to me. I won't run."

"No, you won't," he says as he looks out the front windshield. "But there's more."

"Why am I not surprised?" This is just another clip to my wings, but it won't be forever. It can't be.

"You'll only leave somewhere by asking me first and getting my blessing."

"Blessing?" I ask, angling my body more toward him. "That sounds a lot like getting your permission."

"Exactly," he says with a smirk. "You'll also share your location with me once you get your new phone."

"That's invasive if I'm already telling you where I'm going."

"Call it what you want. It is what it is. You will only sleep in your room, nowhere else."

"Why would I sleep anywhere else?"

"Can you let me finish my fucking rules, or are you going to comment on every single one?"

I stay silent.

"No guys."

"That's a ridiculous rule and none of your business."

"It is my business. No guys."

"And what if I'm already seeing someone?"

A scowl forms on his face as his eyes scrunch up. "Are you?"

"What's your next rule?" I blow off his question.

"Are you seeing someone?" he repeats.

"That's not a rule."

"And that's not an answer."

"Are we done now?" I ask as I open the door.

"For now."

As I step into the tattoo shop, my eyes are irresistibly drawn to the sleek black walls, rich brown hardwood floors, and luxurious dark green velvet curtains, which create an upscale and elegant aesthetic.

The waiting area has two light-brown leather couches and the most unconventional coffee table I've ever seen. The table's base is a nude woman, lying on her back with her legs bent, knees to the heavens, appearing as though she's in the midst of the greatest orgasm of her life.

I avert my gaze quickly from the coffee table before I get caught staring and looking curious, or worse, envious.

As I walk in further, I see a wall off to the far right full of art—mostly surrealist paintings in ornate frames. So many themes, colors, and sizes that you would expect them to clash, but they surprisingly work.

I get lost in the colors and strokes. The talent.

Some of these paintings are truly bizarre and dreamlike. I'm intrigued.

They even remind me of some that Rush used to send, which brings a sad smile to my face. I miss him so much.

It's been so long since I've had the urge to draw, or paint, or do anything artistic, period. Ever since Rush stopped writing, my motivation has vanished like a flickering flame.

Lost in my thoughts, I jump and let out a startled shriek as a hand touches my arm.

"Shit, didn't mean to scare you," Vic says, with wide eyes, holding up those long tattooed fingers. Even his palms have tattoos, which I've read hurts like a bitch.

"No worries. I was just admiring these."

"You like them?" he asks, sounding guarded.

I look back and gesture at them. "They're beautiful, chaotic, and all so unique. All completely different but complement each other so well," I say honestly, keeping my eyes forward on the paintings even though I feel his eyes burning a hole in the side of my head.

"Uh, thanks," Vic says.

"Wait, this is your work?"

"Yeah, some are from my younger years, like this." He points at a painting of a headshot, but the face is distorted and appears to be melting off. "It's been years since I've painted."

Now I'm surprised. Until now, I didn't even know what he did for a living.

I guess I can consider this the one and only thing we have in common.

Art.

"What made you stop? You obviously have talent."

He quirks an eyebrow. "Did you just give me a compliment, Princess?"

"Do not call me that."

"Whatever you say," he says with a grin.

"So, this is how Gage met you? You're his tattoo artist?"

"Yeah, I'm his tattoo artist."

My mind reels at the thought of Gage being released from prison, finding a stranger to tattoo him, then leaving me alone with said stranger, who he hardly knows.

Again, I'm going to kill Gage.

I place my hand on my hip. "So what am I going to be doing?"

"You can start by getting us coffee and breakfast sandwiches." He pulls money out of his pocket and hands it to me. "Here. There's a coffee shop about six doors to the right of us, Sweet Escape."

I stand there, my eyes fixed on his outstretched hand, filled with crumpled bills. If he thinks I'll be his subservient assistant, he's in for a rude awakening.

But maybe he has to gather his supplies and set up his workspace? I wouldn't know since I've never been in a tattoo shop.

I've always wanted to get one, though. My father would've had a coronary if I came home with one. He'd probably cut it out of my skin with a knife as a punishment.

His voice rings in my head. *Your body is a temple, and you must preserve its purity.*

What a joke.

I shift my gaze from his hand, covered in tattoos, to the elaborate artwork stretching across his arms and neck. My thoughts about tattoos differ from my father's.

My body is a blank canvas. I want to adorn it with stunning artwork, and I plan on doing just that while I'm here.

The look on his face catches my attention, especially his raised eyebrow. I rip the money out of his hand. "Coming right up."

The coffee shop was bustling for such a small town. Usually, it would drive me a little crazy to stand in line for so long, but I understand its allure. I'm halfway through my breakfast sandwich and wish I had more. It's incredibly delicious.

"Where's mine?"

I look up at Vic with a tight smile. "In the bag."

He reaches into the bag and pulls out a blueberry muffin, wrinkling his nose in disgust.

"What the fuck is this?"

"A blueberry muffin."

"Yeah, I got that. Where's my breakfast sandwich?"

"They must've put that in there by mistake." I nonchalantly shrug my shoulders as I savor another mouthful of the breakfast sandwich intended for him.

The muffin was originally mine, but the irresistible aroma of sausage, egg, and cheese on a freshly baked English muffin lured me in. I couldn't help myself.

Before I can even swallow my bite, he invades my personal space. His firm chest presses against mine while his hand wraps around my wrist.

My confusion grows when I look up at him. His heated gaze holds mine, and his expression is one I can't decipher.

With a firm grip, he tugs the sandwich in my hand toward his mouth.

I try to resist his pull. It's pathetic how my arm moves so easily, as if I have no control over my body and he's the one pulling the strings.

Shocked, I drop my mouth open as he devours the last bite of the sandwich and part of my fingers.

The bewildering sensation of his lips enclosing my thumb and forefinger causes me to retract my hand and my stomach to flutter, much to my dismay.

The warmth and softness of his lips against my skin is a thought I shouldn't entertain.

"Gross." I wipe my wet fingers on my pants.

"Delicious." With a sly smile, he licks his lips and walks away, leaving me with his woodsy scent and my fingers tingling where his mouth just was.

"Hey, wait. What am I supposed to do all day?"

The bastard says nothing as he walks to his client and starts tattooing. He's good at blowing my questions off, and it's driving me insane.

When noon approaches, hunger and irritation consume me. I've sat on this stool all day. I observed the sky's transformation from the gentle glow of the morning sun to the bright intensity of the early afternoon sun without a single job.

If he assumes I'm just here to cater to his needs, serving him meals and beverages and nothing more, he's mistaken. I'll get a server job if that's the case.

As I stroll back to Sweet Escape, I take my time to glance through the other shop windows. The town lacks an art studio.

"Hi, what can I get you?" My eyes wander to a girl who looks to be around my age behind the counter. Her light auburn locks frame her face, and her oversized glasses highlight her mesmerizing gray eyes. Her hair is haphazardly pulled back into a bun, and her apron is dusted with flour. She must be the one making the delicious food here.

"Hi, can I get another one of your breakfast sandwiches, and... shit, what did he say he wanted?" I say as I look at the menu as if that will help.

"Sorry, I forgot what he wanted. I have to go back to the tattoo shop and ask him. Lucky me."

"Vic, Samuel, or Richard?" she asks.

"Vic."

"I got you," she says as she punches something into her computer.

"Thanks. You're saving me," I say with a smile. I've been complaining nonstop about how mindless this job is all morning, but if I admit I forgot his order, I'm sure he'll give me shit and never give me anything to do. "Oh, what's my total?"

"I'll put it on Vic's tab." She shoos away the money in my hand. I place it back in my pocket and consider it the tip for my services. "In that case, I'll also take a chocolate chip cookie and a bag of baked chips."

While waiting for my order, I finally have a chance to take in the sights of the shop. The walls are a shade slightly lighter than canary yellow, immersing the room in a serene but cheerful atmosphere. A stunning flower and rose arch gracefully hangs above the register, showcasing various shades of yellow. The flooring features a captivating damask print, blending the hues of baby pink, yellow, and teal. An abundance of pillows adorn the cozy couches, inviting comfort and encouraging engaging conversations. The sound of the grinder and the hiss of the espresso machine blend with the murmur of patrons enjoying their day. Sweet Escape truly lives up to its name and reminds me of sunshine and sunflowers.

"Here you go."

"Thanks," I say as I grab the bag of food.

"I put food in there for Samuel too, but Richard gets nothing."

"I haven't met a Richard yet."

"Richard is Axl's first name, but don't you dare let him know I called him anything but Richard."

30

A huge smile graces my lips as I think about my encounter with Axl this morning. The hickeys and the alcohol practically dripping from his pores.

"Ex-girlfriend?"

"Something like that." She scrunches her nose. "What are you doing over there? I saw you grabbing breakfast here this morning."

"I'd say I'm Vic's assistant, but I feel more like his servant."

"Quit." She shrugs as if it's nothing.

"I kind of need a job."

"I'll hire you."

"But you don't even know me. I've never had a job."

"Are you a murderer or a kleptomaniac?"

"Uh...no?"

"Are you asking or telling?" She quirks her brow.

"Telling. Sorry, that question threw me off." I laugh.

"I'm just messing with you, girl. Can you be on time?"

"Yeah."

"Then you're hired. Angie just went back to school last week, and I could use an extra set of hands for the morning rush. Besides, everyone has to start somewhere, and being someone's servant isn't it."

Right away, I find myself liking her. "I'm Rosie, by the way."

"I'm Jess."

"Will the boss be okay with me working here?"

"You're looking at her."

Returning to the tattoo shop, I can't help but feel a rush of excitement bubbling inside me.

I look for Vic, but he isn't at his tattoo station, so he must be in his office. The thought of knocking on the closed door crosses my mind, but I dismiss it when I recall how he saw no problem with putting his lips around my fingers earlier. After thinking about it one too many times while I was perched on the stool all day, I know it was intentional. Why? I have no idea, but it was.

As I enter the room, I notice Vic and Axl conversing in low voices. I make my presence known by placing the bag on Vic's desk with a deliberate thump.

"Thanks. You can go back out there," Vic murmurs without looking up at me.

"Actually," I say, a smile playing on my lips as I reveal the folded paper from my back pocket. "Here." I toss it onto his desk.

"What the fuck is this?" he says to himself while meticulously smoothing out the creases in the paper.

"My resignation. I quit."

"You can't do that."

"And you can't hire someone against their will."

"Damn, Vic. She has you there," Axl says with a laugh.

I gaze over at Axl, and I notice the anticipation on his face as he rummages through the bag for his lunch. "Also, Jess says she only made food for Vic and Samuel. She said Richard can go get his food somewhere else."

Axl's fingers curl tightly around the bag, his eyes boring into mine with a menacing glare.

"I'll be back," he says with a hint of determination.

I don't know what he's done to upset someone as kindhearted as my new boss, Jess, but it must have been severe for her to continue catering to Vic the Dick, as I now call him in my head. As for Samuel, Vic's apprentice, I can't comment on him since he hasn't arrived yet.

As I search through the bag for my food, the scorching intensity of Vic's stare lingers in the air.

"No."

"What?" I look up at him.

"You heard me."

I shrug. "I guess I was waiting for you to reconsider."

"Not a chance in hell."

"What are you getting out of this?" I say as I gesture back and forth between him and me.

"Right now, a massive fucking headache."

"Whatever my brother paid, I'll double it. I just want to live my life here without a babysitter breathing down my neck. I want to be free to make my own decisions."

"Triple."

My eyes widen. "Are you serious?"

Vic stays quiet but smirks. He's going to tax me because he knows I'm desperate. Which is something I would never show to anyone, but I am desperate.

Really fucking desperate, and I don't know how to make it happen because I've never been on my own.

He really is the devil.

"Fine, triple. This will be between you and me only. Do we have a deal?" I extend my hand, but he just looks at it.

"No."

My heart sinks.

"What do you mean, no?"

"You think I'm going against your brother, who's not only one of my best friends but also the next boss in line to the Chicago Mafia?"

There it is. His motivation stems from loyalty. Good for Gage. A desire for future favors, I'm sure, maybe even wealth that can be easy to get from someone like my brother. I'm outmatched when competing with those.

There's only one hand left for me to play. I'm backed into a corner and left with no choice.

"Well, then I guess I'll tell my brother in the past twenty-four hours we've been half naked in a room together with my fingers in your mouth."

Four

Vic

I gaze at Rosie, her self-satisfied smile both intriguing and unsettling.

Gage would chop off my balls if she told him that out of context. Shit, even in context, it doesn't sound good.

She thinks she has me where she wants me, but she's dead fucking wrong.

Standing, I run my fingers along the smooth surface of the wooden desk. "Blackmail?" I say in a low tone as I approach her.

I focus my eyes on her chest, where I can observe the rhythmic rise and fall of her breaths, mirroring my footsteps.

"Is that what you're attempting to do to me, Princess?" As I lean closer, my chest presses against her shoulder, causing her to reach out instinctively to stabilize herself against my desk.

"Ahh, yeah," she says as she looks anywhere but at me. To her credit, she doesn't move. She holds her ground even as I push further into her personal space. She's trying hard to conceal the small smile playing on her lips.

"And where do you plan on working, huh?"

"Sweet Escape."

Of course. Fucking Jess.

If I knew Ax wasn't already over there, I'd send him right now to make her day difficult. Usually, I feel sympathy for Jess with how relentlessly Ax pesters her. But not today. And probably not next week either. Those two need to figure their shit out, anyway. I knew there was always more to their friendship when we were kids. I just never knew how deeply it ran.

I need to approach this argument with Rosie in a tactful and strategic manner. If I give her this small taste of freedom, maybe she'll find contentment in that and not cause me too much trouble. I mean, how much trouble could she possibly get into while working at the coffee shop? It's better than the alternatives we have in town with the bar or strip club.

"Fine."

"Really?" Like sunshine on a summer day, her entire face lights up while a beautiful smile adorns her full pink lips.

I retreat to the other side of my desk, unable to bear the sight any longer.

The desk provides a sense of protection, creating a necessary boundary between us. One that I should remember.

"Yes."

Even as I sit back down, she continues to smile, her eyes sparkling with joy. It's disconcerting to see her smile for something as basic as a human right that she should have, regardless of my approval. Yet my mind's consumed with the notion that I'm solely responsible for the joy reflected on her exquisite face.

I look at her with a critical eye as I've done since she dropped into my life. Attempting to find flaws to make her unattractive.

Her silky black hair hangs to her mid-back and is the perfect length to grab and wrap around my hand multiple times. Her tanned skin appears like the sun has kissed it multiple times, and I don't have to touch it to know how soft it is. It's practically velvet under my rough fingertips.

Her big green eyes track mine as I make the descent down her body with breasts that I'm sure will be a perfect handful. A soft waist I can grab as I'm fucking her from behind with no worry of breaking her in half, and an ass that I imagine my hand reddening until she screams. I don't need to look at it to know how glorious it is. I got an eyeful last night, and I haven't been able to get it off my mind with her small pink thong that showed more than it covered.

I always get what I want, when I want it, but she's the exception to my rule of never going without.

She's the forbidden fruit that dangles just out of my reach. A delectable bite I have no right to taste or savor, because that's what I'd do if I touched what needs to stay just out of my reach.

I knew it would be tough to watch her, but I never expected the self-inflicted torment to be so profound.

"You'll start Sweet Escape on Monday, and you'll continue to work for me on Fridays and Saturdays."

Her face falls the second the words are out of my mouth, and even her disappointment makes me happy.

As long as I'm giving her the emotion that shows so willingly on her face, I'll take it.

"Why?"

"Because as a responsible employee, a notice comes with a period for me to find your replacement and avoid being short-staffed."

"But why do I still have to work here?"

Because I want you close.

"Those two days are our busiest, so we need extra hands."

This entire conversation is the biggest load of shit that has ever come out of my mouth, but I won't take it back. I enjoy watching her steal glances at my coffee table when she thinks no one's looking. Her cheeks get so unbelievably rosy, showing how innocent she is.

"Your furniture does more work in the shop than I do."

"What furniture are you referring to, Princess?" I say with a satisfying smile as the blood drains from her face.

With an annoyed huff, she snatches her food and storms out of my office, her footsteps echoing down the hallway. I use the opportunity to admire the way her ass sways in her black and white polka-dot minidress, the fabric tight in all the right places.

My phone rings as if on cue. Gage must possess a peculiar sixth sense, suspecting my impure thoughts toward his little sister.

Gage

Checking in. Everything good?

Vic

Yep.

Gage

Is she giving you any trouble?

Vic

Nah. All good, man.

Gage

I owe you. Talk to you soon.

I pocket my phone and walk out of my office. Without even realizing it, my eyes search for her.

On the stool I dubbed her throne, she sits with a scowl, arms crossed and legs swinging. She's pissed and well on her way to hating me.

"The looks you keep shooting her way when she isn't looking don't look too platonic. Should I pick out your casket now, or do you want to be cremated and sprinkled in the lake?" Ax says to my right.

"I have no clue what you're talking about."

"Keep telling yourself that. You sure she's safe with you?"

Rosie turns around, her face twisting into a scowl directed right at us or, perhaps more specifically, at me. Her face contorts with anger, and you can almost see the hatred oozing from her pores.

"Damn, maybe I should be worried about her stabbing you in your sleep." Ax laughs.

"I can handle her." I shrug.

My eyes don't leave hers as I walk back to my client. Before disappearing from her view, I leave her with a wink and a smirk.

I'm in complete and total hell, loving every minute of the burn.

Five

Rosie

T rue to his word, Vic makes me work Friday and Saturday with him. And by work, I mean sit down all day and only move to serve him his food.

Jess was understanding and said I could start when I was ready. I assured her, come Monday, I'd be there at the crack of dawn. Monday can't come soon enough.

Sitting here reminds me of the etiquette classes I had to take as a child to become a brainless drone of a wife for my impending arranged marriage.

I remember staring at Mrs. Doubeaux as she practically hammered information into me but not seeing or hearing shit. My mind found faces, animals, and shapes in the crimson damask wallpaper just over her shoulder in our formal sitting room. Twenty hours a week over several years taught me the significance of silverware and its precise positioning. Find the perfect balance between being visible and unheard, skillfully conversing and gathering pertinent information for my future husband's benefit. The epitome of a Mafia Stepford wife, always perfect-ly put together and eager to please.

That was when I got the first itch to run, which only inten-sified as time passed.

"Well, I like this, but maybe we can change a few things. Like this, and this." A customer is busy looking over Vic's design.

I peek at the tablet and internally nod my head. He's good at what he does. I've watched countless customers leave ex-tremely satisfied with their new ink over the past couple of days. However, this customer has made him change the design three times. It wasn't this, or it wasn't that. I get it, though. It will be permanently inked into her skin, so it should be perfect.

I check out the fairly simple butterfly on a rose with a geo-metric pattern as the backdrop, but it's missing more of the feminine touch she's looking for, and the colors are wrong.

I look over at Vic, who's irritated, but hiding it well, from his pinched brow and clenched fist at his side. You can tell this doesn't happen often. Everyone else I've seen so far has loved their designs, and his portfolio on the coffee table is impressive, although I'd never tell him.

"Come back in around an hour. Let me fix a few things."

She walks out, and I stand from my throne of boredom with a stretch I feel down to my toes.

"So, I was thinking..." I say as I look over at him.

"Oh, no," Vic says in a mocking tone as he grabs his tablet and walks away.

I ignore his comment and chase him. "Maybe we can work something out..."

"Not interested," he calls over his shoulder.

I grab his arm before he can walk any farther. He looks down at where my hand touches his skin. "Can you let me finish at least?"

"No."

I continue anyway, not deterred by his dismissal. "Okay, great. So I was thinking I could draw her up something. If she prefers my drawing over yours, I'll get to do something I want at some point and you can't tell me no."

"No," he repeats for what seems like the millionth time before pulling his arm away.

"Why are you such a dick?"

"Why are you such a pain in my ass?"

"Because I want to do more than just sit around all day. I'm sick of it."

"And I'm sick of listening to you bitch and moan."

"Then give me something to do."

"No."

"God, I can't stand you," I say as I rip my notebook and pencil off the counter and stomp to the waiting area.

I gaze at the woman holding up the glass table that mocks me. I'm tempted to paint clothes on her when Vic's busy. With how vindictive and petty I'm feeling, I might just do it. Maybe add a couple of dicks, too.

I look up, and the bastard stares at me with a smirk. He catches me looking all the time with that same stupid smirk that's one step from a blinding and malicious smile.

She's definitely getting painted.

I open my notepad that I have yet to use and go to work.

What I love about art is how you can express and release your emotions, allowing them to flow freely from within and onto the canvas. Right now, irritation and competitiveness are the dominant emotions coursing through me because of his dismissal.

I was only a child when I discovered my deep passion for art, and it only grew once I started college. Professor Skies was so patient and had such a guiding light. It was the first time I felt liberated, no longer stifled by my father's critiques of my paintings. Then, I received a request from a fellow art enthusiast to commission a piece, which cemented my decision. I would pursue my passion regardless of the cost.

My professor taught me to ask the client every question imaginable and watch their movements, what they wore, and their personality. All this plays a role and Vic's missing that one important step.

Again, his design is good, more than good, but sometimes it needs more of a delicate touch. She wore a pink dress and rhinestone sandals with a bag and sunglasses to match. She seemed delicate and sweet even when she continued to turn down his design.

Vic's client walks back in as I add the final details to the petals and the tiny jewels sporadically placed throughout.

She looks over his design with a critical eye, and I see the small frown form between her brows. "This is good, but I don't know. Maybe I should just wait."

I stand and walk over. I understand this is highly inappropriate, and I'm crossing boundaries, but honestly, I don't give a shit.

I want to feel like I have a purpose while I'm stuck here. Hopefully, I can negotiate a deal with him once he realizes my value.

"I have something that might work," I say and receive narrowed eyes from Vic.

"Oh, this is cute. I like the jewels. They could really pop if we did them in different colors, right?" She looks over at me, and I look at Vic. In an instant, my palms turn clammy and perspire. I turn my attention back to her when Vic remains silent.

"I think it will, especially with your skin tone."

"Right, I was thinking the same thing. I like this."

I give Vic a very satisfying fuck you smile and walk away.

Rosie, one.

Vic, zero.

Silence fills the car, adding to the already tense ambience as Vic and I drive back to his house.

I hoped to go out and celebrate my new job with a little window shopping and some kind of chocolate dessert, but he firmly rejected my request with a resounding no. That word seems to be his all-time favorite, always on the tip of his tongue. After winning the client over with my design, his demeanor toward me turned as cold as ice. I'm not surprised. I know I stepped on his toes.

The only saving grace for tonight is the comforting weight of the cardboard box in my hands. I rip the box open with too much enthusiasm and look at my shiny new phone. As I turn it on and go through the prompts to set it up, I catch sight of Vic walking by. Dressed in boots, dark jeans, and a black hoodie; he's looking like nothing but trouble. I run to my door.

"Where are you going?"

"Out," he murmurs but doesn't turn around.

"So you get to go out, but I have to stay in on a Saturday night?"

"Yep. Stay inside. Don't go anywhere or answer the door. I'm setting the house alarm when I leave. There's takeout in the kitchen."

"Okay, Dad," I say.

He keeps his back rigid and clenches his hands tightly at his sides, yet he remains silent as he strides down the hall.

Unbelievable.

I can't believe I semi-successfully ran away from home just to be locked in a house again while he goes off and does who knows what every evening. Starting next week, I will be changing things.

I glance back at my abandoned phone resting on my bed and release a sigh. At least this will occupy my time for a while. The first app I'm installing is for a car service.

"Oh my fucking God. I thought something happened to you. Why haven't you answered any of my calls or texts?" My best friend Alexa yells at me through the phone.

"I broke my phone when I fell out of my window."

Alexa cackles in my ear, and I can just imagine her doubled over with tears in her eyes.

"Not funny. It hurt like hell."

"Maybe a little funny. Are you okay? Where did you end up, anyway?"

"A small town on the border of Illinois and Indiana."

"But I thought..."

"I got intercepted." I sigh.

When Alexa and I brainstormed my escape in the past, the plan was always the West Coast. I'd hop on multiple buses until I saw the sun and beaches. A plane ride, while quicker, would be a no-go because of the ID checks. The plan was never further east or so close to my father's reach.

"What the hell does that mean?"

I bite down on my lip, wrestling with the dilemma of whether to disclose the truth about Gage to Alexa. Although he didn't explicitly mention keeping it a secret from her, his intention was obvious—she was meant to be left in the dark, too.

But I plan to bring her into the light.

During his absence, he didn't acknowledge a single letter I sent. After being released from prison two years ago, he remained silent until the moment I literally collided with him.

My allegiance does not belong to him. He has to earn that.

"Gage found me."

Dead silence fills the phone. "Hello?"

"He-he's back?" she asks in a barely audible whisper.

"Yeah, and he's not the same."

"What do you mean?"

"Imagine him from before. Honest. Sweet. Understanding. Now throw that version in the trash. He turned into a hard man, Lex. You can see the ruthlessness in his eyes, but he did hit one of the guards over the head to knock him out cold to save me, so maybe he's not all bad."

"Which one?"

"Alfonso."

"No way."

"Yeah, he had blood trickling from his head while he was lying on the ground. I even got to kick him in the ribs on the way out," I say with a triumphant smile.

"You should have kicked him in the balls so he's unable to procreate. He always gave me the creeps with his leering and weird comments about our clothes."

"For real. Maybe next time."

"Who are you and what have you done with my best friend? First, running away, and then violence... Please tell me you've already made two horrible decisions but regret nothing."

"I haven't been able to do shit since Gage happened."

"So he's really back?"

"Yep. Just be thankful you haven't run into him yet."

"Yeah, I guess so," she says with a sigh.

I'm sure she's upset that he hasn't found her yet. They were best friends, and he brushed her off, just as he did to me.

"Where are you staying? With him?"

"No, he dropped me off at some friend's house who is now my babysitter."

"A girl?"

"No. A dick. I swear he makes me want to poke out his eyeballs."

"Is he cute?"

"No, he's ugly as hell and a total asshole. I mean, I get he's helping me out, or more like helping Gage out, but fuck, is he irritating. I don't want to talk about me, though. Tell me about you. Are you okay?"

I deflect. He's far from ugly, but the total asshole is spot-on.

While I'm thankful for his efforts to keep me safe from my father's wrath and the countless enemies our family has amassed, I can't help but think that he's being a bit too over-protective and a dick just for the sake of being one to me.

"I'm good, Ro. Real good. You'd like it here."

Luckily for Alexa, her father is understanding and sweet. My brother, Marco's, actions caused his and Alexa's arranged marriage to unravel, resulting in her leaving college, where she and I had been living together until just a few months ago.

For the next few months, she's liberated from the constraints of her future and gets to enjoy herself, thanks to her dad's generosity. As an only child, she will be one of the pioneering female Capos in Chicago once her father and the other bosses pass on the leadership torch to the next generation of heirs. Which is badass and a position I know she will flourish in. Me, not so much. Thankfully, my brothers were born so I don't have to take on that bloody role. Although, I think mine as a bargaining chip for one of the families is just as unfortunate.

I hear a car alarm beep and noise coming from somewhere close. I peek through the curtains as two dark silhouettes stalk to the back. Their figures are bathed in the soft glow of the motion light as they approach the guesthouse.

Vic pulls a giggling, stumbling blonde along. From his side profile, his expression is passive.

Not happy, or sad, or even mad.

Just blank.

Bored.

Vic turns around right before closing the door. Our eyes meet as he looks up at my window, and time stands still. Neither of us moves. Then, a taunting smirk pulls on his face.

What is up with that smug look?

Is it because I'm fucking Rapunzel? Stuck in an ivory tower while he's doing whatever he's doing? The look deserves to be smacked off his face.

"Fuck you," I mouth to Vic before turning away from the window.

"Hey, you still there?"

"Yeah, sorry." I shake my head.

"Can we talk tomorrow? They just delivered our dessert."

"Yeah. Love you, Lex."

"Love you, Ro."

I throw my phone on the bed and look back at the window. My feet take a few steps, and my hands touch the black velvet curtain, but I retract my hand and flop on my bed.

Why do I even want to look outside? Who cares if he brings some girl back here?

He probably has a small dick and lasts five seconds. She'll leave disappointed and unsatisfied. A small smirk plays on my lips at the thought of him lacking in bed.

But I can't help but think of our interactions during the past couple of days. Some of those moments piss me off, while others give me the chills, and worse, flickering in my stomach. Not butterflies, because I seem to detest the guy and reserve butterflies for guys I like. Not that I've ever felt them before.

His stupid, handsome face moves into the forefront of my mind. Who am I kidding? Someone like him, who exudes so much sexual energy with each step he takes, each word he states, and every look or touch he makes knows exactly what he's doing and probably does it well. He could probably write a book on the art of sex and seduction. Not that I'd know anything about either of those subjects. Well, besides books and porn. The latter is more of an educational viewing than anything else, of course.

I just want to know how my life has changed so drastically in the past couple of days. Time will tell if this was for the best or if running was the biggest mistake of my life.

Four Nights Ago

"You can't do this to me. Please don't do this to me. I can't marry Manuel. I don't like him," I plead from across the dining room table.

I turn to Mama, silently begging her to intervene. Since it was arranged for her to marry Papa, she knows my heartbreak. Her sympathetic gaze is filled with tears as she looks at me, while Papa's expression remains passive. He's an uncompromising and controlling man who insists on having his way, even if it harms others.

"You will marry him. This is not up for discussion, Rosalinda."

"But..."

"We've been planning this for an extremely long time. You know this, and you will do as you're told. It's your duty as a member of this family. We all have to make sacrifices." Papa's voice grows louder. He's clearly irritated by me challenging his authority.

I stand abruptly, the chair scraping against the marble floor, while a rage jolts through me like I've never felt before.

I have busted my ass to be everything my father has wanted, and for what? To get thrown into a lifelong situation without my consent. To a guy who makes my skin crawl. Just in the name of strengthening the alliance between our families?

"I never agreed to this. I don't want to be exchanged like some currency. Please don't make me do this. I beg you," I say, looking at Papa while I hold back tears. He doesn't like those; he considers it a weakness and they won't help my cause in the least.

"I'm tired of your dramatics. Marco will drive you back to your dorm tomorrow morning and you will grab all of your shit. Play-time is over. If you continue to be a disappointment, I will make your life a living hell. Gladly offering you to one of the other families in Boston at a discounted price, just to ease the constant headache you cause. Now sit down and eat." He hits the table with his palm, making Mama and me flinch.

"You promised me. You said I could finish out the rest of my semester. What about the art exhibit I have in a couple of weeks? It's not—"

"I don't give a fuck what I said or about your waste of time art exhibit."

Tears well up behind my eyes, stinging with an intensity that I refuse to release. I have thrown my heart and soul into this exhibit. I saw this as an opportunity to prove to my father the extent of my skills. Many nights, as I worked on the pieces, I hoped and prayed for him to appreciate my art. To see me as someone with talent and purpose.

I take one last look around the room. First at Marco, my brother, who keeps his head down, eating food without a care in the world. Then at my mother, who's looking down at her hands in defeat, before staring at my father, who looks pretty pissed at my outburst. What my father says is always final. I know I won't get any help to convince him otherwise.

These are times I wish my brother, Gage, was home. He was always compassionate and would stand for what was right, even if he got hurt in the end.

I can't wait for him to come back.

I decide I'm no longer hungry and stomp to my room. I don't say another word, even when Mama calls my name.

Even when I can feel the glare of death from Papa.

This is the first time I've been so outspoken, and I'd give myself a pat on the back if I wasn't so terrified he'd come after me.

Marco and I came home for our parents' anniversary and a quick dinner, and we'll return to our dorms early in the morning. I was so excited to be home, spending time with my mom, and now I wish I had stayed in my dorm.

Papa's promise of time gave me hope, but now both are gone. I refuse to marry someone I don't choose. I'm running away, and I'll actually succeed this time.

I feel for the texture of my old backpack from high school at the top of my closet. Then, I quickly tear down a few pieces of clothing, the straining and snapping of hangers echo around me.

The plush carpet cushions my hands and knees as I lower myself onto the floor. I tug at the bottom drawer of my closet dresser system, which slides out effortlessly, almost too easily from years of removing it so frequently.

My secret hiding spot. I anxiously grab the discolored white envelopes and clutch them to my chest, treating them like a priceless treasure. These letters are my solace when I'm upset, my company when I feel alone, and my source of joy when I need a smile on my face. I fan them out. Each is equally important to me—two hundred and three letters total. I would receive two letters a month, sometimes three, depending on how quickly the post office delivered them. I run my finger across the writing on the front, feeling the deep indentations he left by pushing so hard.

My very first letter.

Carefully, I unfold the letter with its worn and tattered edges, evidence of the countless times I've opened and closed it.

Dear Rosie,

You don't know me, but I kind of know you. I hope this isn't already creepy. I just want someone to talk to, I guess. I see that you write your brother, but he never writes back, and since you take the time to write to him, maybe you can write to me, too?

If not, it's cool, I understand.

Gage tells me you draw. I do too. Maybe I can send you something? If you want, of course.

Anyway, if you don't write me back, it's okay. I just don't have anyone to write, and it gets lonely sometimes.

- Rush

Despite his abandonment of writing to me months ago, I refuse to let these letters suffer the same fate. I refold the letter and shove it into my backpack with the rest, along with a couple of photos, before looking out the window.

It's now or never.

I float on the water's surface in the late Sunday afternoon sun. My limbs are limp, surrendering to the gentle current. The sun's heat kisses my face while a gentle breeze whispers through the trees, offering me a moment of tranquility I haven't experienced since leaving my parents' house. I thank the credit card gods above for the expedited shipping that had my new cherry-print bikini arriving in less than twelve hours. Thanks, Gage.

I hear someone's steps and open my eyes as I watch Vic pull a different girl to the guesthouse. His eyes never leave mine, and I feel like it's a challenge, so I continue to stare even after they're already inside. I wonder if Gage knows how busy his friend is.

I see a flash of blond hair before a splash breaks the silence. Axl pops his head up from the water.

"I heard you're going to work at Sweet Escape."

"Yep."

"Can you put in a good word for me with Jess?"

I snort. "Not a chance."

"Why not?"

"She may just be the nicest person I've ever met, and you happen to be on her shit list. Seems like you must've done something pretty bad to upset her."

"I'm trying to fix it," he says in a serious tone, devoid of the usual humor I've come to expect over the past few days.

"What have you done to fix it?"

"I apologized."

"Sometimes it takes time and more than just a sorry."

"It's been years. I don't know what else to do."

My lip sits between my clenched teeth as I ponder what to say. I'm mindful of not overstepping the new friendship I'm building with Jess, so I go for a vague response.

"Sometimes it helps to make the other person's life easier. Offering help before she asks, getting her flowers or her favorite food just because. Simple gestures go a long way to show the other person you're thinking about them and you care."

"Okay," he says, looking off into the distance like he's thinking hard. "What else?"

I look at his neck. His hickeys are beginning to fade to blotchy yellows. "If you want Jess as more than a friend, you should rethink your extracurricular activities."

The door opens, and I whip my head to the left as Vic walks behind the girl he just brought back there no more than three minutes ago.

"What the fuck are you doing in the pool, Ax?"

"Having a heart-to-heart."

Vic's eyes meet mine, but he doesn't utter a word as he escorts his friend out. He walks back with a murderous look, and I cluck my tongue. I have this undeniable urge inside me to irritate him and get a rise out of him.

He's been up and down with me for days, which is confusing as hell.

"You know, they have pills for that."

"For what?"

"Your problem."

"Which is?" he asks in a bored tone.

"You seem to have many, but right now, your little friend left pretty quick."

Axl laughs as Vic finally catches up.

"I don't have any problems in that department."

"Whatever you say."

"You've been in the pool since morning. Maybe you should get out and take a nap or something."

"I'm not fucking five, and why are you watching me in the pool?"

"Yeah, Vic. Why are you watching her in the pool?"

"Fuck off, Ax."

"I probably should," Axl says with a sigh. "Thanks for the help."

"Anytime. You owe me a favor." I level Axl with narrowed eyes. Even though I have no desire to involve myself with the Mafia, I understand the value of keeping connections and collecting favors for potential future use.

He nods his head as he gets out of the pool. "Deal."

"No fucking deal," Vic snaps.

"You need to lighten up." I snap back with the same bite as him.

Vic's penetrating eyes lock onto me as he confidently descends the steps and immerses himself in the water. Fully clothed.

Oh fuck.

My eyes widen in disbelief as he menacingly continues to approach me. I stand my ground, unmoving, like a statue, despite my inner desire to retreat. If I wasn't already in the water, I'm sure my palms would be sweating.

"I'll just be going." We both ignore Axl's admission.

Vic stands over me as I look up into his eyes with a giddy smile I shouldn't feel. I remember when I was small, maybe seven or eight, I had this nasty little habit of smiling when I got reprimanded or in tense situations when uncomfortable. It was something I broke as I got older, but for some reason, I can't stop the smile on my face. I bite the inside of my cheek, willing myself to stop. I can't believe he's managed to pull this dormant habit out of me. Perhaps it's the constant verbal sparring between us since I arrived, or maybe it's the captivating sight of his black tee shirt clinging to his body, shaped by the water, that I find myself unable to look away from. Out of my peripheral vision, of course.

"Why are you trying to get on my last fucking nerve?"

"I have no clue what you're talking about."

"Oh, but I think you do. What's with the comment earlier?"

"It was more of an observation. She left quick and without a smile on her face."

"And what does that mean?"

"No clue."

"I don't have any problems."

"Okay."

"I'm fucking serious."

"Okay."

"Since we're here, let's discuss yesterday. We aren't making any deals. You will come to work, and you will leave, and there will be no favors from any of the guys."

"The favors between me and someone else don't concern you."

Vic pushes his weight against me, making me take a step back, the water not helping me stand tall and unwavering as I need.

"Everything you do concerns me. So just be good and stay out of my fucking way, for the love of God."

Stay out of his way? When have I been in his way?

His eyes go wide as I move into his space because he's now pissed me off.

As our bodies press together, my breasts brush against his chest, causing him to draw in a sudden breath and his jaw to tense as his eyes focus on our connection.

"Seems that you're the one in my way right now."

"Don't fucking start something you can't finish, Princess."

"Who says I can't finish?"

"Me."

"You don't know me at all."

"I know you better than you think." He grabs my chin between his thumb and forefinger, giving it a tight squeeze. "I will tarnish your little crown of rainbows and butterflies and send you back to Gage before you know what to do with yourself."

My throat goes dry and itches with a need to swallow, but I remain still.

What the hell did he just say?

I stand there, unable to move, as Vic's thumb glides across my parted lips. As his thumb brushes against my skin, I can feel the softness with a hint of calluses, sending a tingling sensation through my body. And then the damn flutters start.

I'd be tempted to run my tongue against my li, and even his finger, if I weren't so shocked by his words.

"Don't have anything to say now, do ya?"

Vic turns around without another word or backward glance.

I stay in the pool long after my fingers have pruned. When the sun has made its descent and the evening chill has set in.

I sit in the dark water and analyze what he said to where it makes no sense and all the sense.

Tarnish me how?

He has treated me like someone would a bothersome gnat since I arrived.

One thing I do know, it was a warning. One that I should heed, but since being here, I've felt the first stages of freedom, though small, and I'll be damned if I lose that feeling.

Six

Vic

Six Years Old

    As I sit in the dark, cold room, a shiver runs over my body. I grab my blankie and hold it to me as tightly as I can, my small fingers going through the holes in the corners of the fabric.

My tummy hurts. It keeps growling for food.

Mom said she would bring me some, but she never did, and it feels like I've been waiting forever.

Mom and Dad were yelling, and he told me to go to my room. I begged him for food, but he didn't care.

He never does. I don't like Dad. He's mean to me and sometimes to Mom. He falls asleep a lot, and Mom does, too, but every once in a while, she'll spend time with me. She rubs my hair and hums.

Those are the best times.

I wish she'd come back right now.

"Fuck," I growl and slam my palm on my nightstand, trying to reach for my phone that's blaring in my ears. It feels like someone's hitting me in the head with a baseball bat, though I'm thankful for it waking me from the dream that plays on repeat most nights.

"Hey, boss, your nine o'clock just arrived. Just wanted to let you know." My eyes go wide.

"Fuck, I'll be right there. Can you set up my station?"

"Done," Samuel says before hanging up.

I stayed up way later than my ass should have, drinking as my feet dangled in the pool while I looked up at the room shrouded in darkness where Rosie sleeps.

I rub my eyelids with the heels of my sweaty palms and emit a yawn.

Grabbing one of the many protein bars from my top drawer, I polish it off in three dry bites, not even tasting it. Knowing that the bottomless feeling in my stomach has nothing to do with hunger and more to do with the nightmare plaguing my mind.

You'd think after all these years I'd be able to get out of that cold-ass bedroom with a small holey mattress on the floor, but I still get stuck there.

Helpless and hungry.

The shittiest part wasn't discovering my parents died on the way back from a run to score more speed. No, it was being stuck in that house with no food for almost a week. My school finally called the cops for them to do a welfare check after a week of absences. I was malnourished, only surviving off water in the nasty-ass bathroom sink.

I count to ten. Allowing myself to only spend ten seconds in memory land before banishing it to the pits of hell. As I get to one, I close my eyes and inhale deeply before exhaling.

I jump up and stretch, looking back at my very empty bed. It's not often that I wake up alone, since most women try to stay the night. Sometimes I cave and let them. Rachel tried last night after I called her in my drunken stupor, only to literally not get it up for the second time that day.

No one comes close to piquing my interest or making me hard... besides Rosie, which is aggravating. Her comment in the pool was not too far off.

She's both the poison and the antidote to my situation, and I don't know what to do.

I throw on my clothes in a rush. She has her first shift with Jess. I have my client. We need to hurry.

I yell up to her room that we need to leave, like now, then wait in the living room on the overstuffed couch that never gets used. Weirdly, it's called the living room when I do far more living in the guesthouse than I've ever done in here.

Just like every other time, there's an eerie silence in here. One might even call it lonely.

Not long after I got out, I saw this house on the market and found myself in a bidding war with a couple expecting a child. While this house was better suited for a family, I felt an inexplicable longing when I stepped inside. It was the home I should have

61

had as a child, and because of that, I paid well over the asking price to get it.

But here it sits, mostly vacant. Devoid of warmth and laughter.

I check my phone with a sigh. We need to get going. I hate being late.

I ascend the stairs and knock, only to be met with silence on the other side. I open the door to a very empty room.

What the fuck? My stomach drops as I run around the house, looking for her. I pull out my phone and dial Jess.

"Good morning, and thank you for calling Sweet E—"

"Is Rosie there?"

"Good morning to you, too, Vic, and yes, she is. Do you want to—"

I hang up on Jess the second I know Rosie's safe.

As the panic subsides, annoyance takes its place. The second I get ahold of her phone, I'm placing a tracker on it.

I pull over to the side and park in front of Sweet Escape, too fucking pissed to park at my shop and walk over.

The bell above the door announces my arrival, and Samantha instantly greets me a little too enthusiastically. After the shit show the night of Rosie's arrival, I've avoided her. Once Rosie left for the main house, she bitched about her staying with me and told me she should stay elsewhere. First, she and I fucked twice—that hardly warrants her opinion to count—and two, she did it because she felt threatened.

Samantha's pretty, with blond hair and blue eyes, but there's not a whole hell of a lot going on upstairs, and she wanted more. They always do.

"Morning, Samantha," I say politely with a tight smile, not wanting to give her the wrong impression ever again.

"Hey Vic, how've you been?" she asks, leaning over the counter and into my space.

"Not too bad," I say, looking around for the brunette I want to strangle.

"That's great. Hey, I was thinking..."

My gaze halts as I spot Rosie walking toward me from the back with boxes in her hands. "Hey," I say to get Rosie's attention.

"Oh, hey there, Vic," she says, a little surprised before averting her eyes anywhere but at me.

So I guess my little comment in the pool made her uncomfortable. Good. I move closer to her, behind the food display counter and away from her clingy coworker.

"Nothing else to say?"

"Like...?"

"You weren't supposed to leave the house this morning alone. That's not part of our agreement. I'm supposed to drive you."

"Sorry," Rosie says with a dismissive shrug.

"Sorry? That's all?"

"I thought you'd be busy this morning with your company from last night," she says with a bit of a bite to her words.

So she was watching me after she left the pool last night. Interesting.

"Little nosy, don't you think... or maybe it's jealousy?" I smirk.

Her head snaps up. "Not in a million fucking years. If anything, I pity the company you keep."

"Is that so?"

"Four different girls in four days...it's like they all pull numbers and wait their turn."

"You want to pull a number? You seem awfully worried."

"Absolutely not," she says with a smirk. "Just wondering when it's my turn to bring someone to the guesthouse. You know, try out the bed."

My smile vanishes, and my mood sours further, if possible.

She's playing with fire, and she knows it.

She's trying to make me jealous, and it's working.

"You don't get turns."

"We'll see."

"I'm fucking serious."

"And so am I. It's not fair you get to have all the fun," she complains with that same fucking smile she had yesterday. She's practically giddy with the way she's pissing me off. I can't help but feel like I need to get the last word in and win this little battle we seem to always have.

I lean on the counter and narrow my eyes at her before licking my lips, which I know she'll look at. When I know I have her full attention, I give her a hard stare as if I'm looking under her clothes to make her uncomfortable. I gaze down her delectable body, at least from what I can see from behind the counter, then back up, stopping at her eyes that reveal her every emotion.

Irritation, anger, and a flicker of something else.

She squirms under the heat of my gaze as if I'm caressing her body with my hands.

And this is why I need to walk out right now. Why am I doing this to myself? I'm here to reprimand her, and all I can think about is bending her over my knee and spanking her.

"You bring anyone to my house, and I will kill them. Do you understand?"

"Sure thing, Dad," she mutters as she bends down out of view.

I stomp back to my truck and slam the door closed. I'm too irritated to eat even though my stomach groans in protest.

She won't be honest with me, but I know who she will be honest with.

I burst into my office, passing a perplexed Samuel and my most likely furious client, and slam the door. After grabbing a piece of paper from my printer tray and a pen from my desk, I plop down in my seat and stare at the blank piece of paper as I try to come up with something to say besides sorry for leaving you hanging like a piece of shit.

The pen tapping on my desk fills the silence as I wait for inspiration that will not come.

The difference between the letters from before and now is knowing she smells like a mix of flowers and fruit, the notch she gets between her eyebrows when she's irritated, and the groan she makes when she eats like it's the first time every time. She seems even more satisfied with food than I do, which is difficult. Now I know the way her body looks without pants and the way her skin feels. How she breathes in and out while stretching in the gym every morning.

All of this in such a short period is fucking with me, and the resolve I had when Gage asked me to watch over her is almost nonexistent.

One Month Ago

"Yo!" I raise my head from my sketch pad as Gage saunters into my shop.

"What the fuck are you doing here?" I can't help but smile as I jump up and give him a hug.

It's been a minute since I've seen the fucker. He crashed at my place for about a month after he got out and then bounced. He needed safety and anonymity until he got strong enough. It didn't take him long, and I couldn't be more proud.

"Just in the neighborhood," he states while looking around my shop, nodding his head as if approving.

"Yeah, fucking right. It's been too long, bro. What have you been up to?"

"Oh, you know, the usual. Burning down one building at a time." He smirks.

As time went on and we were stuck in our cell, he got more vengeful, plotting moves to take down everyone who wronged him. I was behind him on that fully. Ask anyone how they'd feel after serving years behind bars for something they never did.

"I wouldn't expect anything less," I say with a big-ass smile plastered on my face.

"Listen, I need a favor."

Raising an eyebrow, I ask, "Don't you have your own people to bury the bodies now?"

"That I do." He smirks. "However, I need you for something more important."

"I'm listening."

"My sister, Rosalinda."

My heart beats faster, and a tightness forms in the back of my throat as I think about her.

The one girl I looked at every single day for years, the one girl I fantasized about, the one girl I can close my eyes and see with such absolute clarity. The one girl I promised myself I would stay away from after the night of that party. But she's always been in the back of my mind. She's taken up residence there for years, never to vacate. Her name is all it took for her claws to sink under my skin and poison me with no thoughts besides her.

It sounds insane, even to my own ears, but she gave me hope during one of the most hopeless times I've ever been in. It probably didn't help that Gage told me stories about all of them with the endless time that we had on our hands. He spoke of her being an artist; we had that in common. He spoke of her compassionate nature and sweet personality. His stories reeled me in. Then, I stole her address and wrote to her for years. I'm a piece of shit for doing that behind Gage's back, and if he ever found out, I'd gladly let him beat my ass.

Running guns and drugs cost me many years of my younger life, but I'd do it all again to see her face and write to her. I'm a crazy motherfucker with a screw loose, obviously.

"She's trying to run away in a half-ass attempt to deter my fucker of a father from marrying her off, which he plans to do soon."

My fists clench. The thought of her with someone else makes me see red. Blood red. It's something she mentioned multiple times in letters. She was always adamantly against an arranged marriage, and over time, I was, too.

I didn't want to share her with anyone else.

"Okay, I'm listening."

"I need you to keep an eye on her here for a while. She's sheltered. I don't want her to be taken advantage of, but I want her to live the life she wants until I can figure something out to help her."

"Why don't you want to keep her with you?"

"Someone tried to take me out last week." He points at the graze on the tip of his ear.

"Fuck, it got close."

"Exactly. I don't want anything to happen to her."

"Why me? Wouldn't you want someone further away? Your dad's still pretty close."

"They won't expect her to stay so close to Chicago, and I trust you with my life and hers. I know you'll keep her safe."

"I will."

"You can befriend her, but keep your dick to yourself, as well as every other dick in town."

And there it is. I'm totally fucked.

"When's she coming?" I try not to sound too interested. Too eager. My pulse is in my ears, and my palms sweat in anticipation.

"A month, maybe less. I've been monitoring her text messages. Not sure if I'll have to bring her myself or if she'll come on her own, but take this just in case." He hands me something from his pocket. A photo. I flip it over, and my heart rate picks up.

She's just as beautiful as I remember. Still the same angelic face with that ever-present smile, and again, I'm flying too close to the sun. Feeling the warmth.

I flip the photo over and school my features. Gage doesn't need to see how a mere picture of her affects me.

When I place it in my pocket, it feels like it's burning a hole in my leg. I itch to take it back out and give it another glance. To rub the face in the picture.

"Got it. I'll protect her. No worries." I shrug.

But there are many worries. Big fucking worries. More worries than he will ever know.

"Thanks, bro. I owe you one."

He can trust me with anything... besides his sister.

Fucking kill me.

"That's what family's for." I clap him on the back. "Now, let's give you some ink. I know your ass didn't come all this way just to chitchat with me."

"You know me well. How much time you got?"

"For you, my schedule's wide open."

"Fuck yeah. Let's fix some of this shit you did when we were younger," he says, referring to the not-so-great prison tats I gave him. He was my first canvas.

"Hey, what do you expect, motherfucker? I was limited on supplies."

"Let's start with the first one," he says, looking down at the name of the girl who has been his everything since day one.

"You ever get your girl back?" I ask while I set up.

His face lights up with a huge-ass grin.

"Something like that," he says cryptically. I wouldn't expect anything else.

Fuck it. I'm already in too deep, with no way of making it out whole.

I tried to make her hate me, to make this easier on both of us, but it's not working.

I put the pen to the paper.
Dear Rosie.

Seven

Rosie

The moment Vic leaves the coffee shop, my new coworker, Samantha, comes barreling toward me with a scowl on her face. *Great.*

"So, what's going on with you and Vic?" she asks with an icy stare, something I'm assuming she tries to do to intimidate people.

"Not a thing. He's my brother's friend," I say, keeping it brief. I don't know if they have a past, if she's waiting in line for her number to be called, or if she's just jealous, but I'm not a fan. I don't like mean girls.

"Okay, good. Because he's bad news. I'd hate to see you get hurt," she says, not sounding at all worried about my physical well-being.

I look over at her, and recognition hits.

Blond hair, scowl, and screechy voice. She's the girl he threw on the bed the first night I came. She has to be. I felt like she was a little snappy with me this morning, but I thought she just wasn't a morning person. Looks like she and I won't be forming a friendship anytime soon.

"No worries. I'm not interested in Vic," I say as I resume stocking the rest of the coolers with pastries and ignoring her stare.

The last person I'd be interested in is Vic. Well, he comes in a close second to Manuel, my hopefully ex arranged marriage fiancé. Vic is a jerk and has weird mood swings. Let's not forget about his endless roster of women. Just thinking about that reinforces the reason I'd never be interested in him.

"Good," she all but snaps before stomping away to help a customer. Hopefully, that will suffice, and I'll stay off her radar.

Jess kneels next to me and gives me a reassuring smile. "Don't worry about her, girl. She's harmless, but jealous a certain someone isn't paying her the attention he's paying you."

"I don't want his attention."

"You sure? Every girl wants him in this town. They always have, and if they were getting his attention, they'd be all over him like a popsicle on a hot summer day."

"But not you?"

"Absolutely not. He's practically a brother to me."

"So then Axl...?" I say, wiggling my eyebrows.

He came in this morning and bugged her until she made him food. Then, he paid her in compliments and money three times the amount needed to pay for the food. I watched their entire exchange with a smile on my face. He loves to provoke her, and she always rises to the challenge, creating a dynamic of playful banter. He even brought her a gift. She opened it in her office and refused to show any of us girls, which only intrigued me more.

After he left, her cheeks flushed with a bright shade of red, and she persistently rubbed her palms along her apron as if they were sweaty.

There's a story there, and I can't wait to hear it. I guess he did hear my suggestions when we were in the pool.

Jess scrunches her nose as if smelling something awful. "He's a total manwhore and a jerk."

"But you were something?"

"Unfortunately," she says with a sigh, "we've had moments in the past that I wish I could erase forever. Just thinking about them makes me want to bleach my brain."

"He's still kind of cute," I say with a shrug. I'm privately rooting for Axl, the underdog, with his endless questions on how to fix things with Jess.

I'm a sucker for a happy ending.

"I can't wear this," I mutter as I stare at myself in the mirror inside the fitting room of the boutique a couple of doors down from the tattoo shop.

Char, a friend of Jess's, came into Sweet Escape yesterday, and we got to talking. She runs Burnouts, the local bar in town. When Char mentioned I could work a few weekend shifts, I immediately said yes. I want to escape Vic and his domineering presence while making a little cash on the side.

So here I am, uncomfortable as hell in practically nothing, but Jess says I need seduction attire to fit in. Initially, I was confused about the meaning, but I'm beginning to understand.

Despite feeling completely out of my element and a little anxious, I remind myself that it's exactly what I need and have always wanted. Half of me is worried someone might recognize me, but my father or anyone else looking for me would never guess I'd be working in a bar.

A library or a painting studio? Definitely. A bar? Never.

"What? Why? Back up a little. You should add a choker necklace," she says as she squints through the other side of the phone. We're on FaceTime since she couldn't leave her shop.

"I've never shown this much skin," I say as I stare at the outfit with trepidation. The black leather skirt is a little short, stopping right under my ass with a slit going up the right side of my hip. My bra and cleavage are on full display thanks to my barely-there mesh crop top.

"You look amazing."

"It's not too much? Or I guess, too little?"

"It's modest compared to the other girls, which is better. It leaves things to the imagination." She wiggles her eyebrows, making me laugh.

"Is it silly that I'm nervous?"

"Not at all. You're in a new place doing something out of your comfort zone. But you'll be fine. I promise. Just make sure you wear this outfit. I'll come see you after I close."

"I'd like that. It would be nice to see a familiar face."

"Oh, I'm sure you'll see a couple," Jess says with a huge grin.

The curtain gets ripped open, and I spin around with a shriek. Vic stands in the doorway with a murderous look in his eyes.

"Oh my God. You scared the crap out of me," I say placing my hands over my chest. "Get out of here."

Vic looks down at me before stepping in and closing the curtain of this tiny fitting room.

"Jesus, get out. They're going to think we're... we're—"

"Fucking?"

I slam my hand across his lips to stop any other crazy things from coming out of his mouth. "Shh."

He's still as we stand face-to-face until I feel a wet sensation on my palm, which is pressed against his lips. I pull my hand away and look down at it shine in the dismal light.

"Did you just lick my hand?"

A smile is his only answer. He's trying to irritate me, and it's working.

"Just leave the way you came and stop following me," I whisper-hiss.

"No," he says as he waves his index and middle finger in my general direction. "And no to this outfit."

"Why?"

"Because it's too—"

"Too what?"

"You have nowhere to wear it."

"Yes, I do."

"Where?"

I stop myself before saying something stupid. "Just around the house."

"Fuck no. Put it back."

"I'll wear what I want. When I want. Where I want."

Vic takes a step toward me. "I'm in charge of you, which includes your body and virtue, if it's still intact. If you wear this, it'll be more trouble than I want to deal with. I also know for a fact you'd never wear this. It isn't you."

"You don't know shit, and my virtue's none of your business. Get out now... before someone sees you."

Vic gives me one more look from head to toe. "Hurry up and get back to the shop."

"I'm not on company time. I'm on my lunch, so I'll come when I'm done. I'm also tacking on another ten minutes since you're wasting my private time."

"Fine," Vic mutters before ripping the curtain open with a loud squeal and stomping out the boutique's front door.

"Geez, that was intense. Is that how all your interactions go?" Jess asks.

"Pretty much. He's such a dick."

"You should have seen the way he was looking at you in that outfit. He looked pained." Jess laughs as an alarm goes off. "Crap, there goes the oven. I have to go. See you tonight."

"Okay. Thanks, Jess."

"Always," she says before hanging up.

I look back in the mirror one final time. The outfit is totally too much, but now I'm determined to wear it because he said no.

Who the hell does he think he is?

Besides, it's not like he'll see me, anyway.

Once Vic and I get home after yet another silent car ride, I rush to my room and lay out my clothes. I'm too excited to care about his shitty mood. I swear, he needs a chill pill or a smoke. He's taking his guard job a little too seriously.

I hear him walking down the hall, but pay him no attention. I can feel his presence at my back, but I continue setting out my new clothes. All I've worn are the couple of pieces I threw in my bag at my parents' before I snuck out, so I'm pretty excited to wear something new.

"I'm going out."

"Have fun."

"You're not gonna give me shit about you staying home while I go out?"

"Nope."

"Okay." He takes a step but stops. "Oh, I almost forgot. This was in the mail for you."

I turn around, and my blood drains from my face as Vic hands me an envelope. I know exactly what it is once I see the writing on the front.

I rip it from his fingers and hold the thin paper between my hands and heart.

I look up at Vic with a tight smile. "Thanks."

His head tilts as if he's curious. Probably wondering why I'm holding a simple envelope like it's the answer to world peace. It's none of his business, and I just hope he hasn't gone through the letter. I don't need him telling Gage I've been corresponding with one of his friends for years.

"What is it?"

"Nothing."

"Doesn't look like it from the way you're holding it."

"None of your business."

He doesn't move, so I huff out an irritated breath. "It's just a friend. We like to write each other letters."

"There's this cool thing called a phone. Don't know if you've heard of it. You received these things called phone calls and text messages."

I put my fingers over my lips as if shocked. "No way! You think I can get one after school?" I roll my eyes. "I wouldn't expect you to understand."

He walks away from my room without a word.

I close the door with a kick of my foot and rip the seal of the letter, giving myself a tiny little paper cut in my haste. I suck on the pad of my finger as I grab the letter inside with my other hand and shake it out of the envelope. I've lost my careful handling.

I want to know what he has to say.

I want to know his excuse for dropping me without a goodbye.

We never discussed when there would be an end to our letters. He even continued to write to me when he got out, then, when I went to college, and then nothing.

Radio silence. But the silence was loud.

He became a daily thought over the years. I told him my victories, defeats, dreams. Big and small, he heard it all.

His disappearance hurt like hell. It was like a loss. I mourned him as I did with my brother when he stopped writing. Anyone would have felt as I had once you've spoken to someone for years. I was such a masochist for months after the letters stopped. I went by my PO Box in town weekly, sometimes multiple times a week, just to put my key in the lock, open it, and see it empty.

All I could think of is the last letter I wrote him, testing the water on meeting him. I asked in the early stages of our letters, and he always let me down gently. I stopped asking until my last letter while in college.

I wanted—no, needed—to see the man I'd poured my heart and soul out to over the years.

Would we get along as well as we did through paper? He told me I should reach for whatever I wanted in life, no matter the repercussions. That my art was a gift and not some stupid hobby, as my father would say. Or would we debate, as we sometimes did, on the importance of my love for rom-coms over his action and horror? Him being opposed to them while I was for every-thing: rainbows, butterflies, and love in movies; no gore or death for me. Or him believing it was a necessity to dunk chips in his milkshakes while I thought that was disgusting. Soggy chips, no thanks.

But once the letters stopped, I wish I could hit rewind and go back to before I wrote the last one.

Maybe I pushed too hard to meet him? Maybe he got bored? Maybe he found someone and decided to devote all of his time to them?

I need to know.

I rip open the letter and see one line. One fucking line. One fucking sentence.

Dear Rosie,

You brought heaven to earth in that angel costume.

- Rush

Angel costume?

As I place my hand over my heart, a rush of thoughts over-whelms my mind. I'm transported back to the chaotic college party from months ago. The guy I danced with. It had to be him. He held on to me tight. Even when Marco showed up, I

79

distinctly remember him squeezing me before he let me go, as if he was attempting to savor the moment like a lover would. Like he needed one more second with me. Or at least that's what my mind conjured up.

But why didn't he say anything then, and why is he barely writing to me now?

And how the hell did he know where to send the letter?

Eight

Vic

I need to finish my ledger and supply order, but here I am, watching Rosie dance around the kitchen through one of the many cameras inside my house. I should mention their presence to her. It's the right thing to do, but a part of me relishes in the sight of her dancing freely, unaware of my knowledge. Something I'm sure would stop as soon as she found out. I could say the cameras were solely for her safety, but it would be a lie.

My nerves were at an all-time high as I handed her the letter, and the only thing that brought me comfort was her expression. She was as white as a ghost once she saw it before ripping it from my hand and holding it to her chest.

The letter is the closest I'll ever get to her. Being in her head will have to suffice, because I'll never be in her heart or even in her pants.

If she knew it was me who'd been writing to her for years, she'd probably kill me in my sleep, not that I've given her the chance. I haven't used my bedroom next to hers since she's moved in. I've been too scared that I would wake up next to her.

I've gotten too close at one point already, and it could have spelled the end of my friendship with her brother.

Six Months Ago – Devils and Angels Night

I watch her from across the overpopulated, smoke-riddled room.

Trust fund college idiots downing shot after shot like it's holy water. Assuming it will somehow cleanse them of all their sins and transgressions tonight.

The scent of regrets, weed, and overpriced perfume fills the air. If these are what we have to look forward to for our future world leaders, we're fucked.

But I'm not here for them.

I'm here for her.

The girl I have written to for years.

She knows me better than anyone, and I can't get her or her last letter out of my mind. She pleaded with me to meet her, which I've refused in the past, but this was different. Her letter dripped with depression and loneliness, something I've been familiar with my whole life.

Child with dead parents who cared more about their next fix than their kid, check. Foster kid with abandonment issues and an empty fucking stomach, check. Runaway teen with anger issues and a need for violence and adrenaline, check.

Now, I'm the twenty-one-year-old who just paid twenty dollars for entrance to a frat party with a stupid fucking devil mask on as I watch the angel that I can't get out of my head. She said she'd be at this party if I wanted to meet her.

I never replied. I wasn't sure if I was going to attend until earlier today. I searched high and low for a devil mask and finally found one after five stores.

Her bright smile lights up the otherwise dismal kitchen. I watch as she talks animatedly to a girl from her art classes that I may or may not have followed her to multiple times.

Her head tilts back as she laughs again, showcasing her delicate neck that would look so much better with my hands wrapped around it.

Her angel costume is modest compared to all the other girls wearing lingerie, but she stands out. The fact that she's so covered up makes her that much more alluring and sexy.

I look around to see if anyone else is gazing at her as I have been since she's entered the stuffy mansion. All I see is carbon copy after carbon copy of arrogant, rich frat boy jocks. These guys go for the easy target. They want the kind who falls into their lap with no work. No finesse or skill. They want instant gratification, or they move on to their next unfortunate target. One that will put out and be disheartened when the guy inevitably moves on, maybe even shedding a tear or two.

The difference between these college wastes and me is that I'm a man. One who grew up without the silver spoon shoved down his throat. One who practically died at the neglect of his parents, then went to prison and knows how the real world works and can survive it. Not someone who will join Daddy's firm or corporation and run it when Daddy retires early to spend time with his sidepiece on a yacht. Then run it into the ground because they have no idea how it really works.

I kick off the wall when I see her friend pulling her toward another room. I stroll behind them with a warm beer in my hand that I don't plan on drinking. A passerby in another poorly planned devil costume stops them, his eyes raking over Rosie and landing on her breasts for a moment longer than necessary. His arm shoots out in what she's assuming is a friendly gesture of him squeezing her shoulder as his thumb runs across her exposed skin. The red cup snaps under my grip from the pressure of my fist. The warm amber liquid runs down my fingers as I watch the moment unfold.

What has me continuing to watch while staying rooted in place is how she shrugs his touch off. She shows her disinterest and effectively dismisses him before grabbing her friend's hand and towing her away.

My lip curls into a grin as I watch the Lucifer wannabe sulk as he walks away. The fucker's lucky I won't be chopping off his hand for his idiocy of touching her.

I place the mangled cup on a marble table and follow them to a large sitting room. They pushed the furniture against the walls to make room for a makeshift dance floor. A DJ sits to the far right. The music blares in my ears.

When I got out a year ago, the world felt loud, a sensory overload.

I used to be drawn to and thrived in the chaos and commotion of loud and crazy gatherings. But now I find solace in the peace and stillness. However, I prioritize her needs over my own comfort.

She's everything.

She begins to sway her hips to the beat. I was only planning to watch her tonight, as I've been doing routinely since getting out, but I can't. I won't. My feet take me over to where she is instantly.

Her eyes are closed as she dances, but she must sense me because her eyes open when I'm a few feet from her. She blinks and wets her lips before she tilts her head up to gaze at me. I'm far taller than most of the guys here.

She takes in my red and black devil mask that conceals my identity with curiosity.

Does she know it's me?

She gives me a small nervous smile before continuing to dance. Her back turns, and I take that as my invitation. My front presses into her back. The mask obstructs my nostrils, but her scent still passes the barrier. A sweet and flowery scent envelops me, tempting me into devouring her right here, right now. But I don't. I just keep her close.

No one will get near my sunshine now that I'm with her.

I groan at how her ass grinds against my cock. It gets even harder as I wrap my arm around her midsection, just under her breasts that sway as she dances. Their weight feels like heaven against my arm.

Her hand wraps around the back of my neck, and her nails stroke the skin there, making me close my eyes. A shock wave of goose bumps takes residence all over my skin. It's driving me insane in the best way possible. I savor the moment of her against me.

This is the boldest and best move I've made yet, and I don't regret one fucking moment.

We continue to dance as a slower song comes on. I'm enjoying the change of pace and how it feels like she's practically giving me a lap dance while we're both standing. My arm around her midsection drops lower as I pull her flush against me.

I don't want this moment to end, but I have to tell her it's me. I can't wait.

I bend my neck to her ear when someone pokes me in the back, ruining the moment. I turn around, ready to slit the intruder's throat.

"She's off-limits, bro. Get your fucking hands off her before I break them and you can't ride again."

My spine straightens at his choice of words.

Did he see me arrive, or does he know who I am?

I look over at a face I've looked at for years. But not the one I'm affiliated with. Not the one I trust with my life. No, her other brother, who's clearly pissed at my hands wrapped around his little sister.

I should be going anyway before I do something more fucking idiotic than what I'm currently doing.

I gaze down at Rosie, who's gone still in my arms as she looks at her brother with a mix of shock and embarrassment at her compromising position.

My hand that's wrapped around her waist squeezes her to me one last time as I savor the feeling of her being so close. I slowly pull away and leave, knowing she'll be safe with him. I might hate the guy, but at least I can count on that.

I can't help but shake my head when I think about tonight. I'm a stupid motherfucker for coming out here and getting way too close. If Gage had found me with her, he would have killed me.

She is everything to me, but I can't lose Gage after everything he and I have been through. She could meet me and hate me. Then *leave me just as Mom did. I can't have that. Gage's friendship is safer. Friendships are always safer than something romantic.*

This will be my last time following her. This will be my last time watching her. And this will be the last time wishing she was mine. I won't be writing her back. I can't.

I hear a knock, and Axl comes in wearing a huge grin. "You ready to head to the bar? The guys said there's fresh meat tonight."

The guys are idiots. "Yeah, I'm almost set."

I tilt my head toward the trash bags. "You mind taking these out for me while I get changed?"

"Where's your little apprentice to help with this bitch work?" he asks, referring to his little brother Samuel.

"I let him out early for good behavior, which is a lot more than I can say for your ass. Hickeys are trashy as fuck, by the way," I say, pointing at his neck.

"They're only considered trashy if you can see them."

I raise my eyebrow at him. "Take out the trash, you trashy motherfucker." Ax laughs as I shut down my laptop for the night.

"Hey, they're fading. I'm taking your girl's advice, anyway."

"I don't have a girl."

"Yeah, okay. It seems like it with the way I see you lookin' at her when you think no one's paying attention. I was tempted to rub one out with all the tension in the gym between you two this morning."

Even though I know he's fucking with me, the thought of him touching himself while thinking about Rosie pisses me off. "What's with all the chatter tonight? I thought you wanted to head to the bar?"

Axl rolls his eyes as he hefts the trash bag over his shoulder and walks out the door. I busy myself with changing out of my ink-covered jeans into a pair of fresh ones before going out to the front.

Axl comes back in as I'm turning the lights off and getting my things together. "Let's do this," he says, rubbing his hands together.

"You going to behave tonight or nah?" I ask as I lock the door and walk to my bike, right next to his.

I rarely get the chance to ride with him anymore, as my parole officer constantly reminds me of my club affiliation ban if I want to stay out of prison. But tonight, I don't give a fuck.

I'm wound too fucking tight, and I need this moment of freedom provided by the road.

"Fuck no," he says as he hops on and starts his bike.

Instead of sticking to the main road, we opt to take a long detour through the hills. With only the moon and the faint glow of our bikes' light guiding the way, it makes me feel free. This has always brought me the most peace and put me at ease.

We reach the bar sooner than I'd like and park our bikes next to the other brothers' bikes. It's already packed. Rock music blares, and the smell of beer and smoke permeates the air.

In the bar, my gaze wanders until it rests upon them, clad in black leather kuttes, comfortably seated in the large dimly illuminated booth on the left side. Their infectious laughter mingles with the melodic clinking of glasses.

I make my way over there first, with Axl at my side.

Trey, Marcus, and Julian are in a discussion about who the fuck knows what when we slide into the booth. The three twentysomethings lead the club. Trey took his pop's place as the president, Julian as the vice president, and Marcus as the sergeant at arms.

They don't miss a beat, arguing about dibs on some unfortunate piece of ass. I shake my head. *Good fucking luck to her.* I might have specific tastes regarding the shit I like, but these three will ruin someone. They all like to share and shit. Definitely not my style, but I've kept no one long enough to care.

My thoughts drift as I listen to them bicker. I try to tune them out as per usual until someone comes up to the table and starts grabbing glasses.

That's when the scent hits me, a floral-fruity smell. The signature scent of my obsession.

I inhale deeply and let the scent wash over me. I can't get her out of my fucking mind. I need a drink.

The sweetest voice I've ever heard graces my ears. Smooth and sweet but with a raspy tone when she's nervous. But that's not the voice I get directed toward me. I get the irritated voice.

My head snaps up as soon as Rosie asks the table if they'd like her to get anything else.

I slowly look her up and down. My blood is fucking boiling. So much for the calming ride here.

She's in the outfit from the fitting room that I told her not to get. It shows every curve of her delicate, flawless tanned flesh and makes me want to bend her over and spank the living shit out of her.

She looks delicious, and I hate that everyone gets to see it.

How the hell did she even get a job here, and how did I not know about it? The club owns the bar.

She doesn't know anyone in town, and there's no way she's been sneaking here. I'm always here.

I look around the bar and spot Jess talking to Char. Bingo. Jess must be helping her, even after I told her the very short version of the situation. What a little traitor. And I grew up with her, for shit's sake.

I look over at Ax, who has a smile on his face like he knows shit's about to go down between me and Rosie with her blindsiding the fuck out of me.

I sidetrack him by nodding in Jess's direction as she now talks to some guy in khakis and a polo. Ax gets up right away without a word. *Payback's a bitch, Jess.*

Rosie looks around the table until she spots me, then pauses. Her eyes go wide in shock before shifting her gaze and looking back at the guys. She didn't expect to see me here, which pisses me off even more. How long did she think she could hide working here from me?

"Oh, there's something you can get me, beautiful. What are your plans after work?" Trey asks with a bright-ass smile as he leans in closer to her.

"Just going home," Rosie says as she looks at me. Smart girl.

"How about you have another drink with us?"

"Two's my limit. Is there anything else?"

She's been drinking? I peer into her eyes, which are a glassy green with a hint of red.

She won't be working here after tonight.

"We'll just have another round of beers," I mutter abruptly before she's able to answer.

This is who they're talking about. The fresh meat. Rosie. My Rosie. Over my dead fucking body.

The guys and I have been friends for fifteen years, but there's no way in hell I'd let any of them touch her. The thought makes my heart beat faster and my fists clench.

She isn't under my skin. She's in my veins. The very blood that pumps through my heart.

"Of course. Coming right up," she says and scurries away.

My gaze fixes on her ass; her leather skirt creeps up with each stride she takes. My hands form fists as I look around to see if anyone else is noting the way she looks the way I am. There are a few, and it doesn't help the smiles she gives each customer. Those smiles aren't meant for them.

What am I going to do with her?

"Bro, what was that about? We're trying to ease her into coming home with us tonight. Not scare her away," Trey says while narrowing his nearly colorless eyes at me. They give him a sinister appearance, accompanied by tattoos—mostly intricate sacred geometry pieces courtesy of me—covering his shaved head and the rest of his body. Rosie would never go for someone like him. "She'll be perfect. She's a little innocent, but I'm sure—"

"Dibs," I say for the first and last time.

Since we've been kids, they've always called dibs on girls they wanted, and whoever said it first got the girl, making the other guys back off. The competition was fierce since we live in such a small town, and the options have always been limited. Now, it's apparently my turn.

"Nah, bro, we saw her first. Also, what the fuck? You've never dibsed a chick before," Julian says, looking shocked before blowing a kiss to someone walking by. Now, he is someone she might go for. Julian has that easygoing smile, fuck-boy hairstyle, and diamond earrings you could probably see from space. I don't like the thought of them together.

I shrug. "Now I have."

"Damn, Vic, never thought I'd see the day," Marcus mutters as he takes another pull from his beer. He won't argue with me claiming her because, frankly, he doesn't give a fuck. Where Trey and Julian are demented social butterflies, he's stoic and unapproachable. His imposing, well over six-foot frame, wild shoulder-length hair and beard, and face adorned with tattoos contribute to his 'stay the fuck away' demeanor.

Trey looks over at me. "Why her?"

"She's off-limits."

"How can you say that when you've just seen her?"

"She lives with him," Ax supplies as he scoots back into the booth.

"She's your girl?" Trey asks.

"No."

"Long-lost family?"

"No."

"Then what's the deal?"

Ax stays silent. I told him not to tell anyone who she was. It's safer that way even though I trust the guys with my life.

Ax personally knows Gage and realizes how big of a mistake it would be to touch her. I'm not sure the guys would be as worried, and I'm apparently an idiot who knows and is still tempted to touch the fire that is Rosie.

"She's just mine. Dibs."

"Fine, hands off..." Trey mutters as he looks over at Ax, who's still watching Jess sitting at the bar.

Ax and Trey had a falling out when we were younger–around the time I got popped–over something similar to this, and their friendship still hasn't recovered. It even put a strain on the MC with how much they were at each other's throats. Now they ignore each other and only communicate when necessary. Needless to say, we all take it seriously now.

Rosie returns with the drinks while the guys sulk and just offer a thanks. No more comments from the three stooges.

I let her walk away, knowing it won't be the last time I see her tonight.

"Shit. We gotta go. See you guys later," Trey, Marcus, and Julian all vacate the booth. Probably found a poor soul to corrupt for the night.

"So, you finally did it."

"Did what?"

"Staked your claim," Ax says with a huge grin.

"It was just a statement. No one is going to touch her," I say with a shrug before taking a healthy drink of my beer to extinguish the flame raging inside me when I think about her with another guy.

"Yeah, I'm sure. Looks like your statement didn't get the message," he says with a head nod toward one of the other tables with a couple of guys.

I turn and find Rosie with some fucker's hand around her waist. Her body is rigid, and she's clearly uncomfortable.

I hear Axl curse under his breath as I shove him out of the booth. I waste no time getting right behind the fucker who thinks it's acceptable to touch what's mine.

Tapping on his shoulder, he turns, releasing Rosie. I don't even think before I knock his ass out. He hits the floor with a nice thump of his head, and all hell breaks loose.

His friends rush me, and I feel like I'm in my element. Bring it. I know Axl won't be far behind covering me, so I'm not worried.

This is another statement I must make. No one will place a finger on her ever again.

The other guy is no match. He runs around the table, charging me. What he doesn't know is I've been fighting all my life. Both trained and untrained. He runs right into me, but I expected it, so I grab hold and twist, driving him right into the ground, knocking his breath right out of him. He might also have a broken arm from the crack I just heard. I bend down since he's still conscious, unlike his handsy-ass friend.

"This is our town and our bar. Find yourself somewhere new, or I'll bury you."

Thirty years ago, the club found its beginnings on this very soil, and this bar served as its original clubhouse until the club made enough revenue to find a more secluded and protected plot of land. The townies know not to fuck with us, especially in here, so these idiots must be from out of town.

Both guys grab an arm each while struggling to lift their friend, whose head lolls to the side as he's still in a daze from me knocking him out.

I turn and see Rosie, who looks stunned and as white as a ghost. I take a step toward her when I get intercepted by someone I don't want to be on the bad side of.

"You boys done, or do I need to hose you down to cool you off?" I glance down, and my gaze softens. Charlotte, Trey's dad's

94

old lady and one of the few women I trust. Char's been a mother figure to me since I was a kid.

"Sorry, Char," I say, watching as she shakes her head, causing her short jet-black hair to sway against her neck before she walks away. I'll be hearing about this one later.

I head back to the table where Ax is sitting to grab my phone. I'm ready to go, and Rosie will be, too, once I find her.

"So that was fun. I like this new Vic. He hasn't been out to play in a long-ass time," he says with a grin.

This is my ugly side, and I like to keep it locked up tight. I've channeled my rage into other parts of my life, like working out and sparring with the guys, which won't get me locked up again.

Freedom means more to me than chaos and destruction. Tonight was a slip, but I don't regret it.

Not when it comes to her.

"Don't get used to it. It was a—"

"Statement," Ax supplies with a laugh. "Dude, you're fuckin' screwed, and if you don't see it, you're an idiot."

"And you're a dick. You know that."

"I do," he says, looking like the title makes him happy.

I take a swig of my beer and ignore him while I look around for Rosie.

Nine

Rosie

'Daddy's looking for you, Rosalinda.'

A single sentence from a man with the stench of cheap beer and body odor was all it took to douse my flame and leave me trembling in fear.

It serves as a stark reminder of the things I can't escape.

My family I can't escape.

Then, Vic came, like a dark, twisted knight in shining armor. Though he and I have been at odds, I don't know what I would have done if he wasn't there to save me.

This was a gigantic mistake, but I can't tell Vic that or about the guy's comment. He'd never let me out. I'd be under house arrest, and that's somewhere I never want to be again.

I can't tell him. I won't.

But what if they come back for me? I'm sure once they run back and tell my father what happened, things will get worse.

My lips tremble, and I feel burning behind my eyes at the hopelessness of my situation. I lean against the hall outside the break room on shaky legs while trying to catch my breath. I have to get it together.

"There you are." I lift my head and see Vic advancing on me. He can't see me so shaken. He'll know something's up.

I ignore him and walk around the dark corner, heading to the bathroom to freshen up. My heart nearly flies out of my chest as I'm pulled by the arm and hit the wall with a little thud.

"What—" That's all I get out before Vic's hand wraps around my throat, and his forearm rests between my breasts with a firm hold to keep me from moving.

"Yes, what the fuck are you doing here?" Vic says as he puts a little more pressure on my throat. Not enough to make it difficult to inhale, but to show dominance. Which should unsettle me, but what really unsettles me is how his hand calms me.

My nerves. My anxiety. My crippling fear. The shaking in my hands. It's all gone.

His hand anchors me to the moment and to him, and that's the worst of all.

"Working," I say as I will my body not to think about the newest revelation. "Let me go!"

"No."

"You said I could leave to go to work, and that's exactly what I'm doing. Working."

"Never said you can work here."

"You never said I couldn't. The deal was I could be out when I'm working. It's not my fault you never specified."

"I shouldn't have to. You have more money than all these people combined. Stop picking up stupid-ass jobs. Quit and go home."

"No."

His eyes widen, and he places more pressure against my throat. "No?"

"No!" I scream in his face. I'm sick of being told what to do, and worse, I hate that he's right. But the alcohol coursing through my system is making me bold, bitchy, and slightly tipsy.

Vic looks at me with a sinister smirk on his face that has me regretting the way I just yelled at him.

He removes his arm from against my chest and neck slowly, leaving behind a chill of goose bumps as he steps back.

I look at him, confused, as he just stands there.

In a split decision, I make a dash to the bathroom, but he grabs me by the arm and spins me before throwing me over his shoulder. The air gets knocked out of me, and I'm slightly dizzy from how quickly he threw me upside down.

"Let me down now." *Smack.* The pain that stings my right ass cheek is instant, making me arch my back. "Did you just...?" *Smack.* "Ouch, fucking stop."

"I'll do it again. Stay still and shut the fuck up."

"No, fuck you. Let me down," I say while hitting him against his back and flailing my legs, but nothing gets him to stop walking.

The impact of his next strike lands at the apex of my thighs, eliciting a sharp intake of breath and leaving me rendered speechless as he proceeds down the alleyway.

He's also maintaining complete silence, leaving me to wonder if he's aware of the exact spot he just made contact with.

We stop at a bike, and he flips me over onto my feet. "Get on the bike."

I glance at the long, sleek black bike with chrome metal demon badges near the Harley Davidson logo, then shift my gaze back to him. "No."

He grabs me by my arms and lifts me onto the bike before placing a helmet on my head. "Move, and I'll bend you over my knee and spank the shit outta you."

Did I step into some alternate universe the second I walked into the bar tonight?

This is Vic uncut. He's on a whole other level and still obviously on a high from his fight.

I keep my mouth shut, and my eyes forward as he jumps on the bike, my self-preservation kicking in as I think about how much he seemed to enjoy the altercation and the rage he purged onto those guys.

Not that I ever doubted Vic's capability of keeping me safe, but now I understand why Gage sent me here to him. Rage filled his eyes as he hit those guys, making him appear even darker and more dangerous than usual. He looked ready to commit murder.

I look into the mirror on his handlebars, trying to get a read of the look on his face. Yep, still irritated, but the murder is no longer there.

My fingers run against the smooth leather of the seat. I had no clue he had a bike. It's intimidating, but beautiful.

"What about your helmet?"

"You have it on."

"Don't you want it?"

"It's not required."

"Then why do I have one on?"

"Because if you're dead, you can't be punished. Now, hold on," he yells back to me as the rumble of the engine comes to life.

Did he just say punished?

"My patience is wearing thin," he says.

"Where?" I blurt.

99

He grabs my hands and wraps them around his waist, but I remove them quickly.

"If you don't, you'll fall off."

When I don't comply, he revs the engine, the roar of power filling the air before he speeds off, leaving me gripping his waist. I'm so terrified that I keep my eyes closed the entire ride.

Rush would totally give me shit for not enjoying the moment. The thought of him leaves me feeling confused. I don't even know if I should write him back. Shit, he barely wrote me. Do I just forgive him for dropping me?

As soon as we get home, I attempt to jump off the bike to get away from Vic, but my boot catches on the seat, and I fall to my hands and knees hard.

Despite being known as a graceful, poised dancer, I've been clumsy as hell lately.

I wince and suck in a breath as I survey my stinging bloody palms that took the brunt of the fall. Vic drops to his knees in front of me, and his noticeably bigger, warmer hands grasp mine.

"Shit. You okay?"

"Fine," I say even though I want the ground to open up and swallow me whole. The pain is nothing compared to the embarrassment. I try to pull my hands away, but he holds them tighter and shakes his head.

"Let's get you inside, and I'll patch you up."

Before I can object, he picks me up and cradles me against his hard chest as he walks inside.

"I said I'm fine."

"And I said I'll patch you up." He carries me through the house and into his room before depositing me on his bathroom counter.

He rummages through the vanity and comes back up with a first-aid kit and a smirk on his face.

"What?"

"Your helmet."

"Oh." I raise my hands, but he swats them away, his hands wasting no time in removing the strap. "I didn't know you had a bike."

"I got my first bike ten years ago. I wasn't even old enough to ride yet, but one of the older members, Razor, gave it to me as a present. It was a fucking rust bucket," he says with a spark of nostalgia in his eyes. He looks completely different, and I pause to admire the change. "But once I finally got it running, the feeling of the wind and freedom was incredible."

"That was nice of him. You guys must be close."

"Were. He died a few years back," he says as he clears his throat. "Let me see."

I grimace as I hold both hands, palm side up, for him to inspect. Small pieces of gravel and debris are stuck to the dried rust-brown blood. Vic takes a piece of gauze and wets it under the faucet.

"This might hurt a little." He grabs my hand and rubs the wound gently with the gauze before moving on to the other palm. I'm surprised by his tender touch. It's unexpected.

"Ouch," I hiss as he pulls out a small piece of gravel.

He dips his head and blows on the wound while rubbing the side of my wrist with his thumb. The tender touch makes my heart travel to my throat and close like a vise. Why is he being so sweet all of a sudden?

"Sorry. I'm almost done."

I keep quiet, unsure of what to say. Not wanting to lose this side of him.

While he's engrossed in his task, I seize the opportunity and glance at him. His tongue runs along his bottom lip, just like it does while tattooing. His dark brows, which are the same color as his raven hair and lashes, push into a line as he works. I watch the veins on the top of his hands move as he applies the ointment and bandages. *What is it about men and their veins?*

After finishing, he raises his gaze toward me, his deep caramel eyes resembling the hue of the whiskey I had savored earlier at the bar. They, too, are smooth and give me a warm feeling in my stomach, and I can't look away.

I'm a mess of energy—sexual energy, to be exact. Between the alcohol earlier, the spanking he gave me, his caretaking, and now the dark look in his eyes and his proximity to me, my entire body tingles with awareness and longing. I'm stuck in a daze, watching and waiting for his next move.

Only, I'm the one who makes the move as I reach my hand up and touch the hair that's fallen into his eye. His eyes close for a fraction of a second, as if he's enjoying my hand touching him before they open back up and blaze like an inferno.

As he leans forward, I can feel the heat of his breath against my lips, and I mirror his movement, closing the distance between us.

Our kiss is unhurried and gentle, allowing me to savor his soft lips as they move against mine. Vic pulls back after mere seconds, which prompts me to open my eyes in confusion. His thumb softly grazes my cheek, and I find myself lost in the depths of his gaze, mesmerized by the overwhelming tenderness I see and feel. With a small smile playing on his lips, he leans in and captures my lips once more in a searing kiss.

The bathroom echoes with the symphony of our moans, blending as our hands eagerly explore each other's bodies. I run my hands along his wide back, tracing the sinewy lines of his muscles and experiencing his undeniable strength as his hands glide down my back before grabbing my ass and pulling me closer to him.

Out of nowhere, a loud crack echoes through the bathroom, causing us to freeze in our tracks. The helmet lies on the floor and brings me back to the present.

"Shit," I say as I meet his intense dark eyes. I push him back and hop off the counter.

"Wait," Vic says as I hurry out of his room.

"I can't talk to you right now."

What the hell was that?

It was he who leaned in, but it was my lips that met his. Twice!

That kiss should have felt wrong, but it felt so damn right. I felt flutters of butterflies in my stomach. *Flutters.*

Is this what Stockholm syndrome is? I really hope not. In Baltimore, the underboss's daughter was kidnapped and ended up falling in love with her abductor. She changed after that and even fled to be with her abductor after she was saved. I hope that's not what this is. Although, how could it be? It's not like he kidnapped me, but still. Vic and me? No. We can't.

With the knowledge that Vic is likely to trail me, I forcefully shut my bedroom door and hastily lock it, praying that he interprets this as a clear indication to stay away. I strip off my shirt and skirt quickly.

The door slams against the wall, causing me to jump in surprise.

"Get out!" I say as I try to cover myself.

"No."

"I'm naked."

"You didn't seem to mind at the bar."

"Fuck you."

"Okay," he says as he steps forward with a twinkle in his eye that only promises trouble.

I take a step back and hold my hand up. "Don't you dare."

He searches my eyes, then takes another step forward, bringing his hard chest against my palm. "We can't. We don't even like each other," I say, in a weak excuse to deter him. It sounds silly even to my ears.

"I don't give a fuck." Vic's hands wind into my hair, pulling me to him until his lips are on mine in a crushing kiss.

Vic takes hold of my bottom lip and bites down, requesting entrance into my mouth. I open it slowly with a moan. His tongue is warm, wet, and intoxicating. I hesitantly move mine against his. A moan leaves his mouth and vibrates against my tongue.

I'm floating on a cloud as the kiss turns more urgent. It's dizzying and blissful, stealing my breath. This isn't like our first kiss. This kiss isn't gentle like before; it's consuming and claiming.

Vic picks me up, and I wrap my legs around his waist. He seamlessly continues to devour my mouth with no hesitation and complete expertise. His hand leaves a scorching trail as he rubs up my spine before wrapping his hand tightly around the back of my neck. Pinning me to him, he slowly grinds his hips against my center. My thin thong is no barrier against his hard length bulging through the rough denim of his jeans.

I'm on fire. Burning from the inside out.

I hold onto him for dear life as each grind turns into more of a thrust, each thrust more erratic, more urgent, and rougher than the last. He pushes me into the wall, making me moan louder at his rough handling of me and bringing me closer to ecstasy.

I grab the back of his head, wanting to get even closer to him. I'd be under his skin at this moment if I could.

"Look at me, baby," Vic says breathlessly, the pet name doing strange things to my insides. "You want this. You want me. Look how you're grinding against me. Look at how good we are together," he says near my ear.

My eyes lock onto his as I moan again. This is the most vulnerable I've ever felt but also the most free.

"Tell me you want me," he whispers in my ear as he kisses a trail along the side of my neck before biting down and sucking on the skin above my collarbone.

"I want you," I plead as I hold him tighter. The wounds on my palms are a distant memory. I dig my nails into his back, needing more friction. My breathing becomes erratic the higher I climb. When a wildfire starts at the tips of my toes and works its way through my whole body, I cry out at the intense explosion that wracks me.

As I come down from my high, I open my eyes in shock. I just had my first orgasm ever given to me by someone else against a wall from just kissing and friction.

A couple more thrusts and he's grunting his release and burying his head in my neck as he pants.

I remove my hands from his back that I'm sure are leaving indentions, if not blood. I caress his scalp, enjoying the way his hair feels between my fingers and the sense of calm it brings me. We stay like this for a while as our breathing evens out.

"I want to open my own art studio," I whisper. "My father was never fond of the idea. He had a habit of ruining my paintings by throwing them into the fire if I upset him in any way. That's why I was working at the bar tonight, to save money for a studio. I want to create a place where children can freely express themselves through art, feeling safe and supported. The money you spoke of isn't mine. I'll die before asking my father or even Gage for a handout."

I don't know why I felt compelled to share my dream with him, but as soon as I do, he turns rigid. I realize it was a misstep.

Vic pulls away and looks into my eyes. "Fuck."

"What?" I say as he lets me down onto my very shaky legs.

"Fuck. We just..." He steps back, and his disheveled shirt catches my eye, the collar stretched out from my forceful pull, and the unmistakable large damp spot on the front of his jeans. With a defeated sigh, he lowers his head into his hands and shakes it in disbelief. "Fuck. I have to go."

"Wait, what's the matter?" I hold my hand out to him, only for it to drop when he walks out my door without another word. I hear a door slam, and then his bike starts up before he peels out.

Ten

Vic

Rush,

  Long time no talk. It's a relief to know you didn't encounter a bear or stumble into quicksand, preventing you from getting back to me.

  I guess my first question is, why now? Why not months ago? Why not say something that night? And how do you know where I am now?

  It's a relief to know you're still alive. Maybe I'll talk to you again. Maybe I won't.

  –Rosie

"Who's ready to lose their asses tonight?" Trey asks as he walks in with a blunt hanging from his lips.

"Confident words for someone who lost their Fat Boy last week," Marcus mutters with a mocking smirk.

"I plan on getting her back tonight."

"I'll trade you for your V4R," Marcus says.

"Fuck no! I love the Ducati."

"You should stop betting your bikes, T, or you'll soon have nothing left," Julian interjects.

"The Fat Boy's too clean for you, anyway. She's mine, and I already changed her name," Marcus gloats.

"Don't you dare. Jae is the only name she goes by."

"Jae and Trey?"

"Exactly."

"You're fucking weird."

"All I hear is a compliment," Trey says.

We might be at each other's throats sometimes, but once a week, we come together for our long-standing tradition that dates back to our preteen years. It hasn't always been poker as it is now. As we've grown, it evolved into a safer alternative for the five of us psychos who used to spend this sacred day causing havoc by tagging, fighting, stealing, and partying. Although we still partake in some. It's kept us all close through all the bullshit. Now we bet large amounts of money while smoking blunts and shooting the shit. Even Trey and Ax wave their white flags for the night and leave it to healthy competition.

Strolling in with an air of excitement, our newest member, Samuel, joins our night for the first time. After years of relentless begging, Ax conceded and allowed him to join us, considering he's recently patched in.

The memory of his smile is etched in my mind as they removed his prospect patch and unanimously voted him in as a new member. It probably mirrored the same one I had on my face when I was a teen and got mine, only to lose it a week later.

My luck fucking sucks.

My mood sours until I think about Rosie for the millionth time today. I still can't get the feel of her off me. Not that I want to. But I should. That's why this night is perfect. The guys keep my mind occupied so I don't do something stupid like break down her door and go for round two.

My chair creaks as I tilt it back and look up at her window on the second story through the blinds of the guesthouse.

I haven't spoken to her since running out of her room. I need to figure out my shit.

The first thing I felt that night was relief. I finally gave in to my urges and desires. Then, a form of contentment washed over me as her hand rubbed my head while she was in her post-orgasm daze. Then, the regret kicked in. The *what the fuck am I doing? This can't happen* type of regret. She's not just some chick I can fuck, then ghost like all the others. I felt like a real piece of shit for humping my best friend's sister when I promised I'd stay away from her, and even more so for leaving her confused as hell with a hurt look in her eyes.

Judging by her letter to Rush, it's safe to say she's pissed at the moment. The letter was supposed to give me some insight into her mind and her time here. Maybe she would even talk about me? But I went and fucked it up on both sides. This is all a confusing clusterfuck.

None of this was supposed to happen.

It wasn't supposed to go that far.

It wasn't supposed to go as far as a kiss, but then she did the unthinkable and leaned in for it. She wanted the kiss just as bad as I did.

The thought of getting her riled up and begging for more only to leave her hanging has gone through my head multiple times since she's been here, especially when she gives me shit and tries to drive me crazy.

But then she leaned in and wanted me. Me. Not the me from our letters, but the me who stood in front of her with all my fucked-up parts. Then, she came, and I couldn't help but follow her off the edge. I came in my pants like a fucking teenager. That was a first. The guys would laugh their asses off if they got ahold of this information.

I can't help but go back to the dazed look on her face as she came down from her high. It was beautiful. She was beautiful. Her hair was a tangled mess around her face, and her lips turned swollen and red from our kissing.

"Yo, Vic, it's your turn."

My chair legs hit the floor with a thump and I shake my head. I'm going to drive myself fucking mad if I don't stop this shit.

"You got time for me this week?" Trey asks. "I have a piece I've been thinking about."

"You have room left?"

"Only on my dick. Should take a couple of weeks to finish."

"More like minutes," Ax comments.

"Alright, motherfucker." Trey's chair scrapes across the floor as he stands and unbuckles his pants.

"For the love of God, keep your fuckin' pants on. We've seen your dick enough," Marcus mutters.

"I can squeeze you in. Just get me an ounce of whatever this is." I pass him back his blunt, the relaxed, euphoric feeling hitting me like a fucking train.

"It came from one of my rooms. Been the best run I've had in a minute. I'll bring you a P."

"We're planning to go for a ride next weekend if you're down," Julian says as he puts his cards down.

I shouldn't go. Lately, I've been spending an excessive amount of time on my bike with them, but I can't resist. I miss the powerful sense of brotherhood and the comforting weight of my kutte on my shoulders.

"I'm down."

Before I can stop myself, I lean my chair back one more time. Rosie stands in front of the window while talking on the phone with a huge smile on her face.

Who the fuck is she talking to?

My phone beeps and alerts me to a motion sensor activation on the front left corner of the house despite there being no walkway, just a bush and a fence to the backyard.

"Vic, it's your move. What's got you all distracted?"

"Maybe it's who. Heard you guys got into a fight the other night," Marcus says.

I ignore all of them as I wait for the picture to load.

"You guys expecting anyone?" I ask.

Once the picture appears, I spring to my feet, nearly causing the table to fall. A person dressed in all black with a ski mask is creeping along the side of the house.

"What the fuck's your deal, man?" Ax says as he looks at me, worried.

"Gun. Someone's in the yard. All black with a ski mask." I put my hand out and wait for one to be placed in my hand.

I know they're all packing. I can't carry on my person because of my history, but I have many hidden throughout the house, just in case.

I keep my gaze fixed on Rosie, who remains unaware of the intruder as she talks on the phone.

She better not be talking to a guy.

Trey hands me an anodized gold Glock. Motherfucker would have the loudest-looking gun out there.

"It's my baby. Be good to her," Trey says.

"Marcus, you want to go around the other side of the house?"

"On it," he says, walking out the back door without another word.

I walk out the door of the guesthouse at an even pace. Knowing the person is still on the east side of my house. He's watching me. I can feel it as the hair on the back of my neck stands on end. I turn around as he walks out from the side.

"You walked into the wrong yard, motherfucker."

With the stealth of a ninja, Marcus sneaks up on him from behind and pistol-whips the fuck out of him. The guy falls to the ground with a loud thud.

"Shit. Let's bring him inside before one of your uppity-ass suburban neighbors sees," Marcus says with a huff as he picks up the dead weight.

We move the intruder to the guesthouse, where the guys have already set up a chair and rope. Perfect.

We eagerly rip off his black polyester mask, only to find a stranger in front of us. It's nobody I've pissed off, which is worrisome since he came to my house.

"Wake up, sunshine." Trey smacks his face hard enough that his neck cracks to the side. The man's eyes open to slits, probably feeling the headache from hell from being hit on the back of the head. "I gotta say, you made my night coming to my brother's house unannounced."

The guy says nothing to Trey as he looks around for a way out of this clusterfuck.

"Nowhere to go. Why the fuck are you on my property?" I ask.

The man gazes into my eyes with a piercing stare, his silence speaking volumes.

I'm about ninety percent sure why he's here, and it has to do with the infuriatingly perfect human obliviously talking away on her phone as if someone isn't about to get tortured to death less than fifty yards from her. And if my suspicions are correct, it's fucking concerning how quickly they located her.

I'm just thankful the poker night was here tonight, and I got the alert so quickly.

I fucked up a lot before her arrival, but upping my camera and security system wasn't one of my shortcomings.

"Looks like he's playing the silent game. My favorite," Trey says, "You got a flathead screwdriver?"

I walk to the kitchen and rummage under the sink for my small tool kit. "Will this do?" I hand it to Trey, who looks like he was just given a trophy. This is about to get messy. I reach back under the sink and grab my hidden Glock with the silencer attached before placing it in the back of my pants.

The guy's eyes widen a fraction before he composes himself. Marcus grabs his hand and places it on the poker table.

"We'll give you one more chance. What are you doin' here?" Marcus says.

113

Silence.

"Nothing? Really?" Axl shakes his head. He prefers a quick and direct approach with a bullet between the eyes. Unlike the rest of us, he does not share in our enthusiasm for torturing.

With the flathead screwdriver in hand, Trey forcefully positions it under the guy's nail before wrenching it up. The sound of his nail being torn from the nail bed makes my skin crawl in anticipation. His nail now hangs from a small piece of the cuticle while blood streams from the open wound onto the forgotten cards and table. The man shakes, and a vein bulges from his forehead, but he says nothing.

It's impressive and slightly terrifying.

"Not even a sound? Guess I'm losing my touch, guys," Trey mutters before ripping off the remaining nails from his hand. On the last one, the guy finally cracks and lets out one of the most gut-wrenching squeals I've ever heard. Thank fuck for the soundproof insulation Trey insisted I install when I bought the house.

Trey's smile only gets bigger the more the guy whines. "Talk or I'll start tooth extractions, which hurt a fuck of a lot more than your little hangnails."

"We want the girl."

"What girl?" Axl asks before anyone else gets the chance.

"The princess—"

Without hesitation, I draw my gun and aim it directly at his face.

The overwhelming need to keep Rosie safe compels me to pull the trigger. The absence of remorse engulfs me as the bullet smoothly exits the chamber, whispers through the silencer, and strikes him between the eyes.

"Holy fuck, Vic!" Samuel says.

"What he said. We don't know why he's here, and we were just getting to the fun stuff," Trey whines.

"He said princess, what's that about?" Marcus asks.

Ax looks over at me, and I know he wants to say something, but he keeps his mouth shut. I'll tell the guys about who Rosie is when I'm ready.

I ignore Marcus's question.

"I was tired of listening to him cry like a little bitch. You think you guys can get rid of him before he gets a bunch of blood on the floor?"

"First, you kill the fun, and then you ask for cleanup? What the fuck?" Trey says.

"Sorry," I say with a shrug.

"I guess it's time for some brotherly bonding. Samuel, get the fucker's legs. You too, Ax," Trey says.

"I'll go find somethin' to put him in," Marcus mutters as he walks out the door.

"Best poker night ever. It's going to be hard to top next week, but we can try," Trey mutters.

"Are they all like this?" Samuel asks as he looks down at the dead man.

"No, but I think we should make it a thing," Trey says.

"No," all of us say in unison.

"You guys are no fucking fun," Trey mutters as he hoists the dead man over his shoulder. "Later, Vic."

Eleven

Rosie

I'm assaulted by a mix of vanilla and musty scents as I browse the aisles billowing with books, begging for their second chance at a new home. My eyes scan the titles on each spine as my hand glides against the smooth cedar bookshelves.

The Book Haven is about to become one of my favorite places. It's what I would consider a gem in this little town. They seem to have every book imaginable.

Among my great loves, reading holds a special place in my heart, alongside painting and dancing. They're all art forms and bring you to a place outside yourself and your life. It's a way to feel free, if even for a short time.

I get this from my mama. She has a library I hope to one day emulate with its floor-to-ceiling bookshelves, a ladder that glides across the room, and comfy couches scattered everywhere.

Until I can have a library of my own, this is the perfect place to get lost in for hours.

A refuge that offers a sense of peace.

Few sounds disturb the otherwise quiet old store as I continue to browse.

The wood floors creak as if on cue. I glance to the left, and then to the right, but come up empty in the dimly lit aisle. Only shelves standing still and quiet under the immense weight of all the books crammed on them.

My earlier attempts at finding a book continue until I feel a prickling sensation against my face. Someone's watching me.

My hand rests on a book's spine just as something falls on the other side of the bookcase, but I don't dare move.

My eyes dart back and forth anxiously, but my body remains paralyzed for what feels like an eternity.

The longer I stand there, unmoving like a statue, the more foolish I feel as silence engulfs me again. There's nothing besides me and thousands of books.

My mind is obviously messing with me. I shake my head.

Ever since that fateful night at the bar a couple of days ago, I've been on edge, my heart racing with every little sound. I can't shake the feeling that someone's eyes are fixed on me. The more I think about it, the more I feel the weight of regret for not telling Vic about what that guy said.

When I hear the floor creak again, my heart rate accelerates as a ball forms in the back of my throat.

I grab the book my hand rests on without reading the title and hold it tight to my chest. Quickening my pace down the wall of shelves, I take a hard right further into the back of the bookstore. Passing by many large shelves, I attempt to get lost in the sea of books.

I look around, feeling silly and paranoid when I hear nothing but my ragged breath again.

The bookshelves catch my attention once more, and I eagerly browse the selection of contemporary romance novels. After all of this, I'm in the mood to read something sweet and funny.

As I peer around the shelf, my breath catches in my throat as I spot movement out of the corner of my eye. I crouch down to get a better view and see a white shirt partially covered by a black zip-up hoodie. Then, I smell the telltale sign of cologne. A scent I've become quite familiar with.

One that lingers and travels through the wind to find me.

Suffocating my senses with its sexy, masculine scent.

My eyes narrow, and I rush down the aisle to face him.

He ignores me for days, then follows me around like a creep? I don't get it.

When he first ran out on me, I couldn't help but feel hurt and disappointed. I didn't know what to expect after something like that, but it wasn't him practically running from the scene.

Maybe he was terrified that I confided in him about my dream of opening an art studio. Probably thought I fell for him after the little humping session and was talking about my future.

Once the post-orgasm glow ran its course and he kept his distance, I felt disgusted with myself. I was just another notch for him. I was no better than Samantha, who still hates me because of him.

As I round the corner, I stop dead in my tracks and look at him, casually resting against the shelf, an innocent smile gracing his lips.

"Why are you following me around like some creep when you left me high and dry the other night?" I blurt without thinking.

"If I remember correctly, I didn't leave you high and dry. Maybe high, but not dry," Vic says with a grin. "And I'm not here for you, I'm here for..." He grabs a book. "This."

I peek down at the book he's holding. His long, tattooed fingers splayed against the cover. I try to hold in the laugh bubbling to the surface. The cover captures the majestic beauty of a mountain landscape with a rugged, half-naked man. His dark hair dances in the wind as he rides his horse into the sunset.

I gaze up at Vic with a huge grin as he looks down at the cover with a less-than-stellar expression adorning his annoyingly handsome face.

I nod my head toward the book. "Well, I'm glad you found what you were looking for. Now, if you'll excuse me."

His determined strides toward me make me panic, and I try to turn around. However, his firm grip on my hand prevents me from escaping.

"We're not done here."

I look back at him, narrowing my eyes. "We never started."

He made that apparent when the incident—as I like to think of it—happened, and he left me like a one-night stand gone wrong.

I stride to the front of the bookstore with my only book, the title of which I still haven't seen.

Retrieving my phone from my pocket, I steal a glance. The remaining time for my lunch is dwindling fast.

"Hey, did you find everything you need?" the guy asks from behind the counter.

"Not really, but I'll be back soon."

"Well, I'm always here to help," he says with a little smile.

119

Just as I'm about to answer, the sudden slam of a stack of books on the counter startles me. My gaze swings to Vic, his smile tight and jaw working as if he's holding himself back.

"What's up, Ben?" Vic says in a polite tone that I now know is anything but polite.

Vic's arm falls around my shoulders, and I become motionless, overwhelmed by his touch and possessive gesture. I attempt to shake him off, but he's as resistant as a brick wall. I raise my eyes to meet Vic's. A satisfied smile is plastered on his face. What's his deal?

"Grabbed a couple of books I thought you'd like." Vic's tone is unbelievably sincere for being so fake, making me want to stab him in his gorgeous caramel eyes.

His hand gives me a little squeeze before he retrieves his wallet and slaps a hundred-dollar bill on the counter.

As he bags the books up, I shoot daggers at Vic, who just smiles at my irritation.

"Thanks for coming in," the guy says as he raises the handles of the bag toward me.

I smile while attempting to grab the bag of books.

"Nice seeing you, Ben." Vic grabs the bag from him before I can and ushers me outside.

"Yeah, sure. You guys have a good day."

I stop in my tracks, my heels digging into the ground the second we're on the sidewalk. I whirl around to stare up at Vic. "What the hell was that back there?"

"We went shopping for books. Then, I bought you books. You can say thank you at any time."

"We?" I point my finger between the two of us. "Are nothing."

He narrows his gaze at me. "And the PDA. What was up with that?"

"He was flirting with you and couldn't keep his eyes off your chest. I didn't like it."

"And how is that any of your business?"

"Because I promised—"

"I'm going to stop you right there," I say as I raise a hand. "Your promise to Gage went out the window the second you decided to hump me against the wall."

He cringes and nods his head. "I know."

The moment I bring up my brother, his gaze loses its intensity, and a melancholic air settles between us.

This is why he freaked out the other night. He feels like he betrayed my brother. I'm such an idiot.

That notion definitely stings less than all the other thoughts running through my mind over the past few days.

"Come on, I'll walk you back to work," he says as he turns in the direction of Sweet Escape.

His mood swings are giving me whiplash. Cold and detached, playful and flirty, then territorial and brooding, and then he ignores me, only to repeat the cycle.

I just don't understand.

Jess and I walk up the dimly lit stairs to the middle row. I plop the extra buttery popcorn into my mouth before taking a healthy sip of my Shirley Temple. I sigh with pleasure. The perfect amount of salty and sweet. We find our seats, and I recline the black leather chair back as far as it can go. The tension of the day leaves my body in a flash.

"Shit. Do you have my candy?"

"Yeah," Jess says before discreetly pulling my candy out of her bag. We smuggled our own snacks in because who wants to pay five dollars for one small box? Not me.

I take the Sour Patch Kids, empty them into my popcorn, and give them a shake. Hopefully, they'll be nice and gooey soon.

"What the hell are you doing?"

"Elevating my popcorn."

"That's gross."

"Don't knock it till you try it."

"I don't know about that, but this is by far the best idea after how busy we were today. My feet are killing me," Jess says as she devours her nachos.

"Agreed. We should make this a tradition every week."

"Deal," Jess says as she clinks her slushy with my drink. "They have classics night every Thursday, like tonight, and I'm so down. As long as your guard lets you out, which I'm surprised he did, by the way."

"So am I. I texted him, and all he said was okay."

The mention of Vic has my stomach bottoming out. I haven't told Jess about the incident yet. I'm not even sure how to start. But I have to tell someone. It was big. Maybe not for him, but it was for me. It meant something, but I'm not sure how to feel about it.

I look over at Jess who's reading the trivia on the screen.

"We had an incident."

"An incident?" she asks as she gazes over at me.

"Well, you know how I had my shift at the bar..."

"Yeah, I keep asking, and you keep clamming up. You totally disappeared that night."

"Vic made me leave."

"I figured. I didn't see him either."

"Well, we left, and then we... umm..." I let out a nervous laugh.

"Oh, it's a juicy story. Wait." She reaches over and grabs a handful of my popcorn to throw in her mouth. "Oh, that is good," she says, licking her fingers.

"Told you."

"Okay, continue."

"So, he literally carried me out of the bar, then he spanked me and threatened to do it again if I moved from the back of his bike," I whisper, not wanting any of the other moviegoers to hear the naughty details.

"Wait, he let you on the back of his bike?"

"That's the only thing you're questioning?" I whisper-yell. She didn't even bat an eye when I mentioned the spanking.

"That's big."

"Why?"

"Most of the guys consider it sacred and only let 'the one'"—Jess air quotes—"on the back. Unless you're Trey. He lets anyone with boobs on the back. Stay away from that ho."

"He only let me on the back because he had no other choice."

"Maybe, maybe not. What happened next?"

"Well, then, we got home, and we ended up kissing, and..." Why is it so hard for me to just spit it out? It's my first experience with a guy, so maybe that's why? Geez, I'm a mess.

"Oh, you're blushing. It musta been good," she says with a smile. "You guys hooked up?"

"Well, kinda."

"Kinda?"

"We didn't have sex. We just rubbed against each other until we both orgasmed."

Her smile is the biggest I've ever seen until she's cracking up. "How very middle school of you guys. I love it. Then what happened?"

"He freaked out, and I didn't hear or see him until he stalked me in the bookstore yesterday."

"Well, that's odd."

"That's what I thought. He's so hot and cold with me. Maybe it's for the best since he's my brother's friend, and I'm not even sure if I like him, like him. We just had a moment, and now I feel stupid because I'm sure it meant nothing to him."

"It's not stupid. Did it mean something to you?"

"Maybe... I don't know. I'm lost."

"We all are. That's what having friends is for," Jess says as she pats my hand. "You got to be kidding me."

"What?" I look over at Jess and follow her line of sight. Vic and Axl are at the bottom of the theater steps. *What the hell is he doing here?*

Vic says something to Axl, and he laughs before they split up. Vic makes his way to the set of stairs on my right. He doesn't take his eyes off me as he ascends the stairs. I place the popcorn in front of my face, attempting to block my view of him. I'm feeling awkward about just discussing our incident and then having him materialize out of nowhere. The memories are still at the front of my thoughts.

The heat of his presence looms over me, but I refuse to look up. Acting as if the popcorn container is far more interesting.

Vic grabs the popcorn from my death grip. Yellow kernels of popcorn fly everywhere. My eyes snap up to him. But my glare doesn't deter him. He reaches up to my head, and I slink back into the leather chair. His fingers rest on my scalp for a mere second before he pulls back with a piece of popcorn between his fingers.

"Just cleaning you up." Vic plucks out two more pieces and eats them.

"Stop that," I say, smoothing my hair down only to find one of my Sour Patch Kids stuck. "Shit."

"Let me help."

His fingers go back into my hair, and I look up at him as he delicately removes the sticky mess. Once it's out, he puts the candy in his mouth.

"Mmm... sour and sweet, just like you." I stare at him in shock as he licks his fingers.

I swear, this man has multiple personalities.

Vic smirks at my lack of words before sitting in the chair next to mine. Before I have a choice, my drink is in his hand, the armchair divider is vertical, and there's no barrier between us.

"My drink...?" I ask with my hand out.

He looks down at it before smirking at me.

"No," I say, knowing exactly what he's going to do just as his lips encase the straw and he sucks the liquid into his mouth. His eyes go wide.

"You spiked your drink in a theater that doesn't allow alcohol?"

"No," I whisper, bewildered as I look around with wide eyes, not wanting to get kicked out.

Vic laughs, and the sound goes right to my core. "Careful, Princess, your halo is starting to tilt."

"I have no idea what you're talking about."

"You and I are going to have a lot of fun."

"Now you want to be around me? You're giving me whiplash."

"We'll see," he says as he looks past me. "Ax, taste Jess's drink."

My head whips to my left to see Jess trying and failing to keep her heavily spiked slushy at bay.

I look back over at Vic with what I hope is disdain. "Stalking me twice in the past two days... sounds like you have issues."

"Many, actually. The first being you."

"And what have I done?"

"Nothing you need to worry about."

"Good, wasn't planning on it," I mutter with a shrug as I look back at the screen.

The opening credits begin to roll, and the lights turn down to almost pitch-black.

Vic leans over into my space, his weight pressing me further into my seat, reminding me of when he had his full weight thrusting against me. His lips touch my ear. "Maybe you should," he whispers as he licks my ear, making me suck in a breath of surprise. Goosebumps form on my skin.

My head snaps toward him as he leans back into his seat with another smile. He's driving me crazy, and he knows it.

I lean over toward him, making sure to place my hand on his thigh with confidence I don't have. He looks down at it before we're almost nose to nose. "Keep dreaming, Vic," I say with a sugary-sweet smile.

"I do, of you, every night." My eyes widen at his words, but I know he's just trying to fuck with me. It's just a game. One I intend to play because I'm tired of losing whatever this is.

I lean right under his ear and place my other hand on the side of his neck. I'm sure my touch is throwing him off from the way his breathing has accelerated.

"Sounds more like a nightmare," I whisper. Then I bite the shit out of his neck, making him yelp before pulling away. Hopefully, I drew a little blood.

My satisfied smile disappears as he looks at me with a huge grin. He enjoyed that.

Abort.

I shift closer to Jess, but she's busy dealing with Axl.

"Nowhere to run, sweet little Rosie," Vic says as he kicks his legs up on my reclined chair, moving himself closer to me.

My only win for the night is hearing him groan as he realizes we're watching The Notebook. However, no one mentions the heady feeling you get when a sex scene comes on and you're sitting mere inches from the person you're sexually attracted to. Because, yes, as I sit here next to him, I can't deny that. His personality might be questionable and confusing, but his looks aren't.

My thighs rubbed together more than once as I felt the pulsing ache between my legs, and my heart rate increased as I thought about us the other night.

The feeling of him touching me, rubbing me.

But I didn't dare look over at Vic, who has somehow moved himself even closer to me throughout the movie. First his legs, then his arms. Before I can even comprehend it, he has taken over my chair more than his own. Our bodies press up against each other in a different way. A comforting way. One that has never been introduced to me. A way that if anyone looked at us, they'd think we were cuddling and enjoying the movie together as a couple.

To his credit, he keeps his eyes on the screen, content to sit beside me, and even gave me a tissue as I teared up at the end. Their love was unstoppable, unwavering, and it gets me every time.

Seven Years Ago

Dear Rush,

Hi, I've never written to anyone I didn't know. Well, unless you count school. One year I had to write to a pen pal from a different school, but it ended pretty quickly once we figured out we had nothing in common. But you said you like to draw, so maybe we're off to a good start.

It would be cool if you sent me something. I can send you something in return, although Papa tells me it's a waste of time. I don't think he likes my art very much. Mama does, though, so maybe you will, too? What else do you like to do?

Maybe we should keep this as our secret. I don't want my brother getting mad at you.

Until I hear from you again,

Rosie

Twelve

Vic

"What the fuck is going on in here?" My voice erupts in a yell as I witness Rosie with her shirt pulled up and Samuel leaning over her while she lies on the piercing table.

"Nothing. Get out!" Rosie yells at me while Samuel looks like he got caught with his hand in the cookie jar.

"Like hell." I'm standing over Samuel before he has a chance to get out of my way.

"She was on the books, Vic," Samuel says with his black-gloved hands up in surrender.

"Who put her on the books?"

"Guilty." I look back and see Ax. "My debt is paid."

"Yep. Good doing business with ya," Rosie says with a smile.

"Get off the table."

"I plan to in about five minutes. Right, Sam?" Rosie says as she looks over at him. When did she decide it was okay to abbreviate his name?

"Ah, right."

"No, get up."

"Vic, please." I look at Rosie with those big, pleading eyes, and her plump bottom lip jutted out. I like this look on her.

"Fine." Why the fuck should I care what she does with her body? "Watch where the fuck your hands go, Samuel."

"Chill, Vic, you already told me. I gotta touch her to pierce her, though."

"Well, get it done quick," I say before I look back at her.

She looks like a platter of dessert on this table for me to devour. I know that's not where my head should be. But here I am, standing over her head and breathing down Samuel's neck because I feel territorial of her.

As she moves her arms above her head to give Samuel easier access, the top of her breasts peeks out of her v-neck top. I quickly pull the collar of her white shirt up while pulling the bottom of her shirt down a little farther. It doesn't help that her bra has some kind of pattern on it that can be seen through the white shirt if you look hard enough.

As I gaze over at Samuel, his smirk sends a wave of annoyance through me. I've already caught that little fucker looking at her a few times in the past, and it makes my skin crawl with the need for violence.

"Relax, Vic. What if he messes up?" Rosie says.

"I won't mess up, beautiful," Samuel tells her before looking at me with the same smirk.

If I didn't love him like a brother, I'd kill him.

I reach out and grasp her hand tightly as the needle pricks her skin, causing her to wince. The realization of my lack of control hits me as soon as our skin makes contact. I shouldn't be touching her.

"All done," Samuel says as he helps her up.

"Ah, Vic." I look over at her as she tries to pull her hand from mine.

"Sorry." I let her hand go, feeling a little embarrassed.

She runs to the mirror and looks at her new piercing with a big smile.

She skips back and hugs Samuel, much to my displeasure. "Thank you. I love it."

When she pulls away, he's all smiles and red cheeks. I level him with a glare, and he turns around, making himself busy.

Rosie grabs her bag off the counter and looks over at me with a smile. "Put it on my tab. I'm heading to Sweet Escape to get everyone food real quick."

"You don't have a tab. You won't be getting anything else done."

"We'll see," she says in a singsong tone.

I watch her as she skips out the door, smiling brightly before stopping abruptly to retrieve something hidden in her bag.

I step closer to the window and see a crinkled piece of paper in her hand that she's attempting to smooth out. I step out of the door and look over her shoulder without her even realizing I'm behind her. She has a pen in her hand and is crossing something off.

"What's that?" I whisper in her ear. Rosie's hands go flying since I caught her off guard.

"Nothing."

I rip the paper from her hands before she has a chance to stop me.

"Hey!"

My eyes scan the paper, and I raise my brow. "A list?"

"Nothing gets past you," she says with an eye roll she loves to give me as she tries to rip the paper from my grasp.

"Why do you have these silly things on a piece of paper?"

Her eyes flicker with something close to pain, and I feel like an ass. If she took the time to write it down, it isn't silly to her. I should know this better than anyone, considering our history of correspondence.

"Just give it back."

"Tell me, and I will."

"Those are just things I want to do while I'm free."

"You mean you haven't done any of these things?" I look back at the paper with a frown.

"No. Now give it back."

"What about this last one?" I gaze back at her with a devious smirk.

Her cheeks flush a delightful shade of rosy red, betraying her embarrassment. I reluctantly hand the paper to her, feeling a slight tug as she rips it out of my fingers before folding it and tucking it away in her bag.

"I was thinking. Maybe you can draw for a client coming in tomorrow?"

A radiant smile spreads across her face. "Really?"

"Yeah, I don't have time." A lie. I have plenty of time, but I want to give her this. Despite my frustration that day—between the client and I not meshing artistically and then my constant ache for someone I can't have—witnessing her artistic skills while drawing for that client filled me with a mix of pride and awe. She had a deeper understanding of the client's wants and needs than I did. She has talent, and it would be a shame to see it wasted, especially while she's just sitting in my shop.

"Okay. Be back soon," she says before walking away. "Oh, and Vic?"

"Yeah?"

"Thanks." She looks at me with a sweet smile that nearly brings me to my knees.

I've had disgusted Rosie when we first met, irritated Rosie over those next couple of days, bratty Rosie most of the time, sensual Rosie the night we became more, and now this. Thankful Rosie. This is one of my favorites and almost rivals sensual Rosie. Almost.

I'd love to see her look at me this way more often.

And I plan to.

I incline my head but say nothing. Then, I watch her until she safely steps into Sweet Escape.

I've kept an eye on her every move since the intruder. Who we still haven't been able to identify. I haven't wanted to tell her, though, fearing it would scare her, or worse, she'd tell her brother and he'd take her away. So, I've silently stuck by her side like a creepy fucking shadow.

"Well, you two look nice and cozy," Ax says from his station as I walk in the door.

"No clue what you're talking about."

"You've never been overbearing and protective of any woman. You've been jealous and moody as fuck since she's been here. Haven't seen you with anyone else since the bar."

"I'm watching her for Gage."

"Try again. I've known you for too long. What gives?"

I put my head in my hands and massage my temples. "I fucked up."

"Juicy," he says as he smirks. "How?"

"You remember a long time ago when I told you about a girl I was writing letters to in prison?"

When he connects the dots, his eyes go wide. "No fucking way."

"Yes."

"Does she know?"

I say nothing.

"What about Gage?"

I shake my head.

"He's going to filet your ass." He laughs.

"I know."

"Are you planning on telling her?"

"I don't think I can now."

"Why?"

"Because I fucked up."

"There's more?"

"Yeah," I sigh.

"You fucked her."

I shake my head. "Not exactly."

"So you do have a problem, like Rosie said in the pool."

"What? No."

"I bet I can score you some blue pills."

I massage my temples as a headache forms. "Why am I even discussing this with you?"

"Because I'm your best friend and your servant for the rest of my life."

"You need to quit with that shit. You would have done the same for me," I say as I walk back to my station as quickly as I can.

It's unsettling to see that intense, upset expression in Ax's eyes. The weight of his self-blame has taken its toll on him these past few years, leaving him in a downward spiral. He found solace in partying to excess, numbing his pain with drugs and isolating himself from those who cared about him. The guys said it's been better since I've been out, but he's still not the same.

I guess neither of us are.

Fourteen Years Old

"Fucking go, Ax."

"I can't leave you."

"Only one of us needs to get caught. You have your mom and brother to worry about."

We've been arguing for minutes when time is more precious than ever.

"No, I'm not leaving. You go."

"What about Jess? Her parents just died. If you go away, she'll be all alone."

That statement changes his demeanor instantly.

"But..."

"No buts. Get the fuck out of here," I yell at him just as the sirens get closer. They sound like they're outside.

The other brothers have been long gone. As new patches, our first run needed to go with no hitches. And I thought it did until we heard the sirens, and Julian confirmed so on his computer screen through traffic cams.

We're fucked, and someone needs to take the fall.

There's no time.

I slouch out of the kutte I've worked so hard to earn. This kutte holds hope, brotherhood, and family. Everything I've always wanted.

I hand it to Ax as if it's a priceless heirloom. No way I'm letting these fuckers get their hands on it. He makes his way down the hole, where he'll run through a tunnel for a mile or two, then get picked up.

"I'm sorry."

"There is no sorry between brothers. Take care of everyone."

"Vic."

"Go, Ax," I say as I lock the wooden trapdoor off to the far-right corner of the barn before placing hay bales over it to conceal the secret door. They'll find it. But I want them to find it once Ax is already safe on the other side.

Someone is yelling into a microphone, but I can't make out the words. It's like white noise, and I'm having an out-of-body experience. Everything is going in slow motion, and silence cocoons me. I'm above all the chaos as they ram the door in just as I make my way toward the middle of the barn where crates of AR-15s and AK-47s, and bricks of blow sit.

Men in tactical black gear rush in. Red laser beams target my chest. My hands go up as they stalk toward me.

"Where is everyone else?" Someone shakes me and yells in my ear.

I keep my mouth shut and my eyes forward. I'll never say a fucking word.

"All is clear, sir."

"Fuck!" someone yells. "Rip this fucking place apart. Find them."

I smile, knowing Ax will be safe. It was a simple decision. He has people who love him.

I have no one, and I never will.

Thirteen

Vic

My hands grip both sides of the doorjamb until they ache. I haven't been in her room since the night I thrust my body against hers over and over again.

For not having sex, that was the best orgasm I've ever had. It wasn't boring, as if I was just going through the motions like it usually is. It was raw, real, and the need consumed me. I've never kissed anyone until my lips throbbed, until I was so dizzy from my erratic breathing, and I've never come in my pants like a preteen.

She has ruined me.

Before this, I brought girl after girl home to build a wall between us. I wanted Rosie to keep her distance and be disgusted with me in hopes of keeping me away from her. A stupid-ass plan for sure. Now, I'm living in a continual hell of wanting someone I can't have, but the thought of touching someone else feels like cheating.

I look down at my little angel, who's turning into more of a spicy devil every day. She looks so innocent with her hair splayed out on her pillow like a halo just waiting to be tarnished.

I stroke her cheek with the back of my hand, earning a sigh that gets my dick even harder than it already is. I quickly pull my hand away. I'm not here to watch her like a creep, as she loves to call me.

I rummage through her bag filled with a million makeup products until I feel a piece of paper and flatten out the indents.

~~Sneak out~~
Toilet paper someone's house
Skinny dip
~~Get drunk in a movie theater~~
Get high
~~Get a job~~
~~Go to college~~
~~Go to a party~~
~~Run away~~
Find a new cute town to live in
~~Pierce my belly button~~
Get a tattoo
Find a way to feel like I'm flying
Bungee jump
Paint somewhere beautiful
Get a boyfriend
Make out at a drive-in
Go on the most romantic date ever
Lose my virginity

I can see the progression of her penmanship change and improve through her list, just as it did over the years in the letters she wrote to me.

This list started young. It started off simple. Most of these being something I did as a teen or younger.

The only time I ever felt close to flying was when I rode my bike. Bungee jumping can fuck off. I hate heights. The boyfriend part is a definite no. So are making out at the drive-in or going on the most romantic date ever. What is it with women and romance? And then it ends with a bang. Literally.

When I read that earlier, I was taken aback, and it has been on my mind nonstop. A fucking virgin. I suspected, but I wasn't positive.

That will definitely not get crossed off anytime soon.

I look down at her and think about today. The look on her face as she pulled out her list and her anticipation at crossing it off play on my mind on repeat.

To her, this is more than just a checklist. It's a list of all her firsts, and I can't deny the selfish urge to have her experience them all with me, then watch the happiness bloom across her face as she crosses them off her list.

Her phone rings, signaling an incoming text. I don't hesitate to grab her phone. I've already invaded her privacy. What's one more boundary being crossed at this point?

I tap on the text notification that has Alexa's name across the screen. Rosie's best friend and the center of Gage's universe. He spoke about her constantly. He asked if I had someone, and I didn't, until his sister, but it's not like I could tell him that. So I made someone up since I went from having no letters to having at least one a week. It was the only way for me to prevent him from suspecting, or worse, reading my letters, which were purely platonic but still backstabbing.

I yearned for friendship and the thought of having someone care about me more than anything else. The sexual part didn't start until later, and it just burned brighter as time went on.

The text message thread opens immediately, which means Rosie is comfortable enough not to have a passcode on her phone. This is knowledge I'll shelve because it might be useful later.

She sure as hell won't tell me anything, but I know damn well she'll tell her friend.

I take my finger and scroll to the top of the text thread. It appears to be dated to right after she first got here.

Alexa

How are you doing with Mr. Ugly? Any freedom yet?

Ugly? What the fuck?

Rosie

Nope. Still an asshole dictator.

Alexa

It's a shame. Maybe you can seduce him into giving you freedom. All of your stupid Mafia training classes had to include that to a certain extent, right?

I look down at Rosie. She had to go through Mafia training? What kind of weird shit is that?

Rosie

Even if it did, I wouldn't even touch him with Manuel's dick. I'd probably suffocate him before seducing him.

Who in the fuck is Manuel, and why is she talking about his dick? I'm going to find that motherfucker and kill him. I also find it hurtful as fuck she'd rather smother me than seduce me. She's going to give me a complex about myself or some shit.

Rosie

It's disappointing you never had to do the same training. I could have used a partner in the torture.

Alexa

Not to be a downer, but I don't think you could handle the training I had to do or suffocating the guy, my delicate Ro. Just forget what Gage says and come live with me. I miss you.

Rosie

That's the first place my father would check. I'm going to stay here even though it might kill me slowly. And I miss you, too. Call you tomorrow.

Alexa

My dad called and said your father called him to ask if I knew where you were. Dad, of course, told him no. I guess he was livid, as was Manuel's father. You sure did piss off a lot of scary dudes. You can't see it, but I'm bowing in your honor. I'm pretty proud of you.

Ah, Manuel must be her future intended husband, who will die a slow, painful death at my hands.

Rosie

You can be proud of me once I'm actually free.

Alexa

I'll always be proud of you.

I scroll through memes they sent back and forth until my stomach dips at Rosie's next message.

Rosie

> If a guy told you he would tarnish you, what do you think that means?

Shit. I should've never said that. I was pissed. I brought some-one over to take the edge off, only to not be able to get it up, and then the girl responsible for my little problem—as she liked to call it—poked the bear. Goaded me.

Alexa

> Depends on who said it... tarnish you how? I need details.

Rosie

> My babysitter said, and I quote: 'I will tarnish your little crown of rainbows and butterflies and send you back to Gage before you know what to do with your-self.'

Alexa

> *Damn *flushed-faced emoji*

Rosie

> What?

Alexa

> He wants you bad.

Rosie

> I don't think that's what he meant. It sounded like a warning... or a threat? He also told me to stay away from him.

Alexa

> How was his posture?

Rosie

He was holding my face.

Alexa

Sounds like he wants something he can't have. You can work with that. Buy yourself some freedom.

Rosie

I don't think I can.

Alexa

Why?

Yeah, why?

Rosie

It's hard to explain. I'll talk to you about it tomorrow. I'm going to get some sleep. *purple heart emoji

Alexa

Okay. Good night, Ro. *black heart emoji.

Alexa

Okay, so I met a guy but haven't seen his face, and I might have come when he broke into my house and spanked me senseless.

What in the fuck?

I click the button on the side of her phone to shut it off. Now I feel weird going through her messages. I don't want to see that shit, and if Gage finds out, someone's going to die.

My phone beeps, and I look down. It's like he knows I'm somewhere I shouldn't be.

Gage

How's everything going?

Fucking fantastic. I'm just busy invading your sister's privacy because I can't get enough of her. I also made her come, but don't worry. Her clothes stayed on. Oh, and I'm going insane.

Vic

Great

Gage

Good to hear. I have to get out of Chicago for a minute, but once I come back, I'll come take her off your hands.

My stomach clenches at the thought of her leaving.

Without her here to brighten things up, my life will once again become a dreary, solemn, lonely place. Work, drink, sleep, repeat.

I should be grateful, but I'm not. I'm conflicted. She's wound her way into my nonexistent heart that I've worked so hard not to have. This is why I don't get close. This is why I'm guarded.

She's going to leave me just like everyone else.

Vic

Where's she going next?

Gage

Why?

I shouldn't have asked because it's suspicious and uncharacteristic of me to care, but I can't help it.

Vic

Just wondering if she'll try to run.

Lies. What's one more at this point? I've always prided myself on being an honest person, but not anymore, and never when it comes to her.

Gage

Nah, I don't think she will. I'm arranging for her to marry someone safe. Somewhere far away.

My jaw clenches. I don't want that, but what the fuck am I going to do about that?

Nothing, and I know it.

She'll never want me.

Vic

Ok. Let me know.

Fourteen

Vic

I finish my last tattoo of the day, a piece Rosie drew up yesterday for a female client who wanted a bunch of flowers around a mandala. It looks good, and the customer sat through it like a champ, which always makes it more enjoyable for me.

"Oh, it turned out great!" Rosie gushes to the customer as she leans over my shoulder to check it out. "Here are your aftercare instructions. I hope you love it as much as I do."

I get a strange pull in the pit of my stomach at having her here working with me and not just sitting around like when she first came. I should've let her contribute from the start. But then she wouldn't have taken the job at the bar that night, and we wouldn't have taken what we have to the next level.

Whatever it is that we have.

I walk outside my tattoo shop with Rosie, basking in the chilly evening air. The sun is just setting, and the sky is a magnificent canvas of pinks, oranges, and purples. I stare at it for a beat with thoughts of Rosie on my mind even though she's inches from me.

"Oh, it's beautiful," she murmurs as she tilts her head back and looks at the sky.

"Yeah," I say as I look at her. The sunset is nonexistent. What catches my eye is the radiant sparkle in her eyes, the captivating smile that graces her tender lips, and the lingering memory of her delicate neck beneath my touch.

I grab a stray piece of her hair flying in the soft breeze before placing it behind her ear. My hand lingers, not moving from her head. Rosie turns toward me, her eyes an intense deep green like the forest after a rainstorm.

"Wanna take a ride with me?"

"Where to?"

"Somewhere special."

Taking her bag, I place it in my saddlebag so her hands will be free. Luckily, she's wearing pants and a leather jacket. It's been getting chilly at night.

With her front pressed against my back, she holds me even tighter as we fly down the highway, letting out a little squeal, which makes me smirk.

I want to take her to one of my favorite places when I'm craving solitude and silence.

Ever since I spoke to Gage last night, I feel like I'm on borrowed time with her. It guts me, and I don't know what to do about it.

We get to our destination just as the sun makes its descent.

"Taking me out to the woods? Seems like the start of a slasher movie. Should I start running?" she asks, climbing off my bike and scanning her surroundings.

"Not yet, princess. Now's the time to beg and ask for forgiveness." I smirk.

"Not on your life." She chuckles.

"It's where I come when the world is a little too loud," I say, helping her take her helmet off and pulling her along.

She's thoughtful for a minute, studying the scenery again. I've been here countless times, but I try to see it through her eyes.

Enormous trees and mossy vegetation dominate the space with a small gravel and dirt pathway obscured by fallen branches. When you look up, you can barely see the sky from the overhang of all the tree branches creating a canopy. A light mist from the earlier rainfall drops onto the leaves, creating a calming tapping sound as we walk.

"Oh, it's breathtaking," she says as she walks through the clearing.

The lake dominates the center of the forest, and the trees create a serene backdrop. Dusk is here, and the lake glows with the reflection of the remaining light.

Rosie glances over at me as soon as I catch up to her. "This place is amazing. How's it so empty?"

"We're on private property."

"Whose?"

"Mine."

Her eyes widen. "For real? And you're just now bringing me?"

"Better late than never, I guess."

"You know, if I owned this land, I'd never want to leave," she says with her eyes sparkling.

Be careful what you wish for, princess.

"Come on."

We walk down the dock, and I take a seat at the end, patting the space beside me. She sits down and swings her legs off the side, letting her feet dangle just above the water.

149

I sneak a look at her and notice her eyes are closed, and she's smiling.

I grab her small hand, interlocking it with mine. She looks down at our entwined fingers.

"What are you thinking about?" I ask.

"Do you hear that?"

"Uh...no," I say, confused.

"Exactly. It's peaceful here. Why don't you have a house on the lake?"

"I haven't really thought about it."

"I would. Then, I'd put my easel right at the end of this dock. The scenery is too magnificent not to render paintings of it."

"Maybe I'll bring you back, and you can."

"Only if you do, too."

"Only if you go out on a date with me," I say without thinking. *Fuck. What is wrong with me?*

"A date?" she repeats with wide eyes.

I can't take that shit back now. "Yes. Let me take you on a date."

"Maybe," she says with a shrug before she smiles. Ahh, hard-to-get Rosie has now entered the chat.

"You're the first girl I've ever asked on a date, and you give me a maybe? You're breaking my heart," I say, holding my chest as if I'm in pain.

"The first?" She sounds shocked.

"Yep."

"I'm sure you say that to all the girls."

"Never. And I've never brought anyone here besides you."

"Well, I feel special."

"You should," I say with a smile.

"You're such a jerk," she says with a laugh, then sobers. "Thank you for sharing your lake with me. It's perfect."

She's right. It is perfect, with the crickets softly chirping, the moon illuminating the small waves, and her by my side.

We lie with our backs against the dock and gaze up at the sky. The stars are so easy to see without the lights of the town.

"I've always loved looking at the stars. Ever since I was a little girl, I'd stay out in my mother's garden late into the night just staring at them. Sometimes she or my best friend Alexa would join me," she murmurs sadly.

"You miss your family."

"I do. I miss them so much," Rosie says before clearing her throat.

"What are they like?" I ask, wanting her to open up to me.

"Well, you already know Gage. Probably better than me at this point."

"Maybe," I say carefully, not wanting to open that can of lies and deceit. I've already lied to her too much.

"So, you guys became friends after you tattooed him?"

"Yep. Your family?" I ask, wanting to change the direction of this conversation quickly.

"My mom is always so understanding and loving. Then there's Marco, Gage's twin. He's intense and protective. I love him, but he can be overwhelming sometimes."

"And your father?"

Rosie huffs. "My father is demanding. Very much to the point and no-nonsense. A total asshole, to be honest." She shakes her head as if to remove the negative thoughts. "Enough about my family, though. What about your family?"

151

I hold my breath, knowing that my asking about her life would open the line to talk about my life.

"Not much to tell. Both of my parents died when I was younger. I have no siblings or family left blood-wise. However, I consider the club my family. They've been around longer than my actual family was."

"Oh, I'm so sorry."

"Nothing to be sorry for. It happened a long time ago."

"May I ask what happened, if you don't mind, of course?"

"They were druggies. Their desire to get a fix often overshadowed their role as parents. They got into a car accident on their way to score some drugs and never came back," I say with little to no emotion.

I'll never understand how they could have left a child alone. Their dependency on drugs and selfishness cost them their lives. It's the reason I've stayed away from that shit and never got sucked in, but I can't help but feel grateful. No matter how bad that might sound. Who knows where I'd be or who I'd be if they were still alive?

The puzzle pieces have finally fallen into place. I love my life now, especially with the current company I have.

"That must have been tough, especially for someone so young."

Compassion bleeds out of her, which makes me wish I never opened up. I don't want sympathy or the sad expression currently on her face.

"What do you say we get out of here?"

"Do we have to?" Rosie asks, and it makes my stomach dip with joy. She's enjoying this time together just as much as I am.

As we fly down the road, my mood continues to soar when I feel the moment Rosie breaks free from her mental shackles and embraces the moment.

She's usually stiff and almost uncomfortable on the bike. Not tonight. I can see the smile plastered on her face from my side mirror. Her hands are up in the air like she's praising the bike gods for this moment of freedom. I can't help but smile.

I hope this feels like flying to her, and she can cross this off her list. I can give her this, so she'll think of me every time she sees the list.

She really is special. Something I would be fucking stupid not to hold on to, and that's what I'm struggling with the most.

I can't lose Gage, and I can't lose her. Because if Gage finds out that I'm not only thinking about keeping his sister, but that I've also been writing her behind his back for years, I lose him. If she finds out I lied to her, I lose her.

I'm fucked either way. The heart I've always considered vacant comes to life and bangs against my chest painfully at the thought of losing anyone I care for.

I pull into a small milkshake shack I often frequent after the lake. They're known to have the most random-ass milkshake flavors, like matcha and avocado, but I always stick to the classic vanilla. It's consistently good, and it never disappoints.

"Oh, I love milkshakes," Rosie says as she walks to the window.

I know she loves them. It's part of the reason I brought her. The other is because I want answers, and the only way to accomplish that without bringing on suspicion is to tread lightly.

"Me too. I only get the vanilla, but I've heard they're all pretty good."

"Vanilla?" She looks up at me in horror.

"Hi, I'll have the umm... s'mores mega milkshake, and Mr. Boring will take the vanilla."

And here's my cue. "Can you add potato chips to my boring vanilla, please?"

Rosie scrunches her nose in disgust before her eyes go wide. Bingo.

As we walk toward the table to wait for our order, I tune into her body language, hoping to decipher her current mood. Her only tell of being in deep thought is the bottom lip she's currently nibbling.

"You okay?"

"Ah, yeah. Chips in a milkshake seem pretty random."

"Possibly, but it's delicious."

"Yeah, I'm sure."

"Let me guess, you don't like soggy chips?" I feel bad for baiting her, but I want her to talk about her pen pal.

I want to know what she thinks of me. The real me. After her pissed-off letter, I decided not to write her back. I wanted her to focus on me, not the letter me.

She nods her head before looking at me. "Yeah, I had a friend who liked to eat milkshakes just like that."

Had.

She said had.

The server brings our milkshakes to us. Mine looks as vanilla as vanilla can be, while hers is more of a devious monster. Cookies, graham crackers, marshmallows, and a donut sit on top while chocolate overflows from the sides.

"Wow. I'm never going to finish this." She takes her finger and runs it along the glass to collect the overflowing chocolate, then sticks her finger into her mouth.

She makes the same moaning noise as she always does when she eats, and it goes straight to my dick. Especially now that I know she makes the same noise when I rub my body against hers.

I clear my throat and attempt to stay on track. "What happened to the friend?"

"What do you mean?"

"You said had a friend not have."

"He... we grew apart."

"Was he more than a friend?"

She shrugs. Is it ridiculous that I'm jealous of her pen pal, who is actually me? Yes, yes, it is.

"He was the one I wrote letters to, but it doesn't matter."

"You held on to that letter I handed you like it was special."

"It was."

"Then what happened?"

She pins me with a look that shows she doesn't want to talk about it. "Why do you care so much?"

"Just making conversation." I shrug as if I don't care when, really, I'm hanging on to every word she says. "Thought you might want someone to talk to. You don't have many friends here."

"Are you my friend?" she asks.

"I think I'm more than a friend after the other night, but we aren't talking about that right now."

She looks down at her milkshake. "He left me when I needed him the most."

A deep pain shoots through my stomach at her words.

"Friends, or whatever we were, don't abandon each other without a word. So that's that." Standing, she walks back to my bike. She's clearly done with the topic when I want nothing more than to dissect it, tear it into pieces, and eradicate it from her memory.

I've guarded myself all my life to avoid being abandoned, but it only resulted in making the person I cherish most feel deserted.

I'm a piece of shit.

We get back on the bike, and I take a right at the fork in the road and gun it. I let her enjoy the next couple of minutes before we head into the chaos I know will be present at the clubhouse.

The mile-long driveway is adorned with overgrown tulip trees, their branches reaching out to create a tunnel of greenery, guiding us toward the imposing metal security gate at the end. I catch the prospect's eye, and he immediately guides us in. Nodding in acknowledgment, I carefully navigate my way through the bustling crowd of cars and bikes.

"Where are we?" she asks, a little unsure of her surroundings.

"This is the clubhouse, home base of the Demented Devil's MC. A place I've spent most of my time over the years," I say, looking around with fond memories from my past. I rebuilt my first bike in this hangar. This was the first place I walked into and felt at home.

"Are you sure it's okay for me to just walk in?"

"If it was years ago, no, but things have changed a lot since Trey became president," I say as I guide her through the garage doors and into a flurry of commotion. "Don't worry, you'll be safe with me."

"You sure about that?" I look over and see Ax. He's wearing a shit-eating grin while leaning against the wall.

I roll my eyes at him as I pull her through the hall and into the industrial-sized kitchen, where things are in full party mode. Char is making food fit for an army while dancing to the music.

"Hey, sugar," Char says, looking at Rosie.

"Hi, how are you?"

"I'm good, sugar. You're more than welcome to food and drinks. Make yourself at home," she says with a wink before looking up at me with a knowing smile that says I'm fucked.

I've never brought anyone here. She knows I don't get close to women. She's always said it's a symptom of my childhood or some shit. I trust her, and even Jess, so that can't all be true.

We walk through a long corridor and into the great room, which has multiple leather couches placed throughout. A bar sits off to the right, and a small room off to the left has vintage pinball machines and pool tables.

The clubhouse, nestled on a couple of acres, offers a secluded haven for its visitors and boasts a spacious interior akin to an industrial building. It has two stories, not including the basement. From the second story, you can gaze down and take in the expansive great room below. Not only does the ceiling feature skylights, but it also houses surround sound speakers for an immersive audio experience.

I grab two plates and pile them with food, then grab two waters before leading Rosie to the stairs to sit so we can eat.

"This place is pretty cool," she says, looking around the open area as I hand her a plate.

Some people are milling around, but not as many as usual.

"I like it. We renovated it a couple of years back to bring it up to date." I peek over at her digging in. "I can give you a tour after you finish eating."

"Sounds good to me." Rosie looks around. "So, why don't you wear an outfit like them?"

"That's called a kutte, princess."

"Okay, so why don't you have one? They're your friends. You have a bike and tattoos. Your whole aura screams that this is where you're meant to be."

"Are you feeling me up spiritually, princess?" I ask with a grin.

"No." Her cheeks go that rosy shade of red I love so much. I want to rub my thumb against the color and see if it's as heated as my body feels.

I bump my arm against hers. "Tell me what you see."

"Not on your life."

"One day?"

She gives me a one-shoulder shrug. "Maybe."

Another maybe...it's not a no. I'll take it.

"This was once my home," I say absentmindedly as I look around, feeling the nostalgia hit me. I went from doing homework at these tables to drinking with the guys. This is where I felt full after years of going hungry and feeling empty. "And I was very much a part of this club."

"What happened?"

I blow out a deep breath. "I was a new patch on my first run when something went wrong. I went away, and the only way I could be free again was to let the club go."

"So you did?"

"I did. Mostly, anyway."

"What do you mean?"

"This is still my family, but I'm unable to hang out with them as I used to, and club activities are off-limits."

"Did it hurt? When you lost all of this?"

"More than you know... or maybe you do."

"I do," she says, looking down at her plate.

"As you can see, I still have pieces of my old life, and you can, too."

"What if I don't want my old life back?"

Does that include leaving me behind? Me in the letters and me now? The thought fucking hurts, but her happiness means more to me than my own. It always will.

"Then, you start a new life."

"Does that mean you'll lighten up on me?"

"Not a fucking chance."

"You know, you really know how to ruin a good moment." She scrunches her nose.

"Don't I know it." I sigh.

I point to the rooms above us, explaining we all have our own, then help her stand.

"What do those doors go to?"

"Church."

"Church?"

"Yeah, it's where patched club members gather to discuss important club business, cast votes, or implement changes. Everything important that's club-related takes place within those walls."

"And this door?" she asks as she points at a room with a dead bolt on the outside.

"Just storage," I say with a shrug.

Definitely not for storage unless you want to consider torturing a storage room. I guess we store the dead bodies there until we get rid of them, so it's a half-truth. Our little buddy from poker night is still in there, gradually transforming into a liquid substance.

As we climb the stairs, I move closer to her. It's surreal having her in my space. My home. I'd give anything to wrap her in my arms, but I hold myself back.

Pinging and knocking from the pinball machines assault our ears when we enter. Her eyes light up as soon as she sees the pool tables.

"You wanna play?"

"Sure, let's make this interesting. If I win, you give me a tattoo," she says as she grabs a cue stick off the wall. Wasting no time at all, she chalks the tip.

I grab my own and dismiss her wager.

"When I win, I want complete obedience from you for a week, and every meal served to me on a platter," I say, giving her a smirk.

"When I win, I will expect my tattoo on your first available, and now I want a week to do anything I want, too," she says, her head held high. It's adorable that she thinks she'd win against me. I've been playing for years.

"You won't be winning, so there's no reason to even call it, but sure, you can have whatever you want."

"Whatever I want, huh... probably not the best choice of words."

She's right because I'm supposed to be a loyal friend to her brother. Trustworthy, but right now, I'm willing to give her anything and everything she wants if she keeps talking to me the way she is with that sparkle of mischief in her eyes.

"So, what do you say? You ready to play?"

"More than ready," she says with a determined expression.

"Ladies first." I watch and wait for her to fumble and miss. "You need help lining it up, princess?"

She gives me a look before leaning her deliciously delicate body over the table. After lining it up, she sinks two on her first shot.

"Solids," she says as she looks up at me from beneath her lashes. *Motherfucker.*

"You know how to play?"

"Never said I didn't, *princess*," she says with a smile.

As she goes to sink another one, Trey, Marcus, and Julian walk in.

"What are we playing?" Trey asks as he looks at Rosie's ass. I walk over, effectively blocking his view. This motherfucker has a death wish. All he does is smile at my unspoken protectiveness.

"We're playing pool."

"You guys can play. We just started."

"Actually, the table is full. You fuckers go find a different one," I say, not wanting to share my time with her.

"Don't be silly. They can play with us."

"Yeah, Vic, what she said." Trey grins.

I take a long breath. "I hate you guys sometimes."

"Perfect. Let's start with some shots," Julian says with his ever-present smile.

Marcus polishes his drink off the second it's handed to him. Then, he ignores the whole situation by going back to his phone.

"I heard shots." Axl walks in with a big-ass smile, trailed by Jess. Interesting.

"Yay," Rosie says as she runs over and wraps Jess in a hug.

161

Trey gives one to Rosie and Jess with a grin before shooting his own back. This fucking guy. He's about to be buried six feet under.

Rosie hesitates with the shot in her hand. I wait to see what her next move will be. She turns toward me as if she senses I'm watching her, gives me a grin, then shoots hers back as well. She shudders as the alcohol goes through her body, and I can't hold my groan in.

"Okay, that will be my one and only. I have a bet to win."

In need of something to occupy my hands, I reach for mine and gulp it down like water. Then, I take another, never taking my eyes off her. Feeling the burn go down my throat and into my stomach does nothing to calm the raging fire I feel for her.

"What bet?" Jess says as she downs hers.

"I want a tattoo, so I need to know who is the best, and you'll be on my team."

"I'm not really good at playing games," Jess says as she jumps on a barstool.

"Could have fooled me," Ax mutters behind his shot.

"I'll be on your team," Julian says as he stands beside her.

"Are you good?" Rosie looks over at him with a critical eye.

"I'm good at everything, baby," he says as he moves closer to her, which makes the pool stick groan from the tight grip I'm giving it. He's always been the pretty boy peacemaker of the group, the spokesperson, since he's the most approachable, and I might just have to take his ass out.

"Does that actually work?" Rosie laughs, completely unaffected.

"Always," he says with a grin.

An arm wraps around my waist before I see a face. "Hey, Vic." Samantha attempts to hug me. She obviously isn't getting the hint after multiple unanswered calls and texts.

"Ah, hey," I say, completely thrown off.

I glance over at Rosie and notice the sour expression etched on her face. She's jealous or disgusted. Let's hope it's the first and not the latter since it's taken what feels like forever to get her to look at me without disgust on her face.

I immediately untangle myself from Samantha's grip, but the damage is already done. I can tell from the cold shoulder Rosie's giving me that feels more like a subzero blizzard.

We play for an hour; me holding myself back with every stupid-ass comment the guys make. No, she doesn't need hands-on help to play, and no, she doesn't need more shots even though she takes them anyway because she's irritated with me. They're doing it to rile me up. That much is clear. And worse, Jess eggs them on. This adds fuel to the fire for Rosie, who is now flirting with Julian as they play.

I will get them back for this when they least expect it.

On the flip side, Rosie holds her own and fits in perfectly. Not that I ever had doubts, but it's nice to know with one hundred percent certainty that my family approves because, for a second, I can imagine this going further than a couple of months of her being under my watch.

I can imagine her being here forever.

I decide enough is enough when I see her glossy, bloodshot eyes and a seductive grin I've never seen grace her lips. A grin meant for my eyes only.

I make my way to her in a couple of strides. My fist winds into her hair, and I angle her head back to look up at me. Her eyes go

163

wide, and her plump lips part. I take the thumb of my free hand and rub it against her bottom lip. Her eyes never leave mine. The second her tongue sneaks out and licks my finger, I lose it.

"We're done here," I say, not wanting to wait any longer. I throw her over my shoulder and walk out as quickly as I can.

"Wow, dizzy... bye, guys," Rosie's muffled voice comes from behind me.

"Bye, beautiful. We'll see you soon," Julian says.

"The fuck you will," I say with my back against them as I leave. Three graves, six feet deep, it is.

I walk toward the stairs, her hands clutching the back of my pants tightly. We're getting a bunch of catcalls as we walk by, but I don't care.

"No spanking this time?" she asks as we walk down the hall.

I pause, my steps faltering. "You want me to spank you?"

Silence.

Dead fucking silence.

She's killing me.

Once we get to my room, I flick the switch and close the door with my foot. It leaves us in relative silence besides small thuds of noise coming from downstairs.

"All the blood is rushing to my head." She's a little breathless and slurring slightly.

Shit. I bring her down, putting her on her feet gently before I make her sick.

She sways as if she hears music while she gives me a grin. Obviously feeling the last shot, she took as much as I did.

I pull my phone out and put a song on. She smiles up at me as she pulls me close. Her body moving against mine feels like foreplay. Rosie knows how to use her body. I realized that the first time we danced all those months ago. I don't think she grasps how alluring she was, and is now. She does it unknowingly, which makes her that much more special.

Rosie burrows her face into my chest and moans. "You always smell so damn good."

I decide at this moment that drunk Rosie is supreme to any other version of herself for the sole reason of her honesty. I can't help but eat this shit up.

"What else do you like about me?"

"How you make me feel."

That... I wasn't expecting.

"And how do I make you feel?"

"Alive," she says before bringing her head up to mine. Our lips touch. It's not rushed or even slow. It's somewhere in the middle, somewhere I can imagine staying forever.

I grab her by the ass and pick her up. Her legs wrap around my waist, and she begins to grind against me. I let out a groan of pleasure. Sweet, torturous pleasure.

She kisses me like she dances. Sensual and enticing. Pulling me deeper under her spell.

I shake my head and pull away. This can't happen. I won't be able to stop if I start.

"You should get some sleep. I'll crash in another room."

"Don't leave me in here by myself. What if someone comes in?"

"No one will come in here."

"How can you be so sure? There's no lock."

"Then I'll sleep on the floor."

"You can't be serious."

"I'm dead fucking serious."

"Why?"

165

"We can't have a repeat of the other day."

"Scared you're going to dry hump me to death?" she asks with a giggle. "I'm sure you have more self-control than that. Look, we'll put a pillow wall between us." She throws a couple of pillows in the middle of the bed before plopping down onto the mattress. "See. My virtue you're so worried about will remain intact."

She's fucking mistaken if she thinks her little pillow wall will keep her safe. The Great Wall of China isn't tall enough to keep her away from me. I walk with tentative steps before lying on the other side of the bed.

She pops up from behind the barrier and looks at me with a sweet smile. "See, not bad at all."

"Yeah," I say as I clench my fists at my sides.

I will not touch her.

I will not make this harder on myself.

She isn't mine to keep.

She looks around my room. It's pretty sparse. Just a bed and a few dressers. Nothing personal to show who I am as a person. I keep most of my things at home because I only stay here occasionally. I told Trey he could give my room to someone else, but he refused. Sometimes the fucker is sappy and sentimental.

She lies down, and I can feel the tension growing between us. I rub my hand over my face and try to calm my racing thoughts. I shouldn't have brought her here, especially now that we're in bed together and drunk. It would be so easy to lean toward her and pull her to my side, the dark side. Then fuck her until the sun comes up.

There's complete silence on the other side of the bed, so I close my eyes and inhale deeply, then exhale slowly in an attempt to find enough tranquility to drift off.

"Why don't you guys have names?"

My eyes bolt open, and I look up at her, looking down at me.

"What do you mean?"

"Every motorcycle club has nicknames for its members."

My lips part, and a small chuckle exits as I listen to her explain. "The older members did, but we decided not to."

"Why?"

"It's just not what we wanted, although I understand why clubs do. It's a tradition, helps with anonymity, and creates a shared connection among the members."

"Oh," she says thoughtfully as she looks around. "What made you decide to be part of the MC?"

It's both bewildering and endearing for her to ask me questions about myself. She's trying to get to know me, and for that reason, I answer.

"After my parents died, I was in and out of foster care until around ten. Then, I ran away and ended up coming here. Trey, Marcus, and Julian were friends from school, and they welcomed me with open arms. The rest is history." I leave out some pieces she doesn't need to worry about. A dark past formed the foundation of the club. One that we don't ever discuss.

All of us have lost something precious because of this lifestyle, because of the club. Trey lost his mom, Julian lost his dad, Marcus lost his mom and sister, and I lost years of my life.

I contemplated going nomad while I was in prison. Not being affiliated to one charter in general, but still being part of the brotherhood. It wasn't something I wanted, but I was tempted as fuck to go through with it.

Trey's father, our old prez, brought us down a dark, twisted road, and many lives were lost. It was careless and heartbreaking.

Trey's promise to be better than his father was the only thing that kept me around. They're still one-percenters and do the shit that needs to be done, but greed, power, and vengeance don't blind Trey so heavily that he will sacrifice anyone and anything to get it.

Then, I had another hearing and reached a plea deal for early release. It was either take the deal or serve out the rest of my fifteen-year sentence.

The bargain made me lose what felt like everything at the time, but nothing felt better than walking out those doors and knowing I was free.

She seems thoughtful as she looks over at the chair in the corner, spotting my kutte. "I know a little when it comes to your world. Mostly from shows. The patch right there tells me... things," she says, pointing at my one percent patch on my kutte.

"I would never hurt you if that's what you're worried about. Your brother entrusted me to protect you, and I promise I will."

"But you've done bad things."

This isn't a question but rather a statement. I grab her hand, needing her to not only hear me but also feel me. "I've done bad things. Some may even say horrible things, but I'd never hurt you."

"Too bad you can't protect me from my future," she says with a long sigh. I can feel the sadness radiating from her.

"Maybe I can." I have no right to make that promise, but I will. Anything to get that dejected look off her face.

She shakes her head, resigned.

"I won tonight, by the way. I expect my tattoo sometime next week."

"Barely. I'd hardly call that a win."

"It don't matter if you win by an inch or a mile. Winning's winning."

I look at her adorably serious face. "Did you just quote Fast and Furious?"

"Possibly," she says with a giggle that gets me straight in my gut.

It's so satisfying to hear her laugh so freely in what you'd think is just an ordinary conversation, an ordinary moment. However, she is anything but ordinary. It's special, and it makes me unsteady in the best and worst way.

I laugh with her. "I love that movie."

"Definitely not shocked."

"Let me guess... my aura tells you?"

"I'm never going to live that down, am I?"

"Nope."

"Whatever," she says as she attempts to pull her hand from mine. She forgot it was there, but I didn't. I hold onto it tighter.

"I'll give you a tattoo, but I want *all your firsts*." She blushes and I can't help the smile that tugs my lips. She thinks I'm talking about sex. "Trust me, I want that, but I want every other first, too."

Fifteen

Rosie

My eyes spring open as I hear a moan, and I instantly regret it. My head feels like it weighs a ton. I shouldn't have drunk so much last night.

I try to turn, but Vic's wrapped around me like I'm his life-sized body pillow.

What happened to our little wall of purity?

He'd die if he realized how tightly he was holding me or, more accurately, my breast. I look down at his fingers against my chest and smirk. I wish I had my phone to take a picture and send it to him later.

As I tilt my head back to look at him, I can see the perspiration trickling down his face and hear his faint moans of discomfort. Is he sick?

With all my strength, I move his arm and turn to face him, carefully placing the back of my hand on his forehead to check his temperature. It's clammy and warm.

"No," he says, his brows furrowing into a deep crease as his eyes remain closed. "Please," he pleads, his voice filled with desperation, "come back."

Shit, he's having a bad dream.

Who's he dreaming about? Who does he want to come back?

I tenderly touch his cheek with my trembling fingers as he lets out another moan, his breath tickling my hand. I move to his hair, which has gotten a little longer since I first arrived. It glides between my fingers as I rub his head. The action calms my nerves and seems to have the same effect on him. He relaxes and doesn't make any other sounds.

Whenever I'm trapped in the clutches of my nightmares from the attempted kidnapping, Alexa has always been there to console me, making the transition from slumber to wakefulness much smoother. So I continue to rub through his whole scalp, at least what I can reach, and then down to his shoulder that is naked. *When did he take his shirt off?* I continue my exploration of his skin to his mid-chest until I head back up.

His chiseled abs are on full display as he peacefully sleeps. I yearn to trace my fingers along their defined edges, but I resist the temptation out of respect for his unconsciousness.

Out of the corner of my eye, I notice a flicker of movement, and when I meet his gaze, I'm taken aback by the intensity in his eyes.

"Sorry, you were having a bad dream, and I—ah..." I got nothing.

How embarrassing.

"You were touching me."

"Only your hair," I blurt.

"I distinctly remember your fingers traveling south."

"You were awake?" I ask, mortified.

He says nothing but grins bigger than I've ever seen. It's then I notice how close we still are, and Vic does, too. He rolls away before bouncing up and out of bed.

"Are you okay?"

"Yeah. Can you hand me a bar in the top drawer?"

"Um, yeah," I say, reaching into the drawer filled with the same protein bars stocked all over his house. I hand it to him, and with two quick bites, he devours it before requesting another.

"You sure you're okay? You sounded upset in your dream."

"I'm fine."

"But..."

"I'm fine, Rosie. Just old bullshit from my past."

Understanding crosses my mind. "Your parents?"

"Yeah."

"If you tell me about it, you might not have that same dream again. It can take away its power."

"Drop it and stop with that look in your eyes," Vic says as he rushes through putting his clothes on.

I can't help but feel hurt as he shuts me out. I thought we were making progress and growing closer, but the wall that is his past is tall and unbreakable.

"How about we go by Burnouts?"

"Really?" I say, instantly perking up.

I expected us to go home after work and him to ignore me more. He's been in a shitty mood since I pressed him on his dream this morning. It was stupid of me to push. I know I wouldn't want to be pushed, but I couldn't help it.

I want to know more about him, and I want to fix his pain, or at least understand it.

Vic is usually bossy and a complete jerk, but there are also those rare, tender moments I appreciate. These moments have become more frequent.

He took me to the lake, a place he finds peace, even though he never had to. He didn't have to take me to the clubhouse, which he considers his home away from home, but he did. He's given me more opportunities to draw for clients because he knows I love it. He makes sure I'm always protected and fed. He is a great guy, and I want to give back as a thank you to him.

Vic makes a U-turn, and we end up in front of the bar I haven't been to since my first night.

One that I have very mixed feelings about.

The sound of that guy's words still resonates within me, but it's drowned out by the powerful sensation of Vic's hand gripping my neck as he threw me over his shoulder and had his wicked way with me.

Do I need to see someone over how wrong that is?

Probably.

Vic looks back at the booth where he sat that night. Trey has a girl on his lap, and they look like they're ten seconds from getting it on right in the booth. Geez. I avert my gaze quickly.

"We won't be here long. I'll be right back. Stay here."

"O-okay," I say, a little confused as I watch him head to the back. Why did we even come here if we're leaving so quickly?

173

I head to the bar and order a drink. The drink is barely in my hand before Vic grabs it, downing it in one go.

"Hey!"

"You drank enough last night. Let's go."

"What's the rush?"

"Number two."

"Number two?"

"You'll see," he says with a smirk while pulling me out the front door that Trey and his mystery girl just left through.

Vic salutes Trey, who revs his engine and speeds down the road with his new friend clinging to the back.

Once we're in Vic's truck, he reaches into the back seat and pulls out a duffel bag.

"Put these on." I hold up a sweatshirt and a black mask with holes where the eyes are.

"Are we robbing a convenience store or something?" I say with a laugh.

"Look in the duffel bag on the back seat." I lean back and pull one side open before laughing.

"Is that toilet paper?"

"It is."

Oh my God.

My list.

"We don't have to toilet paper a house. It's silly, remember?" I say, mirroring what he said when he first saw my list.

It hurt when he laughed at it. I guess the idea of toilet papering a house is pretty silly for someone my age, but I started this list as a child. It's something all the other kids did at school on weekends that I never got to experience because of my parents' overprotectiveness. The little girl in me deems it necessary to complete the whole list. No matter how juvenile it may be.

Apparently, Vic is taking it seriously, too.

I can't help but smile.

"We're doing it. Put that stuff on. We're almost there."

I waste no time donning the all-black attire.

As we pull up to a residential area, my heart races uncontrollably. We're really going to do this. I can almost laugh at how silly I'm being. My palms are even in the beginning stages of clamminess.

"Okay, we have to be real quiet and quick. You don't want to go to jail, right?"

I take a deep breath, my eyes going wide. "Jail?"

"I'm kidding. You're so sweet and innocent," he says as he rubs my cheek through the mask, making my heart stop. "We're going to run around the corner to the house. Then throw as much toilet paper as possible. Got it?"

"Yeah," I say with a grin.

We open the doors slowly before getting out. He comes around the back and pulls something out of the back as the duffel bag hangs from his other arm.

"Do you want me to hold something?" I whisper, needing something to keep my hands occupied so I don't throw up out of nervousness.

"Nah, I got it."

We trudge toward a house with a long driveway and trees covering most of the front, giving us the cover we need and helping with our semi-illegal crime. He opens the duffel bag and hands me a roll.

I let the first piece sail through the air like a streamer, and my small giggle feels weird but exciting. I can't believe we're doing this. This is so bad, but it feels good.

Five minutes later, I scan my surroundings while snatching up the last roll. The entire front yard is scattered with toilet paper, creating a chaotic and messy winter wonderland scene.

"Finish that one, then run back to the truck. I'll be there in a minute."

I nod, too scared to use my voice so close to the house.

As I rush back to the truck, a playful chuckle rises in my throat, matching the excitement coursing through my veins as I hop into the cab and rip off my sweaty mask. I'm on a complete high right now. I might cringe about it later when I think of the person seeing it in the morning, but right now, I'm up in the clouds without a worry in the sky.

Vic walks back a minute later with the mask in his hand and a smirk on his face. It's crazy to think that this didn't even affect him. He was calm throughout the whole thing.

Once he opens the door, he gives me a weird look before lunging at me. Grabbing my face, he puts his thumbs in the hollows of my cheeks and kisses the shit out of me. My head is swimming as he ends the kiss as quickly as it came. That... I was not expecting.

"Let's get outta here."

We drive in the opposite direction, away from the scene of the crime. Vic pats his pants before pulling out a cylinder, popping the top, and then pulling something out.

"Can you reach into the center console and get the lighter in there? I lost mine."

I give him the lighter, and he proceeds to ignite something, inhaling deeply before exhaling a cloud of smoke.

I've never seen him smoke, nor has he ever carried the scent of it, but something is undeniably attractive about the way he looks while doing it.

"Number five, I stole it from Trey's stash," he says with a smile before handing me what I now know is a joint.

Getting high was on my list.

I hold it between my fingers before looking at him. "How do you remember everything I wanted to do? You're even numbering them."

"Photographic memory."

"Mm-hmm."

Following his lead, I place the joint between my lips and inhale deep. The citrusy sweet but earthy taste dances on my tastebuds while the smoke fills my lungs. I pass it back to him like I've seen in movies.

Despite feeling lost, I'm determined to exude maturity and competence around him. I don't know when his perception of me shifted to where I care, but it did.

I hold the smoke in until my lungs burn and then exhale. The next thing I know, I'm coughing so hard my eyes water, and I think I might throw up.

"Shit, you're going to be high as hell," he says, looking at me with a grimace. "I should have told you to take it slow."

So much for not looking lame.

"Drink this." He hands me a water bottle that I gulp down to tamp down the inferno in my lungs.

Apart from the fiery sensation in my throat, my head is swirling, and I have a sensation of being adrift. Something similar to the way I feel on the back of his bike or floating in the water. It's kind of nice.

The earlier excitement fades away and brings forth a calmness that's hard to explain.

I grab my bag and pull out my list, but stop.

I can do it later when I'm alone.

"Do it," Vic says in a light voice.

"Do what?"

"You can cross them off."

I look over at him, but he's looking at the road. I open the paper and cross off two more firsts. The joy that fills me when I cross them off my list is indescribable.

It's satisfying but also warms my heart.

"Thank you," I say as I peek over at him.

"Of course."

Sixteen

Vic

I wake up the following morning, wrapped around Rosie. Even in the realm of sleep, I can't stay away from her.

My feelings for her are teetering on the edge of obsession, or perhaps they have already crossed that line and moved into a territory I can't even comprehend.

We could have gone home last night, but I wanted an excuse to lie next to her again.

I was in utter shock when I felt her rubbing her hand against my neck and then lower yesterday. She was trying to console me, rub away my demons, and it seemed to partially work. I felt like a complete ass for snapping at her for asking questions, but I couldn't help it.

It makes me feel weak, and that's the last word I want Rosie to associate with me.

I want her to feel like she can come to me.

I want her to feel protected.

How can she feel that way if I'm the broken one?

I gaze down at her. She's so innocent and was so unbelievably adorable last night while toilet papering the house. I felt her pulse as I kissed her, and it was going one hundred miles a minute.

I tried to imagine the way she was feeling. The absolute excitement and rush she must have felt. It's hard for me to imagine since nothing excites me anymore, well, besides her.

I watch her for another ten minutes, her long dark eyelashes fan against her high cheeks, her hair a chaotic mess, and her chest rising and falling deeply.

I place my hand over her heart, feeling the steady beat. I remove my hand as she stirs.

"Wake up, sleepyhead. We need to get downstairs and eat before work."

Her eyes lazily open, and a smile graces her thick, pouty lips that I want nothing more than to devour, suck on, and bite.

Last night's kiss was an appetizer, and I want more.

Much more.

Trey comes into the kitchen, flanked by Marcus and Julian.

"Morning boys," Rosie singsongs as she looks up from her yogurt and granola.

"Hey there, pretty girl, you done with him and ready to come to the dark side?" Trey says, wiggling his eyebrows.

"Never gonna happen," I say.

"Never say never," he says with a smile.

"What are you even doing here so early?"

"Had to get my other fucking boots," Trey says, sounding irritated.

Showtime.

"Some little fuckers decided to TP our fucking house with a shit ton of toilet paper."

I look over at Rosie. The second she puts two and two together, she practically chokes on her coffee.

"Easy, princess," I say, smirking while rubbing her back that's ramrod straight.

"It took for-fucking-ever to pick it up. When I find them, they're going to pay."

"That sucks, man," I say, feigning sympathy I don't feel.

"It gets worse," Trey says.

"Oh?"

"They lit a bunch of bags of shit on fire and stole my weed."

Rosie's head snaps to me with wide eyes. She didn't know that part of the plan. It was all me. She would have backed out, and I wasn't having that. The three fuckers had it coming with how they've been flirting with her. They deserved it. My only regret is not taping his reaction as he ran out the door to put it all out.

"Who the fuck does that these days? I had to throw away my favorite fucking boots."

"Sounds pretty shitty, man," I say with no emotion. But inside, I can't help but laugh my ass off.

"Not even the worst part. I was fucking the shit out of this b—" I give him a look. He doesn't have a fucking filter. "I was busy doing stuff, and I had to run out with my pants around my fucking ankles. Dick flying everywhere as I stomped that shit out."

"Back up. You didn't tell us you had someone coming over," Julian says.

"You guys were busy on a run. I couldn't wait," Trey says with a sneaky smile.

"Looks like karma bit you straight in the dick since you didn't share, and I told ya we should get cameras. Your ass never listens," Marcus says.

"You know I don't like those. Evidence and all. Besides, I'll be ready the next time," he says with a glint of violence in his eyes.

Rosie mouths, "No," to me, and I just smile.

"You almost ready to go?"

"Yeah," she says quickly like her ass is on fire, and she can't wait to get away.

"Wait, you have time to fit me in today?" Trey asks.

"I have some." I peer over at Rosie. "What are you trying to get?"

"A piece on my upper thigh. You'll be there to hold my hand, right, Rosie? It might hurt, and I need the support."

"She's not your emotional support companion, and also fuck no. We're leaving." I pull her out of the kitchen.

"Bye, guys." She waves, and they say bye in unison.

I'm going to kill them.

I look up to see Trey wince as I rub the paper towel on his inner thigh. I swear the fucker is almost out of skin from how frequently he's been coming in lately.

When I first got out, he helped me get my tattoo shop and fix it up. I tried to pay him, but he didn't want money as payment for his help, only ink. I know it's a form of therapy for him; it numbs his mind, as he likes to say, so I don't mind. He's had anger issues since we were kids. We all do, but I know his run deep. He usually does underground fighting to feed his demons, but they got busted, so this is the next best thing. No one wants a bloodbath on their hands after all, so I'm happy to help.

"Done," I say with a smack on the tattoo I just finished.

He leans over and howls, "Motherfucker!" Then, he winces as he gazes down at the very red area I just smacked.

"Call it even for all the flirting you've been doing with Rosie. You're lucky I don't tattoo a dick on your body," I say, narrowing my eyes.

He takes a second to think about it like he's figuring out a math problem or some shit. Maybe he should lay off the ganja for a minute.

"Fair." He nods before smiling. His smiles are never a pleasant indication of what's running through his head, but I pay him no mind.

I rip my gloves off and discard them in the bin.

"What's on the agenda for tonight?" Axl asks as he leans against the wall.

"Can't, I have plans."

"You've had a lot of those lately. I'm feeling neglected," Axl murmurs with a pout.

"You're with someone new every night," Trey says.

"Not every night," he says defensively.

I give Axl a pointed stare, calling out his blatant lie. He's been as busy with someone as I have been with Rosie. I just hope he's pulled his head out, and it's Jess who occupies his time.

"He only has a new hole every night because he can't have who he really wants," Trey says from the chair.

"I don't want anyone, dick," Axl seethes at Trey.

"Well, I guess you won't mind me going to the coffee shop and getting a drink. I'm quite parched after the tattoo. I'm starving, too. Maybe I'll have a little taste," he says with a devious smirk.

"Stay the fuck away from Jess, or I'll make a mess of your pretty face you love so much."

"He's quite testy for someone who doesn't want anyone, wouldn't you say, Vic?" Trey says.

"I'm staying out of your bullshit." I hold my hands up.

"Go fuck yourself, Trey."

"Don't be like that, bro. We can share."

"I'm not your bro. Our parents dated for five seconds."

"We share a half brother, brother." Trey points over at Samuel, who's trying hard to avoid their shit. You'd think this rivalry would be over by now.

"Still doesn't count."

"Okay, it's been fun. I'm out," I say with a salute before walking out the door.

"Wait up," Axl calls to me as I'm getting on my bike.

"Where are you going?"

"Bike ride. It's supposed to be a clear night."

"With Rosie?"

"Yeah," I say with a smile. Just the mention of her name lifts my mood.

"Care for two more to join?"

"You and Trey...? No thanks."

A look of disgust crosses his face as if he's caught a whiff of something foul. "Nah, Jess and me, dick."

"How do you plan on getting her to agree? Last I checked, she still hated you."

"I'll take her love, her hate, and everything in between. One day, she'll wake up and realize I'm the only one for her."

"The best thing you can do is to settle the fuck down. Jess needs someone stable. You're all she has left. Don't fuck it up, Ax," I say.

He's going to lose the best thing that ever happened to him if he doesn't pull his head out of his ass.

He laughs. "When did you become so knowledgeable, oh wise one? Was it before or after you fell for Rosie?"

"I didn't fall for her."

Infatuated. Obsessed. Addicted, yes.

I don't think I'm in love. I don't have that in me.

"Maybe you aren't so wise after all."

I say nothing, but roll my eyes.

"All I'm saying is you deserve some good after all the shit you've been through. I owe it to you to see that it happens."

"You don't owe me shit. Stop saying that."

"Don't let her go. Work it out with Gage, sell your soul, whatever. Just...don't let her go."

"Why are you getting all sentimental on me?" I narrow my eyes.

I hope he's not falling off again. Ax has been doing good. He isn't drinking as much, and he seems happier, lighter.

The same way I've been feeling.

"Because I know what it's like not to feel like you're good enough, only to push the goodness away and lose the only light you've ever seen," he says.

"You deserve it just as much as I do. Nothing has come easy for us, but that doesn't mean we aren't deserving of happiness," I say.

"Maybe," he says, just as unsure as I am about what I just said.

It's hard to ignore the constant cacophony of self-doubt in your mind, a relentless scream that echoes your worthlessness.

It's your darkest companion that sticks to you like a shadow, never straying far from your side.

It's there on your worst days, lingering like a dark cloud, and still has the power to dim the brightness on the best days.

"There are no maybes. I love you, bro, but you have to let all that shit go." If only I could take my own advice. "Let's go see the girls."

Seventeen

Rosie

The coffee shop has been slow today with every local at the town fair. Carnival rides, rigged games, and
deep-fried food take priority over the coffee shop. Left to our
own devices, Jess and I dance around the shop as we clean,
fueled by the freshly brewed espressos running through our
veins.

"I think I'm about ready to close up for today," Jess says with
a sigh as she removes her apron, accepting the reality that we
won't make any more money today.

"Sounds good to me! I'm exhausted anyway," I say, holding
back a yawn. It looks like the espresso didn't do the trick.

"Vic's been keeping you pretty busy," Jess says with a smile.

"Maybe," I say with a shrug, my mind going to a dirty place
without even trying. What is this man doing to me?

"Are you blushing? Damn girl, you got it bad, don't you?"

"I don't know." I sigh. "Well, yes, I do. I like him a lot. More
than I should, and because of that, I'm scared. I've never been

with anyone before him, so I'm trying to keep my expectations realistic."

"The first guy... ever?" she asks with wide eyes.

"Yeah, I've never dated anyone before," I say, feeling embarrassed.

"Holy hell, you're telling me..." she says, pointing at herself for emphasis with complete shock on her face. "Vic's the first guy you've been with ever, like ever, ever?"

I nod.

"That's like jumping in the deep end when you don't know how to swim."

"Yeah, I'm starting to realize that. Then he goes and does sweet things for me that he doesn't have to, and deep down, it makes me want him that much more. I swear I'll get my heart broken, but I don't even think I'd mind at this point."

"Okay, we're closing and going to the fair. You need a night off, maybe a drink or two, and some deep-fried Oreos." She pushes in the chair.

She looks over at me just as I grab my bag. "If you ever want to talk about anything, I'm here. I've been around these boys my whole life, so I know quite a bit more than I want to, actually."

The temptation to get a little insight into Vic's life is too much to pass up. He's a vault, and my curiosity compels me to delve deeper, eager to unravel the mysteries within him, especially after his nightmare.

"So you knew him when he was a teenager?"

"Yeah, and even before that," she says as she locks the door and leads us to her car. I get into the passenger seat, and we head to the fair.

"What was he like when he was small?"

She looks out the front windshield with her lips pressed into a thin line. "He was quiet and kind of sad. I once heard him talking to Ax about his shitty parents, about how they abandoned him, and how he had no one. It broke my heart because Vic was always sweet to me, like a big brother. The whole thing was such a big story. His father was from a wealthy family, and all the secrets came out when he died. Drugs, child abuse, child endangerment."

"What?" I ask horrified.

"Yeah, the article read that the little boy was severely malnourished, sick, and left alone for days."

My heart pounds violently in my chest, and suddenly, everything falls into place. His weird fascination with stockpiling food, the need to eat as soon as he wakes up, and always making sure that I've had enough food. A lone tear leaks out of my eye.

"Once he got older, he changed drastically. Got into a lot of trouble. Stealing, fighting, drinking. It probably had to do with being in foster care and then with the MC. Then, he went away for a couple of years and came back different again." Jess looks over at me as I take it all in.

"Why did he go away? He said something went wrong, but he never said what. Did he kill someone?" I whisper the last part.

It freaks me out a little to think of him murdering some innocent soul. I could never get over the fact of my father doing that. Alexa could always separate the two worlds when it came to her father, but Alexa's father differs greatly from mine. He's always treated his family with love and care. Leaving the monster at work and not bringing it home. My father, not so much.

"No, nothing like that," she whispers, as if we aren't the only ones in the car. "The day that happened, I overheard Trey on the phone talking to someone. I guess they were transporting guns

189

and drugs. Something went wrong, and it was supposed to fall on Axl, but Vic took the fall instead."

I'm relieved to hear he didn't hurt someone. I sound like a bad person, but guns and drugs don't hit any nerves. I've been around both my whole life, so I'm pretty desensitized.

"Okay, detour! Let's have a quick drink, then we'll go to the fair," Jess says.

"Deal."

We pull into the bar parking lot, which is just as empty as Sweet Escape.

"Hey, girls," Char says from behind the bar. "Why aren't you at the fair with everyone else?"

"Girls' night... A quick drink and then we're headed there," Jess says.

"I got just the thing."

"Make it strong, Char!" Jess yells to her.

Char slides the drinks across the worn wooden bar top. "You're in luck. That's the only kind I make... and it seems like you two will need it. Don't look now, but Victor and Richard have their eyes set on you two." She tips her head to the front door.

We both turn to see Vic and Axl advancing in our direction. I forgot to text Vic about my plans to leave with Jess, so I cast him a sheepish smile.

Why does he always make me so nervous?

"Shit, down that shot quick, girl," Jess whispers in a rush while downing her shot and bringing mine to my lips.

"Ladies..." Axl says with a predatory smile aimed at Jess.

Jess tips the glass and starts pouring it into my mouth, the cool liquid seeping from the side of my lips and running down my chin.

Vic moves into my space, takes his thumb, and runs it down the line of liquor on my face before bringing his thumb to his mouth. As his lips encompass his thumb, he moans.

Holy hell. My insides are on fire, and it's not from the shot.

I'm jolted back to reality as Jess nudges me. "Will you come with me to the bathroom?"

"Yeah, we'll be right back."

When we hit the hall a few steps from the bathroom, Jess turns toward me. "Let's ditch them."

My brows scrunch at her. Axl and her have been semi-friendly lately. "Why? Is everything okay?"

"Yeah, I just... Axl and I had an incident, as you like to call it."

"Really?" I say with a smile. Apparently, my little pep talk with Axl helped.

"Yeah, but I don't know how to feel about it. I need to get away and have a breather from him. It seems like he's always around me, you know."

"Okay. How do we ditch them?"

The moment the hushed words leave my lips, Vic walks into the hallway. He's apparently impatient tonight.

"Run!" Jess yells and pulls me down the hallway to the exit at the side of the bar. I can't help but giggle as I catch sight of Vic's predatory expression, a mixture of mischief and intensity. It's a challenging gleam that transforms his whole face.

The moment we pass the front of the entrance, we catch a glimpse of the guys rushing out of the bar toward their bikes. Jess flips them off while I smile and wave.

"They're going to catch us." I laugh as I look behind me, but a van comes behind us, and I lose sight of the guys.

"We'll lose them at the fair," Jess says while taking a hard right down a deserted residential street.

I look over at Jess, who has a crease between her brows. "Are you okay?"

"No," she says with a sigh, "Axl...Axl's presence has always been intoxicating to me. Because of that, I make really reckless decisions when he's close. Hence the incident we had the other night."

I nod. I'm starting to understand that feeling all too well.

"Has it always been like that? For you two?"

"When we were younger, his mom was often absent, so he'd spend his time at my house with me. We were inseparable for a long time. But things happened, and now everything is messed up." She shakes her head. "Memories that were buried resurface. Always the good ones that leave me breathless and craving more. Only for him to leave, as he's always been good at, which brings on the bad memories that also leave me breathless but abandoned."

My heart breaks. "Oh, Jess, I didn't know it was like that. I'm so sorry."

"It's okay," she says then shakes her head. "No more drinks. It makes me sappy as hell. Let's go hide."

The guys are nowhere to be found when we leave the car but I bet they're close.

We walk through the gate and right to the battered goodness that promises a stomachache but will taste like heaven. We eat a couple of deep-fried Oreos as we make our way deeper into the fairgrounds.

Multiple booths offer tossing and shooting games, but none with any chance of success. We pay for a couple of tickets and head to the rides and attractions. Our first stop is the Ferris wheel.

We wind through the maze of metal barricades until we reach the front. As we wait, we hear a whistle, and both of us turn. We spot the guys toward the back of the line. Axl blows kisses at Jess while Vic stares at me like he plans to eat me alive.

The gate opens, and we rush onto the lift. After we're buckled, the Ferris wheel moves counterclockwise to accommodate the rest of the people in line, giving Vic and Axl the opportunity to look back at us as we go around in a circle.

Axl tries to get Jess's attention, but she pointedly ignores him while I can't take my eyes off Vic. He keeps mouthing things I can't decipher, so I laugh and blow him kisses.

When the ride stops, we exit first. We walk to a maze, and as we give the attendant our tickets, I look back to see the guys still stuck on the ride.

Vic's eyes never leave me. I give him a wave as I'm pulled into the attraction.

The room we stumble into is dark and cold, only illuminated by the neon lights and lasers. I link my arm through Jess's as we walk into the middle of a section that houses three tunnels. Each has a different theme: under the sea, the forest, and outer space.

"Where do we go?" I ask Jess.

"I did something like this last year. Each tunnel has optical illusions and false passages. Only one tunnel should have a way out. Which one do you want to go through first?"

I look around, feeling the hairs on my back rising. "You pick," I mumble as I feel eyes on us. It's probably just Vic and Axl.

"Let's do the outer space first."

I take one last look around as we walk in. "Okay."

Neon space wallpaper adorns the walls with floor-to-ceiling mirrors placed at intervals. We take a right and end up in a hallway with no way out. We turn around and head back the way we came.

I see someone out of the corner of my eye run by in black clothing.

"Did you see that?"

Jess looks around. "See what?"

"Nothing. Let's hurry and get out of here." I don't like this anymore. There was definitely someone.

I walk with her through the rest of outer space without finding an exit, much to my dismay. We make it back to the beginning and head into the forest, which is the middle. It's even darker in here and reminds me nothing of the forest Vic took me to. This one has an eerie feeling to it. My nerves are on high alert as we walk through a maze of glass panes.

"This place is kind of creepy," Jess says right before she smacks her face into one of the glass windows. We double over in laughter. "Shit, that hurt," Jess says as she rubs her head.

We turn around and stop in our tracks when someone in a ski mask stands in our way. My eyes go wide as I break out in a cold sweat with my heart in my throat. This is who I spotted in the other tunnel.

We were followed.

All my fears come rushing back, and I feel like the little girl holding her canvas painting.

I took numerous courses and classes in self-defense from a young age, but looking at this tower of a person, I don't think I stand a chance, especially with Jess by my side. I squeeze her arm as she looks at the guy in a mixture of panic and surprise.

"What do you want?" I yell, feigning confidence I don't feel whatsoever.

My breathing increases, and I try to keep a hold of the moment. *Please don't break down. There is no one to save you this time*, my mind reminds me.

"Who sent you?" I ask, but I know. My father will never let me go so easily. I'm a pawn in his game of chess. He needs all the pieces to get what he wants.

A shattering noise assaults my ears seconds before we're grabbed. The instinct to fight takes over, and I thrash about, desperately summoning any of the self-defense training I should have taken more seriously when I was younger.

I cry out as he pulls my hair into a vise grip. The force he exerts is so strong that I can feel the hairs being pulled from my scalp.

"Be careful with that one," the captor who has Jess states.

I look at Jess lying limp over the other man's shoulder. Her auburn hair cascades down the guy's back, and her glasses are gone.

"Take me, but leave her. She has nothing to do with this," I plead.

This is all my fault.

Her connection to me put her in danger, and I'll never forgive myself if something happens to her because of my negligence. I should have told Vic about the guy in the bar even though he would have never let me leave his sight. I can't believe I prioritized my pride and selfishness over recognizing true danger.

I'm met with silence as they find the exit and bring us out back. The second I take a breath and attempt to scream, a nasty, leathered hand effectively blocks the scream coming from my mouth.

His disgustingly hot breath fans against my neck and ear. "If you scream or cause a scene, I'll kill your friend."

That has the fight leaving my body. We walk in the cover of darkness behind tents and trailers. This kidnapping was thought out. It wasn't some spur-of-the-moment decision. That much is clear.

What little breath I'm able to gather from the glove over my mouth is coming in ragged as the thoughts of hopelessness kick in. I feel like I'm going to have a panic attack. My hands are numb but tingly, and my vision is going into a black tunnel. *Please don't let this happen now.* Jess is still unconscious, or worse, so I need to stay awake.

As we approach the black paneled van, I desperately fight back, kicking and thrashing with all my strength. I'm praying it will grant us enough time for Vic and Axl to find us.

All the horror stories kick in like a grotesque slideshow, reminding me of our likelihood of getting out alive once we're moved somewhere else. It's almost nonexistent, especially on the off chance that this isn't my father's doing.

My captor pulls on my hair even harder, and I emit a silent scream as more tears gather in my eyes.

The guy holding Jess throws her in the back of the van and advances on us to help the guy holding me. They both take an arm, leaving my mouth exposed. I try to scream but can't.

It's like being in one of those dreams where you try to run, but you can't.

You try to scream, but you can't.

You try to wake up, but you can't.

I'm stuck in this state that I can't get out of as tears leak from my eyes at what's to come for me and my friend.

They throw me into the back of the metal van with a hard thud. I scream as my wrist cracks from landing at an odd angle while trying to catch myself. A burning and throbbing pain radiates from my wrist to my elbow.

As soon as they slam the van's doors shut, I crawl to Jess's unmoving body.

I grab her shoulder and turn her over onto her back. A cut on her forehead is oozing blood, and she also has a bloody nose.

"I'm so sorry, Jess. Please wake up," I whisper repeatedly.

Tears run down my face as I succumb to sobs. I place my hand over her chest and feel her heartbeat and the rise and fall of each breath she takes.

This is all my fault.

The van begins to move, and I know we're fucked.

Tears continue to slide down my cheeks as I think about the past couple of weeks.

Running away was never a mistake.

Staying in this town, even though I wanted to flee, was never a mistake.

I made friends, got a job, crossed off firsts.

Met Vic.

It was all worth it, and at least I have that.

I wish I could have said thank you.

I wish I could have said goodbye.

I wish I could have kissed Vic just one more time.

Eighteen

Rosie

I count the turns as the van careens around corners. Right, left, right, then straight for around seventeen minutes before right, and then left? It all becomes a blur.

The silence is abruptly interrupted as a phone rings loudly, piercing through the metal partition that divides the front and back. A sickeningly deep voice fills the air, making my stomach turn. "You have her?" my father asks.

"Yes, and her friend."

"Excellent. Kill the friend. I only want my daughter."

I place my hand over my mouth and shake my head as I hear my father's orders. This can't be happening.

One of the men in the front lets out a shrill scream seconds before the van veers sharply to the right. In the midst of the chaos, the piercing sound of two loud pops reverberates through the air, reminiscent of a gunshot, right before the screeching of the van's tires. My body is catapulted into the air, then it all goes black.

As I come to, a persistent ringing in my ears overwhelms my senses while my eyes struggle to adjust to the darkness of the starless night. I place my arm at my side to hoist myself up and instantly regret it when I feel like I'm on a motion ride. I fall back onto the dirt and wild grass under me with a thud.

What in the hell happened?

I angle my aching neck to the right and see Jess lying a couple of feet from me. Shit.

Rolling to my side with a sense of unease, I crawl toward Jess's limp body. I place my index and middle finger under her jaw and feel the thump, thump of her heartbeat. Thank God she's still alive.

I move to a kneeling position and cast my gaze in every direction. We're on an isolated road, surrounded by darkness, with no streetlights, cars, or buildings in sight. The perfect place to do unspeakable things to someone.

The van is tipped over on its side, with one of the back doors swung wide open. Did I crawl out? And what about Jess? How the hell did we end up over here?

As a faint noise reaches my ears, I immediately hit the ground with my stomach pressed into the earth. I focus on regulating my breathing and tightly close my eyes. When I don't hear any steps advancing my way, I slowly open my slitted eyelids.

Standing by the van, a slender black figure who is neither of the two men from before gazes across the vast landscape before walking to the front of the van. The sound of glass shattering reaches my ears, followed by the distinct noise of something being dragged.

I hear a huff as the figure drops something hard to the ground. I squint as I try to make out the pile, only to realize it's one of the men who took us. The figure retreats to the front of the van again before dropping what I can only assume is the other man next to the first. The figure rips something with a grunt, and then a light comes on as they hold a phone over their bodies.

The light from the phone creates enough visibility that I can finally see the face attached to the figure. My breath catches in my throat, causing them to turn their gaze toward me. Their face is hidden behind a white mask except for eye holes resembling a river of black tears and lips painted crimson red.

The masked person looks back down at the men before flipping them both over with an ease I find terrifying and taking a few photos of their faces.

Are the photos a trophy for the kills? Alexa and I went through a phase when we watched only murder documentaries for months. This would be considered a trophy or something, right? Or maybe they were on a hit list, and tonight was their unfortunate night?

They walk down the road without a backward glance, and I start to believe they won't be coming back until I see headlights coming at an alarming speed back toward us.

I scramble to my hands and knees, and shake Jess.

"Jess, please. Wake up. We have to leave," I beg, but she remains unconscious.

The car skids to a stop a few feet from us, and the masked person jumps out. In the offset light from the headlights, I watch them grab one of the men and pull him toward the car. When they get to the second one, they drag him by his arms and let his head rub against the dirt and rocks. As the light hits the back of his neck, I glimpse a tattoo. A circle with a slash through it. Odd. I've never seen something like that before.

The masked person reappears and gazes over at me before advancing in my direction, which makes me squeal and try to cover Jess's still sleeping form.

They get two feet from me and put up both of their hands in a calming gesture, and that's when I realize the person has long nails poking through the end of black gloves.

It's—it's a woman?

She looks over both of us with a hand on her hip.

"Thank you," I murmur. I don't know why she did what she did. I'm grateful, but still slightly terrified she might kill us next.

She just flops her hand at me as if it was no big deal before placing her finger over her mouth in a shushing gesture and walking to the driver's side of her car.

All I can see from her back is blond-looking hair in a tight bun. And as I squint, I see the same tattoo on the back of her neck as the guy.

My eyes widen in shock. Did she just kill someone she knows?

The car's headlights gradually fade away as she accelerates and swings the car around. The silence is shattered by another vehicle's engine growing louder and closer with each passing second. I look back toward the other car and let out a sigh of relief when I see Vic's truck speeding toward us, its engine roaring. I turn my gaze back to the other car, but it has vanished without a trace. Like it never happened.

"Fuck! Rosie, baby, are you okay?" Vic says as he and Axl make it to us.

Axl drops to Jess's level. "Jess. Wake up. Please wake up," he says while moving the hair out of her face with a gentleness I never thought he had.

"I'm okay," I say with exhaustion clear in my voice. The terror-induced adrenaline seeps out of my body, and a bone-deep chill replaces it. "It all happened so fast. The guy knocked Jess out in that maze. She needs to go to the hospital."

Vic helps me up and wraps me into a tight hug as Axl picks Jess up and holds her tightly to his body.

Vic grabs my hand as we walk, and I yelp. "You're hurt?"

"I got thrown into the back of the van on my wrist," I say, sniffling at the immense pain I now feel that wasn't there in the face of danger.

Vic holds my arm and wrist delicately as we walk. "It's okay, I swear."

"It's not okay. I thought you were dead. You both vanished, and Jess's car was still there. I want to know everything after we get your wrist looked at, and where the fuck is your phone?"

"I left it in Jess's car," I mutter as I look at the ground.

I'm just full of stupid decisions.

The on-call doctor meets us at the clubhouse because the guys have one on retainer. He looks at Jess first. She woke up during the ride here confused and was complaining about her head hurting. The doctor confirmed she has a concussion and gave her some stitches but instructed her to go to the hospital for more testing.

I walk away with a sprained wrist but nothing more, thankfully. It's not lost on me how much worse things could have gotten.

Vic and I enter a room I've never been in before. A large oak table dominates the center, with multiple chairs where the guys currently sit. This must be the church he was talking about.

Julian's fingers move across the keyboard with lightning speed as Trey and Marcus lean in to see the screen.

Trey looks up as we enter. "How're our girls?"

"My girl," Vic mutters.

"I'm okay," I say with a tight smile.

As time ticks by, the weight of my impending freak-out becomes heavier. A moment I've been dreading since Vic found us. I just don't want to do it in front of everyone, so I put on a brave face, camouflaging the torrent of emotions swirling within me. They want answers, and I have them.

Julian continues to type while Marcus looks over at Vic. "The car you saw speeding away had no tags or identifying marks from what we could see. Someone scrubbed the video footage from the servers as we were looking at it. Whoever did this is good... too good."

"And the number that texted me the location?" Vic asks.

"Burner, apparently. I can't find shit," Julian says, sounding disappointed.

"What about the van?"

"Samuel is towing it here as we speak."

Marcus looks over at me. "We're going to need answers," he states as he crosses his arms over his chest.

Out of the three of them, he's the scariest because he's the most stoic. His eyes bore into yours with an intensity, not creepy, but like he's analyzing you.

I once asked Vic, and he said it has to do with his past. He has trouble trusting people. His intimidating presence still leaves me slightly unsettled despite feeling sympathetic toward him. Then, I found out he's the club's enforcer, which means he's very good at keeping order and killing people. Scary.

"Is Axl planning on coming down?" Trey asks Vic.

Vic shakes his head. "Nah, he's with Jess. I'll update him later."

All four of the guys look at me, but Vic is the one to break the silence. "Start from the beginning."

Taking a deep breath, I examine my quivering hands, a telltale sign of my anxiety that prompts me to tuck them away behind my back.

"Well, we were going through that maze thing, and I felt someone's eyes on us. It wasn't until we went through the second tunnel that someone in a ski mask caged us in."

My stomach turns as I recall the feeling of staring up at the man who took me.

"Go on," Marcus says.

"At first, there was only one person. Then, another appeared and broke the glass to grab Jess. Then, the man in front of me grabbed me."

Tears escape my eyes and trace a path down my cheeks. Vic wraps his arms around me, but I pull away. When I see the hurt in his eyes, I place my hand on his chest. "I have to finish this, and then I never want to talk about it again."

I look back at the guys. "They brought us both out to a black van, threw us in, drove away, and then someone saved us."

"Who?"

I pause. Our savior preferred to keep her help to us a secret. That much was clear, and I can't help but feel a sense of loyalty to her.

I shrug. "I have no clue."

"What did this person look like?"

"I-I, uh... couldn't tell. She had a mask on."

As soon as I say she, I grimace.

Shit.

Trey raises a brow. "She?"

"Ahh... yeah, she."

I wish I would have thought this through prior to their line of questioning. Although I doubt they'll ever find her.

Trey narrows his eyes. "So you're saying a girl outsmarted two likely trained men?"

"Yeah."

"We don't know the who, but maybe we can figure out the why," Julian contemplates as he looks at Trey from above his laptop.

"Don't look at me, fucker. I've been keeping my nose clean," Trey says.

Julian narrows his eyes. "Are you sure about that?"

"One hundred percent. Life's been fucking boring lately. But this... this gives me something to look forward to," Trey says, rubbing his palms together. An evil smirk adorns his lips, and I look away.

"You're such a dick," Vic says from my side.

"I can't help it, bro. There's some chick in town who can allegedly take down a couple of guys. I need to find her, stat. And you guys all know that I've made changes since I've taken over. Pop's rule was bloody and vile. I won't put us back through that shit. We lost too much," he says with a sigh.

"You piss anyone off lately, Vic?" Marcus asks while ignoring Trey.

"Nope, I've been pretty preoccupied," Vic says while looking down at me with a small smile.

"What about the guy on poker night?"

Vic goes rigid. I look up at him. "What guy?"

"After you moved in, someone came to my house," Vic says, looking guilty.

"Why didn't you tell me?"

"Because I didn't want you to worry."

He's right, I would have. That still doesn't make it right. But I also didn't tell him about the guy at the bar.

"So, maybe he came back?" I ask the room.

"Unless he can crawl out of the soup drum he's in, I doubt it," Trey says with a creepy smile.

My eyes go wide. Did they kill the guy? I look up at Vic, but he's looking at Trey.

"Well, I got nothing, but I'll ask the other guys and Ax. Shit has to be connected, though," Julian says while closing his laptop.

The guys review possible suspects while I stand there, looking at Vic. Not saying anything could get them hurt, and I've already gotten one person hurt so far. I can't let that happen again.

I wait three seconds, mulling over what to do, and then sigh. "Wait... they were coming for me."

"Why would you think that?" Marcus questions with a quirk of his brow.

"Because I heard my father on the phone with the men."

My throat gets tight at the memory of his gruff voice with a hint of excitement at the prospect of me being taken and brought back to him.

"Your father?" Marcus raises an eyebrow.

I watch Vic still, and an expression I can't decipher pulls onto his face, but it disappears just as quickly.

"Pretty sure you couldn't piss off anyone bad enough to get yourself kidnapped," Marcus states.

"I did. I pissed my father off." I bite the inside of my cheek until it's painful, weighing my options, then say fuck it. Goodbye to my anonymous life. "I'm Rosalinda Gallo Moretti, and my family..."

"Is the highest-ranking Mafia family in Chicago," Trey says, narrowing his eyes at me, then Vic. "You knew this?"

"Yeah, she's my friend's sister."

"Gage?" Trey says, putting the pieces together. "I thought he looked familiar when he was crashing at your place."

"No fuckin' way. Her?" Marcus points at me with shock clear on his features, which is semi-insulting. I guess I don't really scream Mafia princess when you look at me. I don't have the attitude or confidence most have.

Trey looks back over at me. "Your father is a piece of shit, by the way."

"How do you know her father?" Vic asks.

Trey shakes his head. "We'll discuss it later. I think we're done here, boys."

"See you later, princess." I flinch at his words.

"Can you possibly act like you never got that piece of information?" I ask with a grimace.

I like the anonymity of being Rosie, the unknown girl. She was fun and carefree. Uncomplicated. I want her back. Not what the guys know now.

Trey regards me thoughtfully before shrugging. "I'll think about it. Vic, later."

Vic nods at him before grabbing my arm. I walk out of there more confused than when I entered.

As we ascend the stairs and approach his room, I steal glances at him. He keeps his eyes forward and chews on his lip as he looks at his phone, lost in thought.

As he gazes at me, his eyes soften, but there's still something in his eyes I don't like. He looks upset. "You must be exhausted. Why don't you get some sleep? I'll be right back."

He turns around and shuts the door without another word, which feels like he's shutting me out as well.

Tears free-fall from my eyes as I rummage through Vics's drawers for something clean to wear.

I feel utterly drained, with a heavy weight pressing down on my chest and an unending stream of tears.

The realization that death was a real possibility hits me hard, and the thought of Jess being harmed because of me is even more devastating.

Nineteen

Vic

The second I walk back into church, I spot the guys all lounging on the leather couch. I take a seat and look at Trey expectantly.

"Here," Marcus says as he passes me the bottle of Jack, "you're gonna need it."

I grab the neck of the bottle and chug until the liquor hits the inside of my stomach and warms me from the inside out.

With a long exhale, Trey runs his hands over his face. "When Pop first started the club, he wanted to make a name for himself, the club, and leave a legacy," Trey says with an eye roll.

He and his father never had a common understanding or viewpoint.

"He wanted the territory one of the rival clubs had, so he made a deal."

"I already know this," I say with a sigh. I just want to get this done and go lie in bed with Rosie.

"You do, but he never told anyone the who."

"Rosie's father," I say.

"What better way to get to the top than to get hired by the Mafia, right? Pop ran guns and drugs for him for years, then shit started to get weird," Trey says as he looks over at the guys. "First, with people dying or going missing."

"Then," Julian says, "the first run you and Ax went on got fucked. I swear to you nothing on the monitors showed anything. I would have never let you guys stay there as long as you did if I knew."

I look over at Julian. He looks upset. "You think this was your fault?"

"I should have figured out the pigs were tipped off before it happened."

"You couldn't have known, man. Shit happens. It's not your fault," I say to Julian. I didn't know he held guilt over that day.

"Shit was fishy as fuck after you got arrested, so I started snooping around more. Pop was furious and went off the deep end. I figured out it was Hector, Rosie's father, who employed the club through the years."

"So, you're telling me Rosie's father is the reason I got caught?"

I always knew the run was too clean to become so fucked up otherwise.

Trey nods.

"Why the fuck would he do that? From what Gage has told me, he practically owns the police force."

This is so fucked up.

The need to expel the liquor as it churns in my stomach is almost unbearable.

"Whispers flew about his oldest son, Gage's twin, getting in trouble. Hector's hush money wasn't enough to fix the last fuckup his son made, so he handed them the club to clear his son."

My heart beats in my ears. I paid the price for Rosie's brother's fuckups.

Then, I landed in the same cell as her brother, Gage. Coincidence? I think fucking not.

Rosie's father is the reason I ended up behind bars.

"I found out something else," Trey murmurs as he looks at the ground. "The night your parents died, it wasn't an accident. They were murdered. They owed too much money, and the time came to pay up. Rosie's father made the call, and the club carried out the orders."

As he utters the final word, a heavy weight settles on my chest, making it difficult to breathe. The club killed my parents.

"Who?"

"Razor and Tiny. I'm sorry I didn't tell you sooner. When I saw how broken up you were when Razor died, I didn't want to make anything worse. But shit's coming out, and I didn't want you to find out any other way."

My mind is reeling. I spring up from my seat while my heart pounds in my chest. I need to get out of here and get some air.

"Whoa. Where are you going?" Julian asks.

"Bed."

"You okay?" Marcus asks as he grabs my shoulder and squeezes.

"Never been better," I manage to say, my voice quivering as I struggle to stay upright.

I walk back to my room in a daze, and the worst part isn't Rosie's father or idiot brother. It's knowing Razor is the one who killed my parents.

From the moment I arrived to live at the club, he made me feel like I belonged, treating me as if I were his own. He taught me how to ride, fight, shoot, and kill. It's a twisted irony that he assumed the role of my father when he's the very person responsible for the death of my parents. Did he feel the weight of the guilt for turning me into an orphan? Is that why he spent so much time with me?

I press my palms against the rough edges of the doorframe, feeling the coolness seep into my hands as I rest my forehead against the solid oak door.

No matter what I know now, it can't alter what has already happened. I can only hope that the future holds more compassion for me and that I can still discover fragments of happiness along the way.

I quietly turn the door handle and peer in to see Rosie lying on the far side of my bed. I quickly shed my clothes and slip in behind her. Unable to resist, I reach out and pull her against me. Relief and a sense of security settles in, which is weird after everything I've just learned.

I caress her cheek, needing to feel the softness under my fingers, but stop when I feel wetness instead.

Alarm bells ring in my head.

"Why are you crying, baby? Are you hurting?"

"I'm fine," she says as she rubs the sheet across her face.

"The fuck you are. Why are you crying?"

"I don't know."

"Look at me."

"I can't," she says as she sniffles.

"Look at me, Rosie." Her emerald-green eyes swim with more tears, and I wipe them away with the pad of my thumb. "Everything will be okay. You're safe."

"I never told you about the bar. This is all my fault."

"What about the bar?"

"That night, with that guy. He mentioned my father. I never told you."

I think about that night. How she was white as a ghost while that fucker's arm was around her. I thought it was because she was uncomfortable. I should have pressed her on it, but I wasn't in my right mind that night.

Jealousy was at the top of my list, and I failed her because of it.

"That other guy came to the house, and I should've heeded the warning and kept better tabs on you," I say with a sigh. "It seems we're both keeping things from each other."

"Never again. I'm so sorry," she says as she cries harder, and it guts me for so many reasons.

I still have an enormous piece of the puzzle I'm keeping hidden from her, but I know she can't handle my identity right now.

"Please, don't cry."

"Are you mad at me?"

"Why would I be mad at you?"

"I thought—" she takes a deep breath—"that you were mad at me. What about that thing with my father? You looked upset."

"You thought wrong," I say with a small smile. "And you don't need to worry about that. I should be the one who's sorry. This is all my fault."

"You can't protect me from everyone all the time, Vic."

213

"I can try."

I look down at her lips and then back up at her eyes, asking for permission.

I want to make her forget, and I want to forget, too.

So, I angle my head and kiss her as deeply as she kisses me, taking my breath and all thoughts away.

Twenty

Rosie

T he sensation of weightlessness in the water eludes me. Dark thoughts and despair hold me captive, suffocating my every breath.

For the past week, I've felt like a stranger in my own skin.

I feel lost and alone.

I feel heartbroken for the Rosie of the past who thought she could be herself. I am not myself.

I haven't left the safety of Vic's home. I haven't gotten ready, gone to work, or even talked to anyone besides Vic.

I can't help but replay the events of last weekend in my mind, like a twisted horror movie montage.

I can't feel Vic caressing my lip as Jess spilled the drink on me or the laughter I shared with Jess as we ran from the guys.

All I feel is a cold sweat over my hollow shell as I think of the guy in the black mask who grabbed me. How I was so paralyzed with fear that I couldn't help my friend.

I feel responsible. I am responsible. I should know better.

I grew up in this life. This is all my fault. Jess is fine, according to Axl. I'm a terrible friend. I don't want her to see me. I can't even look at myself in the mirror. It's bad enough Vic gets to see this version of me who barely talks, eats, or takes a shower. It's the version he's rolled with since coming back the morning after the attack.

He brings me food three times a day, makes sure I'm safe, and he holds me. Sometimes it isn't about the big grand gestures; it's about the simple things, like knowing he has you and he will catch you if you fall. Which I have done more often than not. He just picks me up and wipes my tears, which have yet to stop.

I poke my finger in the water of Vic's pool and bring it a few inches above the surface. Small droplets hit the water, and a giant ring branches out before disappearing into the depths of darkness surrounding me.

A rustling sound catches my attention, and I hold my breath. I went around the house and switched off all the lights on the outside, even the ones that would turn on automatically with any movement.

Vic would be pissed if he knew this, but I wanted to see the stars.

I wanted to find a piece of myself in the pile of pieces that I know I am. I've always loved gazing at the stars, but I feel nothing when I look at them.

The sound of footsteps intensifies. "Vic, is that you?" I call as I see a dark figure walk into the water.

"Shit, I didn't know you were out here. I thought you were in bed."

"I couldn't sleep."

He gets closer, and his eyes narrow before going wide. "Are you fucking naked?"

I ignore his question.

"I can't even float anymore." My voice cracks.

"Let me help you."

"You can't," I say as a tear falls into the water.

He grabs my hand. "Come here. Lie flat." His forearms support my back and right below my butt.

I should feel a mix of excitement and nervousness at the prospect of him seeing me naked, but all I feel is hollow and numb.

"You're stiff as fuck. Close your eyes and let the water hold you." His voice is close to a whisper.

I close my eyes, but the sensation of being pulled into utter darkness intensifies, so I quickly open them again and lock gazes with him.

"I can't."

"Try for me one more time."

Despite my desire to keep them open, I obey his insistence and close my eyes.

His timbre is gentle and low as he speaks. "You're walking through the forest after a storm. You can feel the soft mud beneath your feet and the cool mist in the air. The scent of damp leaves and brush fills your nose. A variety of olive, khaki, and brown earthy hues color the space. Your steps quicken as you're drawn to the glowing light at the end of the path. The path leads you to the edge of the forest, where the sunlight reflects on the surface of a massive lake. The water is clear and crisp, with a rainbow reflecting on its surface. You walk farther into the clearing and down the dock. With your head tilted toward the sky,

217

you sit on the dock and take a deep breath. The scent of freedom fills your lungs as you inhale deeply."

Gracefully gliding across the water, I take a deep breath in as he instructs and feel an overwhelming sense of peace wash over me.

He did in two minutes what I haven't been able to do all week.

I feel myself falling, not because of the trauma, but because of the man holding me.

"Can you be there with me? On the dock?" I whisper while keeping my eyes closed, not wanting to break the spell.

"You want me to be?"

"Yeah."

"I see you sitting alone, your hair dancing in the wind, and I can't resist the urge to join you and savor the moment together. Once I sit, my hand intertwines with yours, and we enjoy the view."

Vic hums, and I begin to feel calm until his arms leave my body.

"Don't let me go."

He pulls me close again. "Never."

"I'm floating again."

"You are."

"Because of you."

"No, baby, it's all because of you."

I tilt myself closer to him, and my breathing increases as a very free, hard bulge pokes me. "Are you naked?"

"Let's act like I'm not."

"What if I don't want to?"

"That's dangerous, princess."

"I trust you."

"You shouldn't."

"But I do."

As I gaze into his eyes, a tingling sensation burns in my chest and travels to my belly.

I want him.

I want more.

"I want you to be my first," I say before I lean up to give him a kiss.

He pulls his head away and looks at me. "Not right now."

The tingling and burning vanish as embarrassment washes over me.

I wish the darkness could swallow me whole. I can't believe I just threw myself at him, and he rejected me.

I try to move out of his arms, but his grip tightens.

"Why?"

"Because you aren't you yet."

I nod as my heart drops into my stomach. He sees me as damaged.

"I'm broken."

"You're not broken, baby."

"Then, why?"

His gaze locks onto mine as his hand gently brushes against my face.

"I want to see the fire in your eyes as I touch you. Hear the ecstasy fall from your lips as I thrust into you. I want you to hold onto me, not because you're scared, but because you can't get close enough, because I can't get deep enough. I want you to feel me in every way. I want to consume you."

My breath catches in my throat. His words caress every piece of me inside and out. But I want more. I need more.

"But I want to feel you now."

Indecision mars his features as he contemplates my words. He bites his lip as he looks into my eyes. He moves us to the stairs and then out of the pool. The feeling of weightlessness hits me at the same time as goose bumps pebble my flesh from the slight breeze.

"Are you going to take me in there?" I ask as I point at the guesthouse where he takes all his conquests.

He shakes his head. "You'll never belong in there."

He carries us through the house soaking wet, but neither of us cares. I'm lost in his eyes and the small smile he keeps giving me. Is he just as nervous as I am?

Vic places me on his bed and looks down at me with another expression I can't decipher.

"I've been waiting for this exact moment since I first laid eyes on you," he whispers as he trails his finger from my bottom lip down my chin and onto my neck. "Imagining you naked…" His finger travels between my breasts. "At my mercy to do with as I please. I tried to do the right thing. To stay away from you. But I can't, not anymore. I won't." His eyes gaze into mine as his finger stops right above where I need him most. "Tell me you want this just as bad as I do. That you want me to taste you. To please you."

"Yes."

"Tonight, I plan to savor you as I should have done from the start." He pulls my legs apart and rests them over his broad shoulders as his tongue meets my center.

I let out a surprised breath as his tongue explores me. This sensation surpasses all my wildest expectations.

As his caramel eyes meet mine, they seem to burn with intensity, matching the heat between us as his tongue explores my folds.

"God, you taste so fucking good," he says as he kisses the inside of my thigh before burying his head between my legs again.

The sensation of his tongue caressing my throbbing clit sends jolts of pleasure through my body, causing my hips to jerk and my fingers to grip tightly onto his hair.

In seconds, he's turned me into a quivering mess as I beg him not to stop. He grabs my nub and sucks, making me see stars as I hold on to his head and ride it out.

As I come down from my high, I make a promise to myself. From this day forward, I'm choosing to cherish my time with him.

No matter how long or short that time may be.

Twenty-One

Vic

> Something came up. Should pick up my sister in about a week.

I read Gage's text repeatedly as I watch her naked sleeping form. She started sleeping in my bed at the house days ago. I was against it until she had a bad dream that gutted me—whimpering and crying in her sleep.

I know what it's like to feel the terror of being stuck in a nightmare, only to wake up alone and still feel its misery sinking its claws into you.

So, now, I lie in my bed with her until she falls into a peaceful slumber, and then I quietly slip out to watch her. Only tonight, I went further than a stolen kiss or harmless cuddle of comfort with barriers of clothing and blankets between us. She tasted phenomenal on my tongue, and though we didn't have sex, I hope it gave her a piece of what she craved.

I know I should regret being with my best friend's sister, but I don't. What I feel is a sense of soul-crushing despair that our time is coming to an end.

My selfishness prevented me from telling Gage about the kidnapping, knowing he would rush to pick her up. I want her to stay here forever. I don't want to go back to the way things were before.

Bitter. Sad. Alone.

Filling my time with poor decisions that leave me feeling more empty than when I started.

The quiet no longer brings me peace if she isn't by my side.

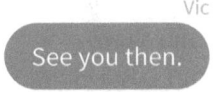

Vic

See you then.

I place my phone on my nightstand and pull her close.

I've let her fall into a silent destruction over the past week. She went through a traumatic, fucked- up event, and it wasn't even her first, from what she told me, but I can't watch her live there forever.

Endless tears, sleeping all day, and shutting out the world aren't what she was made for. She's meant to flourish in the sunshine with her breathtaking smile and infectious personality.

When she asked me to be her first, my heart soared, but also plummeted. I want her to desire me out of genuine happiness and readiness, not as a means to compensate for her emotional distress. I've been there. It often leaves you feeling worse in the end, and I'm not that much of an asshole to take something so sacred from her when she isn't thinking clearly.

When I denied her request, she shut down; her face filled with disappointment and sadness. Her self-perceived unworthiness shattered my heart, and I couldn't leave her feeling that way.

223

I'm making it my mission to put this beautiful angel back to-gether, and then I will tell her the truth. I just need time, and so does she.

"Wake up, princess," I say as I brush a few stray strands of hair from her face.

It was a restful night for both of us, a welcome change from the restless sleep we'd experienced all week.

"Come on, sleepyhead."

I'm determined to stay focused on my mission, to help her cross off her list of firsts and to get her to fall for me.

"But it's so warm and cozy in here."

"I guess I'll tattoo someone else today, then."

In an instant, her beautiful emerald eyes open. "I'm in a very vulnerable state. Don't mess with me, Vic."

"Never. Get ready and we'll head to the shop."

With a burst of joy, she springs to her feet and starts dancing around the room. I haven't seen happy Rosie in so long.

"You know what you want?"

"Ah, yeah," she says as she runs to her room and comes back with a paper. I look at the mostly simple design. A blooming lotus flower with birds ascending from the pinnacle and some kind of symbol at the bottom.

"What's this?"

"A unalome."

"A what?"

"It's a symbol of enlightenment."

"Meaning?"

"It's nothing."

"Then why add it?"

"Just because..."

I raise an eyebrow for her to continue.

"It's a reminder that I'm the one who holds the reins of my fate and existence. My destiny shall not be decided by anyone other than myself. A unalome."

"I like that. Maybe I'll get one, too."

"I don't think you have any room to add it."

"There's one place I can think of..."

Her cheeks instantly go red as she looks at my crotch.

"I was talking about my leg. Get your mind outta the gutter, princess," I say with a grin.

"You sure you want this on your ribs?" I ask as we walk into my shop.

"Yep."

It's going to hurt like a motherfucker, especially for her first tattoo.

"Can I tweak a few things?"

Her eyes light up. "I was hoping you would."

I motion for Rosie to stand in front of me while I sit on my leather stool. I grab her hips, my fingers running along her exposed silky skin, before angling her to the side so I have better access to the area I plan to tattoo.

Blood rushes in my ears as I think about my hands being on her for different reasons.

My hands linger on her hips for a second longer than necessary before slowly brushing away, leaving chills in their wake, which makes a small smirk appear on the side of my lips.

After cleaning her skin with gentle strokes, I press a piece of transfer paper against her side, making sure to capture every intricate detail. I grab the edge of the paper and take it off before going over the whole design with a critical eye, leaning right, then left. It has to be perfect. This is the most important tattoo I've ever done.

"Perfect."

She walks to the full-length mirror on the other side of the shop. A genuine smile graces my lips.

"It is perfect."

Rosie skips back to my station and lies down on her side. We get right to work, and the second the needles brush against her skin, she winces. This is going to be a long-ass day for her.

We stay in relative silence for a while. Her in her head and me in mine. It becomes almost peaceful as I'm lulled by the buzzing of the tattoo machines.

"Gage texted and said he's coming to collect me soon. Looks like you're going to be rid of me and back to your life."

I look over at her, and she has a look I don't understand on her face.

"Is that what you want?" I ask, leading the conversation away from me and life after her.

I know what I want, but what the hell does she want?

"I don't know that I have a choice," she says, resigned.

"Bullshit. You always have a choice."

"If I did, I wouldn't be here."

My stomach plummets, but I school my features. "So, you regret it?"

But what I really mean by it is me. *Does she regret me?*

The bell rings above the door before she can comment further.

"I heard someone was getting tattooed," Trey says as he looks over my shoulder.

"How's it feeling, Rosie? You need someone to hold your hand?"

I shake my head. "You're a stupid fucker if you're still flirting with her after knowing who her family is."

"What's your excuse?" he fires back.

I ignore him. "Why're you here?"

Trey smiles like he knows I'm changing the subject.

"Waiting for Ax. I told him I'd meet him at Jess's, but he declined."

"Shocker." I laugh.

"He needs to chill. She's like my little sister, for fuck's sake."

"You seem to enjoy fucking with him about her."

"Serves him right after breaking my fucking nose."

"Why'd he break your nose?" Rosie asks through a wince.

"He thought I was trying to poach Jess."

"Were you?"

"Fuck no. I was doing him a favor. Though I doubt his stupid ass will ever see it that way. Ah, speak of the idiot," Trey says as Ax walks to the door.

"Should I be worried? You two never do anything alone together."

"We bought Samuel a bike for his birthday. It's pretty fuckin' clean. He should be stoked," Trey says with a smile. "Are we still on for tomorrow?"

"Yep."

"See you guys then."

"What's tomorrow?" Rosie asks through another wince as I rub her side with a paper towel to clean the ink off.

"Nothing. We're done."

Rosie sluggishly rises from the chair and makes her way toward the mirror. I have no doubt her adrenaline is wearing off after the lengthy session, and she'll be in need of some rest soon.

Her face lights up with a mixture of excitement and awe, exceeding all my expectations.

I hope she looks at this ten years down the road with the same expression and not the regret she seems to have.

As I walk up behind her, I hold my breath, patiently waiting for her to acknowledge my presence while her eyes remain fixed on her own skin. As if she can sense my gaze, her head snaps up in the mirror, meeting my eyes. I'm caught in a trance as I advance on her, our eyes never leaving each other.

Something raw and animalistic burns through me as I see her with the design we created together, with my own personal touch.

My fingers graze the side of her neck, and I feel her pulse beating strongly under my fingertips. I pull her flush against me so that she can feel just how turned on I am by her. She lets out a surprised squeal as I turn her around to face me.

To my surprise, she reaches her lips to mine and initiates the kiss.

"I regret nothing about being here with you, Vic. Nothing."

Twenty-Two

Rosie

I sit on the back of Vic's bike as we fly down the road. The sunshine I haven't seen in what feels like too long is beating down on me and bringing me back to life. But despite the beauty of this day, there's a shadow cast by the hourglass in my head, reminding me that Gage's arrival is just days away.

Right here is where I want to stay, feeling the sun's rays on me while the breeze caresses my body in this small town that feels like my sanctuary with my hands wrapped around this beautiful man.

Vic gives my leg a squeeze as if he can read my thoughts, which brings me back to the present.

This is the first ride I've been on with all the guys from the MC, and I can't help but feel a little badass as I sit here with them. They give off an I *don't give a fuck* air, and I can't help but admire that.

After years of playing the part of the good girl, it's exhilarating to let go and not worry about what others think or how they perceive me. I've tried since I arrived to slough off the old me, and it finally feels like I am.

Trey, Julian, and Marcus are in the front, with Trey leading the way. Vic says it goes by order of rank. Vic and Axl are behind them, with Jess and me on the back of their bikes, and then more guys behind us.

When I voiced my concerns about Vic getting in trouble for riding with them, he shrugged it off. I can tell he misses this. His happiness has been undeniable all morning.

I look over at Jess, who sits on the back of Axl's bike. She wraps her arms tightly around him, and a huge smile graces his lips as he says something to her through their mics. She, of course, rolls her eyes before giving a small smile. From what Vic told me, they're attached at the hip these days.

It was hard to see her. I still feel immense guilt for what happened, even more so when I saw the stitches that are barely beginning to heal across her forehead.

The weather is chilly, but there isn't a cloud in sight, just light blue skies in the late morning.

The desire to stretch my arms wide and experience the wind caressing my skin is overwhelming. After about twenty minutes of watching the trees on both sides of the highway zoom by, I say fuck it. I squeeze my legs tighter against Vic and lift my arms in the air as I always do on the back of his bike.

Feeling the wind fly between my fingers, like a bird flying high with no thoughts of coming down from the clouds.

All of my worries fade away. The pressure on my chest is not as heavy. I almost feel like myself again.

This feels like living.

AMARIE COLLINS

We make a right and come to a halt on an arched metal bridge, joining a truck and a small group of people. As I dismount from the bike, my legs tremble like gelatin from the long ride. When I stumble, Vic reaches out his hand to steady me.

"Whoa there." He chuckles while his eyes sparkle with amusement.

Embarrassment from almost meeting the floor again colors my cheeks, so I blurt the first thing that comes to mind. "You know you're kinda beautiful."

"And you're kinda perfect," he murmurs as he rubs my hand with his. The gentle touch accompanied by those words stirs a profound yearning for him within me. "You ready?"

"For what?"

"I remember someone saying they wanted to bungee jump."

I squeal. "Are you for real?"

"Yep."

"You did this for me?"

"Of course. Let's go, baby," he pulls me over to where the guys are setting up.

"You shouldn't have, Vic," Trey says as he gets buckled in. A huge smile graces his lips. "Later fuckers" is all he says before doing a back flip off the bridge.

He's definitely a little unhinged. Trey disappears over the side, and I look up at Vic with wide eyes.

"You scared?"

"A little."

"You'll be safe."

"Are you going to do it, too?"

"Fuck no."

"Why?"

232

"Vic's scared of heights," Axl says with a laugh.

"Fuck you, Ax."

I can't help but smile. Vic fearing something makes him almost seem more human. I've thought of him as someone who's immune to that feeling.

It sounds bad, but I find comfort in him fearing at least one thing.

I look over at Jess, who's close to Axl's side. "What about you, Jess?"

"Uh." She looks over at Axl, who shakes his head, then she looks back at me. *Weird.* "I'm with Vic. I don't like heights."

"You're up," Vic says.

I look over to the ledge where they're waiting for me. Second thoughts race through my mind. Vic threads his fingers with mine and pulls me over.

The guy clips me in as I look up at Vic with trepidation.

"You can do this," he says while watching the guy. "Watch those fingers, buddy."

When the guy stands back up, Vic narrows his eyes at him. "Are you sure everything is secure and safe?"

"Yes, sir."

Vic holds his stare for a moment longer before looking down at me. "I'll see you when you get back up. Have fun."

My gaze slides over to the other side of the bridge, where some of the guys are jumping.

"Vic, I can't do it. I'm scared," I whisper, shaking my head as I look down. My feet won't move as fear paralyzes me, and the weight I thought was gone from my chest reappears.

Vic's face softens as he rubs my cheek.

"Okay," he says before looking behind me. "Can we go tandem?"

"Yeah. Let me get you a harness." The guy says.

My eyes widen when I figure out what he's doing. "But you don't like heights."

"No, I don't."

"You don't have to do this."

"But I do." He rubs my cheek softly before kissing my lips. "For you."

My heart soars at the sacrifice he's making for me. I don't know when he deemed it okay to kiss me in public for anyone to see, but I love it.

We unlocked a new level in our relationship after the night in the pool. One that left me feeling light, and dare I say loved? Not in love, because I know Vic would never want that, but cared for.

With him securely fastened to me, we walk toward the edge. Our bodies intertwine as I securely hold his waist with my arms, while his arms provide a comforting embrace around my shoulders.

I can hear Vic's heart pounding in my ear, its rhythm erratic. I'm filled with an overwhelming sense of gratitude toward him. His selflessness grants me the opportunity to experience yet another first.

"Alright, guys, whenever you're ready."

"Are you ready?" I ask as I gaze up at Vic.

,"No," he says with a nervous laugh, his eyes vulnerable. "But for you, I'll do anything."

That's all the answer I need. I go on my tiptoes, give him a peck on his lips, and then lean over the edge.

We free-fall off the bridge that has a river running through the bottom. I scream loud enough for everyone to hear as the weightless feeling hits me, and my stomach drops. Vic's arms tighten around me as we move back and forth at the bottom of the bridge like a bunch of rag dolls.

"That was—"

"Awful."

"It wasn't that bad."

"With you, it wasn't."

"I appreciate you," I say as I kiss his chest.

Another first and core memory this beautiful man has given me.

We split from the pack of bikes and off toward another high-way. Different shades of green zoom past us as we fly to our destination.

It's getting colder, so I burrow even closer to him, feeling his muscles bounce as I wrap my chilled hands around him. He takes one hand off the handlebars and gently rubs mine back and forth, spreading warmth through my entire body.

I love when his hands are on me.

Before I know it, the ride is over and I look around. "You brought me back to the lake!"

"That I did. We came a little earlier than last time, so we can stay longer if you'd like," he says while grabbing my hand and leading the way.

"I still can't get over the beauty of this place. Thank you for bringing me back."

We head through the clearing, and I can't help but inhale a breath of surprise.

Lanterns line the dock over the lake, and at the end are two easels with blank canvases.

I look over at him in shock. "You did this? For me?" I say with tears in my eyes.

He just grins and pulls me along.

"When did you get all of this up here?" I ask as I look at all the supplies.

"Don't worry your pretty little head about that. I want to see you paint."

"It's been a long time," I say. I've sketched, but it was with clients' ideas before the kidnapping.

I'm scared my creativity is gone.

"No doubts. Put the brush in your hand and ignore everything else. Even me," he says with the push I need.

I take a deep breath and square my shoulders before grabbing the supplies I need.

Soft music plays from behind me and I can't help but sway and get lost in the moment of doing the two things I love at once. I've always been the type to need music and a bit of chaos around me to get my vision onto paper.

I'm in that element, and I let the moment take me. Deep strokes of black, browns, greens, and white dominate the canvas. I don't stop until the sun is almost down and we're surrounded by only the muted light of the lanterns and the moon.

I didn't even notice how chilly it was until now.

Vic comes up behind me, wrapping me in the warmth of his embrace.

"It's breathtaking, just like you," Vic says against my ear.

"Let me see yours."

I look over at Vic's canvas, and my head angles to the side. It's a beautiful and simple red rose, but it looks familiar. Weird. But a rose is just a rose. How else would you draw one?

Get out of your head, Rosie.

Enjoy the moment.

I turn around in his arms and sway with him to the soft music that's playing.

This is what living is.

This is what I ran from home to have.

Moments like this.

The freedom to choose my memories.

We sway until we hear lightning in the distance, bringing us back to the present.

"Shit, we better go before it gets bad. I don't want to ride with you on the back while it's raining," he says in a rush.

"What about our paintings?"

"I'll handle it. Let's get the fuck outta here."

Vic grabs my hand as we walk into the forest. I lean closer to him for both warmth and safety. The branches sway ominously in the wind, foreshadowing the impending storm. As we hurry, the scent of damp pine and moss fills the surrounding air.

We make it to his bike, and Vic turns around abruptly, making me bump into his chest. I look up into his eyes, confused.

"Go to the back of my bike, spread your legs, and lean over it. Place your chest on the seat," he instructs me with a stern voice.

I quirk my eyebrow. "What? Why?"

"It's time for one of my firsts. Get on the back of my bike, baby." A dark grin adorns his face.

He leans down and crushes his lips to mine in a hard kiss. The gentle Vic from the lake is gone, and I love it.

His hands go straight into my hair, and he pulls hard, eliciting a moan of both pain and pleasure from me.

He turns me around; my back against his hard chest. His mouth runs from my collarbone to my ear, kissing and sucking, giving me goose bumps and making me shiver. His hands move down my front, flicking the button on my jeans open.

"What about the storm?"

"Fuck waiting. Fuck the storm. Fuck everything but my hands on you. My mouth on you," he says in my ear while he keeps moving his hand south.

He sticks his hand in and rubs my clit roughly through my panties. I buck my hips, unable to stay still. It feels so good.

"I can feel how wet you are for me. I'm going to fucking eat you alive," he says in a raspy voice, breathing as heavily as I am.

A whimper is my only response. I'm mindless and on sensory overload.

He stops rubbing me and slides my pants down, including my panties. One hand on my hip and the other on the middle of my back, he pushes me down until I'm lying on the seat face-first. I move my head to the side to peek back at him, but from the angle, I can't see much. All I can do is feel.

He grabs the back of my neck, giving it a tight squeeze before he smacks my ass hard. I yelp. The sound echoes like a tree falling on the forest floor.

Oh God. It stings so good.

"Please," I whimper.

"Please, what?"

"I want you," I whisper, knowing I've never been more sincere.

"And I want you." He takes his time moving down my body, building my anticipation. Both of his hands grip my thighs and spread them apart. His face above my center, he breathes me in before groaning.

If he doesn't do something soon, I might die.

Just when I think I might shed a tear out of frustration, his mouth comes down on me. Warm and wet. Licking, kissing, sucking me. My legs buckle when he licks me from the bottom to the top, just over my puckered hole.

"Oh God, yes," I say on repeat.

"You like that, beautiful?" he asks. "You want more?"

"Please."

"I love when that word falls from your lips," he says before returning to my center.

He licks faster, with more pressure, sticking his tongue in a place no one has ever been. In and out, in and out. Driving me to the brink, then stopping, making me huff out a breath of despair.

"Wait, no, don't stop," I say without thinking. I'm too distraught over the thought of being left hanging to worry about sounding needy.

His hand grips a handful of my hair, making my back bow and my chest come off the seat before he sticks two fingers inside me.

I yelp at the intrusion, my eyes going wide. Feeling him stretch me, his fingers going in and out. He scissors me wider to make room for his fingers. The position has me grinding against the end of the seat, my clit stimulated with each move.

The wind picks up, and I can feel its icy touch on my overheated skin.

"You're so wet and tight. You hear the sounds your pussy makes for me? I can't wait to be inside you," he says while pumping into me faster, making my legs shake and hitting something that has me seeing stars before I scream out my release.

He's still slowly pumping, wringing out the last bit of my orgasm before withdrawing his fingers.

I lie on the back of his bike, breathing heavy, hair in a chaotic mess all over my face, too spent to move.

I'm wondering if this is it. *Will he finally give me what I've asked for?*

He takes something out of his saddlebag before I feel him wiping me down. Then, he pulls my panties and pants back up. I push my hands against the bike to get up before turning around to look at him. Confused.

"You ready to go?"

"But I thought..." I leave the rest unsaid.

"When we get home."

Home, I think as my heart swells.

But there's something I want to do.

I drop down on both knees in front of him. His head tilts to the side, looking down at me. "Are you sure?"

I nod, too nervous to talk.

"Have you done this before?"

I shake my head.

"You're so perfect," he says. "Unbutton my pants."

Trembling, I reach out and touch the rough denim of his pants, my eyes fixed on the noticeable bulge straining against his zipper. As I awkwardly fumble with the button of his jeans, my inexperience becomes painfully obvious. I finally win the war and unzip his pants before looking back up at him.

"Pull them down."

I slide down his pants and black boxer briefs. My eyes widen when he springs free. He fists himself a couple of times, and I can't keep my eyes off the way his hand looks as he pleases himself.

"Open your mouth and stick out your tongue," he says as he places the tip at the opening of my mouth.

I open wide while maintaining eye contact with him. It feels so intimate, and I love it.

He places his tip against my tongue and thrusts in with a groan. "Fuck...so good."

More thunder strikes, and it sounds right above us.

"We gotta hurry."

I nod.

"I'm going to take over. If you need me to stop, tap my leg, baby." He threads his fingers between the strands of my hair, anchoring me to him before thrusting in harder, deeper until he can't go in any farther. He hits the back of my throat, making my eyes water, but I continue to lick and suck. He groans with each thrust, and I can't help the moan that follows.

I'm making him feel just as good as he makes me feel.

"Look at me, baby. I want you to swallow. Can you do that for me?" I look up at him, tears in my eyes, skin flushed, feeling more turned on than I have ever felt.

I give him a small nod, and he explodes with a deep groan. I swallow as he pulls me to my feet and presses his lips to mine.

"Let's go home," he says, making butterflies swarm in my belly and something deeper take root in my heart.

About ten minutes into our ride, the telltale sign of drops hit my back and shoulders. Shit. More come, and I can't help but laugh. I've always loved the rain.

Tonight can't get any more perfect. Vic guns it down the highway, much to my delight. From the huge grin I can see in the side mirror, he's enjoying himself as well. I move my hand under his shirt and rub his lower stomach, loving the way his muscles move and tighten under my touch. I was once nervous about touching him, but now I want to feel all of him.

"I'll order us some food while you change," Vic says as he helps me take my helmet off in the garage.

As soon as I enter my room, I strip off my damp clothes and grab one of my longer shirts. I pull open my top drawer, then close it, opting to skip underwear.

I want him, and I'm done waiting.

I find him in the living room, where he rarely sits. His phone in hand while he types.

With every ounce of courage I possess, I stand in front of him.

"Food should be here in about thirty—"

Before he can finish, I swiftly position myself on top of him. A mischievous grin spreads across my face as I savor his surprise at being caught off guard.

He traces his hands along my waist before caressing my ass. His hands pause as he realizes I have no underwear on, and he moans his approval.

Drawing closer, I lean in and capture his lips in a tender kiss.

A wave of nervous excitement washes over me, and my stomach flutters with a flurry of butterflies.

A chaotic swarm, buzzing with energy.

A kaleidoscope of color and feelings.

This feels right.

I pull back and go for his pants. His eyes go wide. "Are you sure?"

"Surer than I have ever been in my entire life," I say as I pull at the drawstrings.

He shifts his hips and pulls them down to his knees. I gulp as I look down at his dick that's long and thick with a mean-looking vein on the side.

"Umm." I glance up with trepidation. It looks way bigger in the light.

"Don't get scared now, baby. I promise you'll love every minute of it."

That's all the reassurance I need. I sit up straighter as he grabs himself and lines the head with my entrance.

"Look at me. I want to see your eyes the moment my cock is fully inside you. Owning you like I've always wanted to. Bringing you pleasure no one else has. Only me."

"Only you," I breathe before putting my hands on his shoulders and squatting back in his lap.

We don't break eye contact as I drop fully onto his length. I let out a pain-filled groan while Vic leans into me with a deep moan. Holy hell, it hurts. He's stretching me so much.

I wrap my hands around his neck as if that will ease some of the pain.

"Are you okay?"

I exhale. "I think so. It just hurts."

"I know, but it won't hurt for long." He rubs my back, which calms me and soothes some of the discomfort.

He pulls back and slowly circles my clit, making my walls clench around his hard length in painfully sweet satisfaction.

"I'm gonna start moving. You can tell me to stop at any time, and I will."

I nod into his neck as he continues to rub my clit.

He lifts me with his other arm as if I weigh nothing before slowly bringing me back down on him.

Each stroke he takes builds momentum, and they're harder than the last.

He's breathing heavy in my ear, mirroring my own breaths. All I can do is hold on and take what he's giving me.

The searing pain subsides and brings forth a mixture of both pleasure and pain.

Every time he pulls out, I wait with bated breath for him to slam back into me again.

"You feel so fucking good, so fucking good."

I moan into his neck. Unable to form a coherent response, I feel a burn building in my stomach from the friction of my clit against his stomach while he hammers into me.

"God, I can feel you squeezing my cock. Come for me, baby."

He holds me tighter against him, and I see stars. The orgasm sweeps me away in the most intoxicating way I have ever felt.

"You're so perfect," he says as he kisses my forehead.

He stands with me in his arms, his length still buried inside me as he walks us down the hall and into his room. He throws me on the bed, and I let out a surprised squeal.

"Are you too sore?"

I shake my head. It's tender, but I never want this moment to end.

"Good. Lose the shirt. I want to see all of you."

I pull off my shirt, and my nipples pebble under his gaze. He crawls over my body and takes my nipple into his mouth, sucking while squeezing my other. A moan pulls from my lips as a shock of pleasure goes through my body.

He grabs my legs and lifts them onto his shoulders. "Put your hands against the headboard and don't move them."

I lay my palms flat, making my breasts rise higher.

The moment I look back up at him, he slams into me.

Hard.

"Oh fuck," I chant over and over.

It turns him into an animal as he powers into me. He's thrusting so hard you can hear the smack of the headboard against the wall, drowning out my cries of pleasure.

Vic's eyes roll in the back of his head. He must feel the pull of euphoria calling to him as it is doing to me.

He reaches between my legs and rubs my clit one, two, three times before I'm screaming. He follows me over the edge, bucking his hips wildly before coming to a stop, my release mixing with his.

He peers down at me, and I can't help the smile on my face. "What?"

"No wonder it makes people crazy. That was amazing."

"You're so perfect." He falls to my side and pulls me closer to him.

My hands go into his hair. I know how much he enjoys the way it feels.

"My mom used to rub my head like you're doing. It's one of the few things I remember about her."

This is the first time Vic has willingly talked about his family. My heart clenches as I think about what Jess told me.

"Do you miss her?"

"I miss the thought of who she could have been if not for her selfishness. Maybe it would have made me different."

"I don't want to imagine you being different. I think you're perfect the way you are."

"Even my fucked-up parts?"

"Everyone has them, Vic. You just have to find the people willing to see them as beautiful."

"The only thing beautiful here is you."

I smile at his subject change. I'll take the hint and just be grateful he's beginning to open up to me.

"You make me wish we could stay in this blissful moment forever."

"We can."

"We both know that's not true," I say with a heavy sigh as I think about all the things I promised myself to forget until it was time.

Gage.

The arranged marriage.

Leaving Vic.

The last one hurts the most.

"It could be."

Twenty-Three

Rosie

As I stretch, I'm acutely aware of the soreness permeating every inch of me.

Last night was a whirlwind of excitement, beauty, and perfection. It went beyond anything I could have wished for.

Vic is just full of surprises. Perhaps his emotions run deeper than what meets the eye. Hopefully, he's experiencing this connection just as strongly as I am.

I have to talk to him. I don't want to build up my expectations only to be disappointed in the end.

But how could I not after the date on the lake? It was magical. I wish I could tell Mama all about it. She would be swooning.

This is the life I would have hoped for if I thought it was possible, and it's all because of him.

I can imagine waking up every morning next to Vic, working with him, laughing with him, experiencing more firsts with him.

Falling more in love with him.

I tap the side of the bed, but it feels cold. Where is he?

An iced coffee sits on the nightstand beside a folded paper. I go for the coffee first, take a big sip, then grab the piece of paper. I can't help but grin at the idea of receiving a hand-written note from him rather than a quick text message. It's adorable.

Blood roars through my ears as my coffee falls from my hand and lands on the floor with a crash.

I take in the handwriting sprawled across the white paper. I've seen this writing before.

You could show me thousands of handwritten notes, and I'd still be able to distinguish it from the rest.

How the pressure exerted practically engraves the letters into the paper.

How the letters smudge from him being left-handed and not giving it enough time to dry.

The way he never crosses all the way through his t's.

No.

This—this can't be.

I run to my room and throw open my drawer, collecting the letters from Rush. I lay them out, side by side, and it's clear as day. Hysterical tears threaten to spill from my eyes.

There has to be a plausible reason for this.

Maybe they have the same handwriting? I mean, that can happen, right?

I run back to Vic's room and head straight for his nightstand drawers, opening all six but finding nothing.

This is silly. What am I doing?

I sit on the bed and blow out a breath before looking at his closet.

My intuition is telling me something isn't right.

I enter the closet and open his top drawer, filled with black boxer briefs. My hand dives in, sifting through the contents, making a mess but coming up empty.

The second drawer houses socks, and I show them just as much care as his top drawer. My fingers graze against something that crinkles, and I pause.

I pull out a paper bag. Since this was hiding in his drawer of the home he lives in by himself, it can't be good.

I open it, and I see paper bundled up in a rubber band.

Before I pull them all the way out, I know. I just know.

These are my letters.

The first tear falls before I even process I'm crying.

On the top sits a picture of me, worn at the edges as if it has been touched a million times. It's an old one from college.

Way before I came to town.

Way before I thought I knew him.

Way before I fell for him.

Under the letters is the final nail to my heart, a black and red devil mask I've seen before.

The sudden onslaught of nausea floods my body, leaving my stomach unsettled and churning.

"No," I say to myself as I shake my head. "This can't—"

I can't believe this.

The sound of footsteps reaches my ears just moments before I catch sight of him.

I'm rooted in place. A statue ready to crumble. My grasp tightens around the lies I hold.

He swallows as he looks at what's in my hands before gazing back up at me.

249

Regret is the first emotion that flits across his face before determination steps in. His eyes seem to burn with intensity as he takes a step forward.

"Don't come any closer," I choke out, my words catching in my throat.

"I can explain," he says as he steps forward anyway.

"Were you ever going to tell me?"

"Yes."

"When? Because it sure as hell wasn't after we met. Or after we kissed. Or even after I gave you my virginity. So, when? Once I became yours?"

"You are mine."

A hysterical giggle bubbles out of me. I'm so fucking close to falling apart, but I refuse to do so in front of him.

"No, I'm not. I'm the idiot who told you everything when you asked even though you knew everything already."

"I wanted to hear the words from your lips. Not on paper."

Suddenly, a wave of crushing realization washes over me. The person I wrote to for years isn't real.

Every written letter, every smile, every laugh, every tear shed. Fake.

"Rush doesn't exist. He doesn't—"

"I do. I'm right here," he says as he points at his chest.

"You ruined one of the most important things I had left," I say as I throw the letters at him. He and I both watch them land on the floor.

A tear slides down my cheek, and I smack the traitorous thing away. Vic takes another step forward, but I take another back. "I said don't come any closer to me. You should have told me right away."

"When? Before or after I threw Samantha on the bed? That night, you were disgusted with me. I could see it in your eyes. I knew I fucked up and lost what we could have had."

"That's where you're wrong. I never expected you to be a saint, and we never moved past the more-than-friends category, anyway. You were my best friend," I say as my voice cracks.

"I still am," he says with sadness in his eyes.

"No, you're a liar," I say with a sniffle and point at him. "Rush was my best friend. He would've never lied to me. Deceived me. Manipulated me. How could you?"

He shakes his head. "Please, just let me ex—"

"No!" I scream, too heartbroken to hear any more. "I don't want to hear it."

"It's not what you think. I never meant to hurt you. I care about you."

"Which one is the real you, Rush or Vic?" I say as I look at him as if it's for the first time.

I dreamed of meeting Rush for years. Imagined what he would look like, what he sounded like.

I finally got my wish, and it fucking hurts.

I give him five seconds to give me the answer. Neither will make me feel better, but I have to know.

He runs his hands through his hair and takes a big breath as if lost in his thoughts and not sure what to say.

I shake my head. "Your time is up. I'm leaving."

I rush past him and snatch my phone off the nightstand, my fingers trembling with urgency. Prepared to sprint the entire distance back home if necessary.

"Please don't go. I can't lose you."

The desperation in his voice is clear, but I don't care. I can't.

"You just did."

As his head falls forward and his gaze stays fixated on his feet, I seize the opportunity and dash through the house, my footsteps reverberating against the walls until I burst into the chilly downpour outside.

Twenty-Four

Vic

W hy do I always fuck shit up?

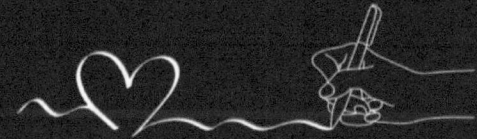

Fifteen Years Old

The clink of bars sounds, and I open my eyes from the bottom bunk. A kid walks through with bedding and an extra pair of clothes. He looks around the same age as me. Haunted-ass eyes with the look of pain and vengeance. A heady combination, one that will ultimately lead to destruction.

Welcome to the fucking club, man.

The door closes behind him in a haunting noise that always makes me anxious and gives me claustrophobia. Trapped, locked in, caged.

"What's up, man? I'm Vic," I say with a head nod.

"Gage," he says, looking around.

"You can take the top bunk."

"Thanks."

"You get more letters, man?" I ask Gage.

We've been cellmates for a couple of months now. Thankfully, we get along a lot better than the last fucker. I put him in the hospital for stealing my shit. I got time added and was in the hole for two weeks, but it was worth it.

Gage is cool, though. Quiet, clean, and someone I've learned I can trust. He's honest, which is hard to find in people.

"One from my sister," he says, holding up a letter and a photo.

I reach to take the photo with a wince. My side is still tender from the shiv that was embedded in my ribs when I tried to save Gage in the day room a week ago. He had five on him, and blood was fucking everywhere. I'll always remember the sight of him rising from the ground, his body covered in crimson wounds, yet he held his head high even though I'm sure he was in a fuck ton of pain. He earned my respect and many others' that day.

My attention is instantly seized by a girl in the photo. Her dark hair, captivating green eyes, sun-kissed complexion, and beaming smile make it impossible for me to look away.

Just the sight of her makes my pulse jump.

"That's Alexa, my sister, Ro, and my douche of a brother, Marco."

"That the Alexa you've been talking about?" I ask to take the focus off my looking at the brunette, who's unfortunately his sister.

"Yep," he says, taking the picture back and looking at it longingly. The poor fuck is hopeless when it comes to her.

"You think she'll wait for you to get out?"

"She doesn't have a choice. She's mine," he says with unwavering confidence.

He hops back on his bunk, probably to stare at her picture more.

I've never met a girl who has had a hold on me like his girl has on him.

My thoughts fly back to the photo of the goddess with green eyes. I wonder how her voice sounds, her laughter, her screams. How soft her skin is, and what her smile would feel like aimed at me. Only me. I shake my head to banish all the devious thoughts of his sister from my mind.

He's my friend, and I feel like a dick for thinking of his sister that way.

You're in here, and she's out there, Vic.

She's bright sunshine, and you're pitch-black night.

You are the bitter cold, while she is the radiant heat.

Despite repeating it to myself for years, I'm unable to resist the temptation of stealing a quick glance at the photo Gage placed by his pillow on the wall, both day and night.

Despite repeating it to myself for years, I still continue to write to her. Falling deeper into the sunshine she is. Warm, comforting, and free.

Present Day

"Back the fuck up. What do you mean, motherfucker?" Gage yells through the other end of the line.

"I fucked up, man. I lied to her, and I need to figure out a way to fix it," I mutter as I peer out my window into the pouring rain.

It feels as if a vice is squeezing my throat, making it hard to speak. Tears burn my eyes, something I haven't felt since the day I was saved from my birth donor's condemned apartment as a child.

"Where is she now?"

"I don't know. She bolted. I need to go find her," I say as I rush through my house, which feels barren without her.

She belongs here, by my side. I have to get her back.

"Absolutely the fuck not. I'll figure it out. Just... just stay away from her," he says, ending with a sigh.

"I can't do that. I can't let her go."

I won't recover if I lose her forever.

"You have to. There are more pieces at play than just you."

"You'll have to kill me before I let anyone take her from me," I say, thinking about the arranged marriage he spoke of.

"I should kill you, anyway."

"I love her," I say as I rub the moisture from my eyes. This is the first time I've admitted it.

I love her so fucking much it hurts.

"Don't bullshit me."

"I'm not. Please, Gage," I beg, something I'm not accustomed to doing.

"She's not someone you throw out when you get tired of her, Vic."

"She's my forever."

"You stupid motherfucker. If you hurt her, I'll bury you, no matter how close we are."

"Noted."

"You still have shit to answer to." I nod as if he can see.

I fucked things up with him, too. I have a lot of shit to fix.

"I know. I'll do anything."

"It's gonna cost you."

"I'll pay with my life," I say as I hold the phone tighter to my ear.

"I was hoping you'd say that," he says, and I can practically feel his Cheshire cat smile from the other end.

Twenty-Five

Rosie

I run through the pouring rain until I get to the forest line just beyond the houses where Vic lives. I can feel the freezing cold seeping into every inch of my body, numbing my skin and chilling me to the core, yet I pay it no mind.

Everything feels distant and empty except for the overwhelming pressure in my chest.

How could he deceive me with every word, every action, every touch, every kiss?

Each breath I take feels shallow and strained, leaving me feeling suffocated and unable to regain control of my breathing.

As I pace the edge of the forest line, I try to focus on the earthy scent of moss and dampness that permeates the air. In my struggle to stay present and avoid being consumed by a panic attack, time loses its structure, melding into a confusing blur of emotions.

I don't know where I go from here.

I feel so damn alone.

What made me believe I could be happy? How could I have been so naive? I was a fool to hope for more.

The sudden ring of my phone startles me. I hesitantly look, only to see Jess's name.

"Hello."

"Rosie, Vic called and said you might need me. Are you okay?"

No, I'm dying inside.

"Can you pick me up if you aren't busy? I'm outside of the houses Vic lives in."

"Can you share your location?"

"I will."

The moment her car pulls up, I jump in. "I'm so sorry for the inconvenience... and your wet seat."

"Never apologize for needing help. Here." She shrugs out of her jacket and hands it to me. "You must be freezing."

"Thank you."

"I made you a hot chocolate from the shop. Chocolate helps everything."

I grab it and take a gulp. It's warm, and the chocolate tastes delicious as it melts in my mouth.

"I swear I don't deserve your friendship."

"Don't you dare! You've been a great friend to me." She looks over at me. "Do you want to talk about it?"

"I wish I could erase this morning and go back to last night."

"Oh shit, it's one of those..."

"He lied about everything, Jess. Everything," I say wiping away a stray tear.

"He told me."

"He did?"

"Yep. I'm not sticking up for Vic whatsoever, but when I spoke to him, he sounded devastated. I've never seen him act like he does with you."

"It still doesn't excuse him."

"Agreed. But if you care about him like I think you do, just give yourself some time to think about everything. I'd hate for you to have regrets later. Memories are precious and so is the time you spend with people."

"You're right."

"And now that I've said all that, I will totally be your girl and slash the tires on his truck with you. But I refuse to go near his bike because I'm not suicidal," she says with a grin, which makes me smile.

"Thank you for being such an amazing friend. Meeting you was one of the best things I did since moving to town." I pull her into a hug.

"I could say the same about you. Someone pulled in behind me."

I look out the window and pray it isn't Vic. I can't handle seeing him right now, but all I see is a suit.

"Ugh, my brother Gage," I say with a sigh. "I better go."

I pull Jess in for another hug, feeling like this might be the last time I see her.

I could fight Gage on this, but what's left for me here?

Nothing.

Because it was all a lie.

"Call or text if you need anything. Like I said, I'm here for you... always."

"Thanks, Jess."

I get out of Jess's car and walk toward Gage.

"How'd you find me this time, big brother?" I ask as I try to distract him from my tear-streaked face, bare feet, and shirt combo I have going on. I must look like a mess.

"Vic told me."

Lovely.

He closes my door, and I stare out the window into the pouring rain. The weather is a mirror image of my emotions right now. Dark, gloomy, and cold.

You always hear about the highs that come with meeting someone and falling for them. The stolen glances that set your body on fire. The giddy feeling you get when they send you a text and the anticipation of their words, the butterflies you get when their hands are on you. Searing your flesh with scars even after their touch is gone.

But no one likes to speak of the lows once all of that is ripped from your grasp.

The soul-shattering emptiness where those feelings used to lie.

A part of me longs for the blissful ignorance of never noticing that something was off.

I regret ever opening that drawer and uncovering the painful truth.

I didn't lose one person.

I lost two.

I could have been in bed right now, cuddling in his safe, warm arms. My curiosity got the better of me, and I got burned, just like I thought I would.

Gage closes his door, bringing me out of my thoughts. As we make our way down the road, I catch movement in my peripheral, and my head turns automatically. The moment I think I see something or someone, it's gone, and so are we.

"We have much to discuss, little sister."

"Later."

"Of course," he says, dropping the subject and leaving me to my thoughts.

I close my eyes and will myself to wake up from this horrible dream.

We get to Gage's townhouse, which is on the outskirts of Chicago. He's living right under everyone's noses. Alexa would freak if she knew how close he lived to her.

Gage has been living lavishly. His home has black-and-white accents, glass walls, marble floors, and light sconces that turn on as you walk by. I don't blame him after where he's been in the past years.

I make my way up the staircase made of cable ties and stone that seem to float mid-air. I pick the first open room on the right and settle in. Jumping on the bed face-first, I think about how much more messed up my life is. I'm not entirely sure how long I'll stay, considering Gage planned to get me from Vic soon, anyway.

Gage comes in later with Thai takeout for dinner. We sit on the bed as he hands me a white container and a pair of chopsticks. I open it and smile, seeing as he ordered my favorite, chicken pad Thai. I can't believe he remembered. The delicious aroma hits my nose, and my mouth instantly salivates. As I take a bite, a comforting warmth spreads through my body, making me feel a bit better. Comfort food always hits the spot.

"Thank you for this," I say, holding up my food.

"That's what brothers are for," Gage says while grubbing down on his own food container. "Let's talk about today."

"I'd rather not, and I'm sure he told you, anyway."

"He did, but I want to hear it from you."

"He lied," I say with a nonchalant shrug, but inside, my heart feels like it's crumbling.

"About what?"

"Everything." I inhale deeply as if I'm trying to catch my breath. Tears sting the backs of my eyes, and I will them to retreat.

Gage stops at the threshold, looking at the wall. "Do you love him?"

"I don't think it matters anymore."

With tears welling in my eyes, I position the lighter beneath the paper, feeling a mix of sorrow and determination.

What was once a treasure now feels like a list of lies.

Deep down, I held onto a delusional hope that Vic would reach out to me. Write me a letter. Show me he cared by doing something thoughtful. He hasn't. It's been a week. He just gave Jess my stuff to give to Gage.

"What's that?" Gage asks from behind me.

"Nothing," I say as I put the lighter down.

He leans against the counter with his arms crossed over his chest, with a concerned look.

"Tomorrow's Halloween. I was thinking maybe you'd want to get out and join the living, or the dead, I guess you could say, at my club."

"Thought I wasn't allowed there."

"You can as long as you stay in the front bar area. I think it would be good for you to get out, Ro. You haven't been out all week, and I know you've been sad."

Compassion drips from his voice. After spending almost a week here, I notice bits of Gage's old self resurfacing. It's reassuring to know he hasn't lost himself completely to the ruthless and materialistic nature of our world.

"I'm not sure if that's a good idea."

"It'll be fine. You can dance and enjoy yourself, take a night off from your thoughts. My men will watch over you to make sure you're okay." At my reluctance, he adds, "I also remember a certain girl loving the holiday back in the day. You can't let your younger self down."

The bastard has me there. I've always loved dressing up for Halloween.

As I take in Gage's Halloween costume, I can't help but scrunch my nose. It's eerily similar to the one Marco wore at that college party.

The one Vic showed up to but didn't say—*no, I'm not doing this to myself. Take him out of your mind for the night, Rosie.*

I opted for a burlesque costume with a Gatsby flair, much to my brother's dismay. The silver corset is wrapped tightly around my midsection, giving me exceptional lift and cleavage. Sequins, rhinestone, and tassel embellishments hang from the skirt, and a headpiece sits atop the crown of my head and drapes over my skull. I paired it with a smoky eye and dark maroon lipstick. I feel confident and beautiful tonight. A drastic change from how I've felt all week.

"You look pretty, Ro."

"Thanks. I'm glad you talked me into going out."

"Everything will work out. I promise you."

"Yeah, well, I don't know if getting my heart stomped on was supposed to happen, but I'll take your word for it."

"Not everything is as it seems. Just give it time."

I swear he thinks he's helping, but he talks in riddles that only he understands. I feel like I'm always missing pieces of the story, and I probably am. He may be the same as I remember in some aspects, but in others, he holds a completely different identity, full of secrecy and deceit.

It's a short drive to his infamous club. After using my internet searching skills and taking a trip down a rabbit hole on the dark web, I discovered Gage owns a high-end, ultra-secret sex club.

The establishment accommodates various forms of debauchery, including entirely new and intriguing ones, while I have no intention of ever exploring others. My face was on fire as I googled all the different kinks the other night. Talk about diving into an alternate universe.

We walk through the back and enter his office, filled with sleek black leather and glass decor. I sit at one of his couches off to the side as he speaks to a couple of bouncers who are all decked out in black attire and creepy carnival masks. Black, red, and white are the dominant colors of the masks, and each has intricate designs.

I'm just glad none of them are in ski masks. Those will forever be a source of terror for me.

As my brother meticulously goes over their game plan for the night, a sudden warmth spreads across the side of my face, making me uneasy, as though someone is intensely watching me.

As I turn my head, I catch sight of one of the masked men staring directly at me, his head tilted in curiosity. Sending a wave of embarrassment through me, I give a tight smile before turning my head.

Now that was fucking creepy.

"Ro," Gage calls to me, and I make my way over to him, noticing the creepy one remains while the others have already left.

"This will be your security for the night. Act as if he doesn't even exist," Gage says while sending a huge smile toward the guy.

I can feel the weight of the guy's gaze behind the mask as he observes me without saying a word.

I give him another tight smile before looking at my brother. "Can I go enjoy my night now? The dance floor and a drink are calling my name."

"Stay in the bar area and take it easy on the alcohol."

"I will," I say, feeling my face turn red with embarrassment. The conversation about my findings of his club is still pending with Gage. Probably forever. "But last I checked, you're not Papa, and

I can drink what I want, when I want." With that, I storm out of the room without a second glance.

I stop in the hallway and look left, then right, then left again. Shit, I don't know where the bar is.

I feel a presence behind me as a hand finds my lower back and sends a chill up my spine. My new babysitter doesn't say a word as he guides me to the right.

It makes me think of Vic and how much I still miss him. My eyes roll in exasperation, a futile attempt to shake off the lingering belief he might actually care even though his silence speaks volumes.

We continue to walk in silence as we make our way through a series of doors. I can feel him staring at me, but I don't dare glance up at him.

I hope my brother screened him because he's giving me the heebie-jeebies.

We head through one last door and into a large room covered in orange lighting and sparkly marble floors. The orange lighting that moves with the bass hits the disco balls at the bar, creating what looks almost like fire embers all over the place.

I walk to the counter and beckon a bartender over, eager to place an order to make me forget.

Shot after shot goes down like a harsh prayer, beseeching my mind to have amnesia until further notice.

I ask for my fourth, but the bartender declines my request at my brother's orders. I roll my eyes before telling him sorry and thank you. It's not his fault my brother is a killjoy.

One of my favorite songs comes on, and my legs take me to the dance floor without a second thought. I close my eyes and move to the music. The alcohol hits my bloodstream, making me feel warm and relaxed.

At that moment, I make a promise to release all the negativity burdening and suffocating me.

My broken heart.

Shattered dreams.

Unknown future.

One song fades into another as my body glides around the dance floor with ease. My mind feels lighter than it has all week.

A guy comes up to dance with me. He has a friendly smile from what I can see besides the fangs. He's two steps away from touching me when the babysitter I totally forgot existed intercepts him.

"Sorry, Dracula..." I giggle, and my babysitter turns around and looks down at me with caramel-colored eyes.

Twenty-Six

Vic

H ere we are again, a full circle moment. She's dressed in a costume that has me unable to look away while I'm hiding behind a mask. But there's nowhere I'd rather be.

It's been pure fucking torture to be on the sidelines while watching guys eye-fuck the shit out of her all night. After the last fucker came up to her, I decided the game was over.

She goes still as she takes me in. I've missed this look on her face. The one that tells me she doesn't know whether she wants to kiss me or kill me.

She turns around to storm away, but I grab her. My front molds to her back. My arms wrap around her.

"I've missed you, baby," I say as I inhale. Her sweet scent fills the air, and I close my eyes, savoring the memory of her smell.

"What are you doing here?"

"Watching you."

She huffs, "I should've known it was you. You're good at deceiving me."

She attempts to pull away, and the thought drives me mad.

"Please don't pull away."

"Why, Vic?"

"Because I've been dreaming about holding you since you ran."

"Then why haven't you said anything?"

"Because I was giving you time."

"Time to what?"

To come back to me.

"I-I don't know," I say with a sigh.

I'm so lost and don't know what to do.

How to fix this.

Us.

"You should have told me. I feel like it was some fucked-up game."

"You were never a game. You were—you were everything," I say as I clear my throat.

She attempts to peek up at me, but I hold her tight, locking her in my embrace with my chin resting on the top of her head. I don't want her to see me on the brink of crumbling.

"Were you ever planning on telling me the truth, or were you just going to keep me in the dark forever? Maybe once Gage came to collect me, you'd start writing to me again, and I'd never know that the guy I fell in love with was a fucking liar."

The club and everyone in it fades away as her words wash over me.

She fell in love with me? Me.

I grip her tighter as my heart beats painfully in my chest.

She jerks out of my hold and faces me; tears rim her eyes. Fuck me. I hate the look on her face. She looks down, and I grab her hand.

"I'm sorry."

"Sorry for lying, or sorry for getting caught?"

"I'm sorry for everything. Let me make it up to you."

Her brows scrunch together. "How?"

"Anything you want," I blurt.

A small smile appears on her lips, accompanied by a subtle twinkle in her eye. "I already told you that's a bad choice of—"

Rosie's complexion drains as someone unexpectedly dashes into her field of vision. I turn and see Gage running after a girl in an angel costume.

With an indecisive expression, Rosie glances back at me with a sad smile before sprinting in their direction. I scramble to catch up to her.

The girl in the angel costume and Rosie exchange a look before holding hands and running out with another girl in tow who looks like... poison ivy? This night keeps getting weirder.

I catch up with Gage as he heads to the front of the club. By the time we make it past the threshold, the girls are already jumping into a car and speeding off.

"Motherfucker!" Gage yells into the air and holds his head.

"What the fuck happened?"

"She ran when she figured out it was me."

Fuck. That's not good. Seems like his plans for 'Operation: Get Her to Fall for Me' are failing epically. The poor fuck looks crushed.

Trey, Marcus, and Julian run out a second later. Tonight, they were compensated exceptionally well for their duties as bouncers, while Axl has remained mysteriously absent all night. They would have done it for free had he only asked.

This is the ultimate playground for them. An unlimited amount of sin.

Trey removes his mask. "Which one of you fuckers made poison ivy run? We'd just barely started having our fun."

Twenty-Seven

Rosie

R unning to Alexa and away from Vic triggered a pang of
sadness in me. A reminder of the void created each time
I part ways with him.

Despite the anger running through my veins all week, the
touch of his body against mine triggered a rush of memories,
as if we were long-lost lovers finding each other again.

I needed to keep it together; he lied to me and betrayed
me. But my traitorous body has a mind of its own. It wasn't
on the same playing field as my mind, which is idiotic after he
crushed my soul.

"Will someone please tell me what the fuck is going on?"
Poison Ivy asks from behind the wheel.

"Jenna, Rosie. Rosie, Jenna," Alexa says while breathing in and
out heavily. Her light blue eyes are wild, and her dark brown hair
is a complete mess, adorned with leaves and branches. "Back
there... well, that was Gage. Oh my God, that was Gage," she says

before putting her head in her hands and continuing to say, "Oh my God."

Gage's stupid devil costume and the need to keep her in the dark makes a lot more sense. I feel pretty stupid for not thinking he'd keep tabs on her, too. He seems to be quite the puppeteer in both of our lives as of late.

"Nice to finally meet you, Rosie," Jenna says while still driving like a bat out of hell.

"Nice to meet you, too," I say as I rub Alexa's back.

Jenna and I engage in small talk as we keep a watchful eye on Alexa as she runs through twenty different emotions. I've learned to let her purge, as she likes to call it. She needs this moment of vulnerability to herself without questions. But best believe I will hit her with them once she's ready.

"So, when are we going back? That place is insane, and those guys in masks were intense. I'm surprised my panties didn't dis-integrate from how wet I was and probably still am," Jenna says, wagging her brows.

Alexa whips her head toward Jenna before shoving her arm. "Are you seriously thinking about going back while I'm in crisis mode?"

"Hey, I'm driving here, and yes, I want to see those three again. I'm just pissed I didn't get one of their numbers. You think Gage knows?"

I can tell by the grin on her face she's attempting to ease Alexa's tension. I can't help but appreciate her for being a good friend.

"You're contemplating being with all three?" Alexa says with wide eyes at Jenna.

"There's no contemplating. I'm totally into it. You think he knows them?"

"I don't care who he knows. No way in hell will I ever see or speak to him again."

"Not even for me?"

"Nope."

"Come on."

"I can barely handle one guy, and you're trying to go for all three... You're crazy."

"I take that as a compliment."

"You shouldn't. But I still love you."

I'm thankful Alexa could find a friend who's had her back since she left. It makes me think of Jess. She would've thought tonight was wild. I make a mental note to text her and plan something for us soon.

As we walk into an apartment, Jenna yells something about wine before walking away. I take a seat on the couch as Alexa comes out in pajamas with a bundle of clothes in her hands.

"Thought you might want to get comfy."

I grab them and then wrap my arms around her, squeezing her tightly. "I'm sorry for whatever my brother did. I had no idea he even knew where you were."

"Me neither. I'm such a fool," she says with a sniffle.

Jenna saunters in carrying three bottles of wine, a box of chocolate under her arm, and wearing superhero-themed pajamas, which I find hysterical.

We sit cross-legged on Alexa's bed, a bottle of wine in our laps and a takeout container between our fingers. We listen to "Bad at Love" per Jenna's demands on repeat until we're truly drunk off the wine.

"Okay, spill. Who was that guy earlier? He looked upset when you left," Alexa says.

"It's a long, shitty story."

"Spill, Rosalinda." My eyes widen at her nerve.

"Don't you dare full name me, Alexandria."

"How dare you!" She screams and then we all laugh until Alexa jumps up, cursing under her breath and scanning her surroundings with wide, panicked eyes.

"Cameras."

"Huh?" Jenna and I murmur in unison.

"Fucking Gage. He put cameras in my room before I knew it was him."

Okay, that's fucking weird.

"So, you were putting on private shows for the devil?" Jenna's eyebrows go up and down as she twirls her long blond hair around her finger.

"What? No! I was flipping him off most of the time."

"Rightfully so. That's creepy as hell," I say, looking around.

My brother is insane. I didn't think he'd have the nerve to carry out something like this.

"Do you know where they are?" Jenna asks as she springs from the bed and looks around.

"If I did, I would've already gotten rid of them, genius."

She nods her head before continuing her search. "Right... Be right back."

Jenna runs back within seconds, some sort of box in her hands with antennae on the top. "Sorry, boys," she says in a singsong voice before clicking a button to turn it on.

"What's that, Inspector Gadget?" Alexa peeks over Jenna's shoulder.

"Something that won't allow any devices to work." We give her a questioning look. "What? I'm scared of skeevy landlords watching me dance around naked."

With the invasion of privacy taken care of, we take our respective seats back on the bed and continue to drink our weight in alcohol.

"Okay, spill."

"Everything was great until it wasn't."

I start with the easy details.

"Wait, wait, wait. You told me about a piercing, never about a tattoo! Who are you, and what have you done to my best friend?"

"Why do you keep saying that? It makes me sound like a prude."

"It just means you busted out of that sweet little quiet shell you had, and now you're a little vixen! Let me see it."

I pull my shirt up, and both Jenna and Alexa squint.

"Oh, I love it! What is this?"

I roll my eyes, "It's a unalome—"

"I know what that is, genius; what's this?"

"What's what?"

"Holy shit," Jenna says while laughing.

"What?" I say as I try to peek at my side.

"R.V.W.?" Alexa questions.

With a jolt, I spring up and hastily glance in the mirror. "That motherfucker."

"He practically branded you with his initials. How did you not notice?" Alexa asks.

"Because I'm an idiot, apparently."

"His possession is kinda hot," Jenna says with a shrug.

"More like insane. Only you would find romance in something so dark and twisted," Alexa says while I continue to look at Vic's initials on me.

Again, there were clues, and I missed every single one.

"Plain old roses and chocolates are played the fuck out. Get a tattoo of my name to show me you're serious, or stab someone in my honor. That's romance," Jenna says.

"You know, you're more of a Harley Quinn and less of a Poison Ivy. I feel sorry for your future husband," Alexa says.

"Ugh, as if anyone could hold me down."

"True that. Okay, continue," Alexa says as she looks at me.

"Fuck the PG shit... we want the juicy details." Jenna wags her eyebrows and rubs her palms together.

"He wanted all of my firsts, so we did everything I haven't done yet, which was a lot, obviously."

"Oh really. Do tell more," Alexa says.

"Damn, girl. Your face got bright red."

I roll my eyes. "I'm talking about the things our parents wouldn't let us do. Skinny-dipping, toilet papering a house, which somehow turned into burning bags of shit. Don't ask, I'm still scared. Getting high, bungee jumping."

"And..." they prod.

"And we did the deed," I say, covering my face.

Jenna snaps her fingers. "Details."

"Not on your life." I giggle.

"Well, I find it adorable he wanted you to experience new things with him," Alexa says, playing both sides of the coin. Damn her. "He also made you more spontaneous and adventurous. What happened?"

"He lied about who he was."

"I don't understand."

"I never told you, but Gage's cellmate started writing to me, and we continued to talk even in college."

"What?"

"I should've told you, but I wanted something for myself. I know that sounds selfish, but I did."

"What does this have to do with Vic?"

"Are you slow from your meltdown earlier? Homeboy was the pen pal," Jenna says.

"Oh... No fucking way."

"I didn't find out until the bitter end. He asked me questions about myself as if he didn't already know, and my stupid ass was more than willing to answer them." I shake my head at my idiocy.

"Why didn't he just tell you from the start?"

"The night Gage dropped me off, he literally threw a girl on the bed I was sleeping in by mistake. He said he knew he lost me then."

"What a stupid excuse. He could've still told you."

"Yep."

"So, what now?"

"I don't know. My heart fucking hurts. I fell for him hard, and the scars from his betrayal still burn."

"I'm so sorry, Ro," Alexa says.

"Do you think there's a chance you can forgive him?" Jenna asks.

I think about it for a second. *Do I forgive him? Can I forgive him for the lies?* The feeling of his arms wrapped around me still clings to my memory. It felt so good, so right.

Like home.

He feels like home.

From the top of the highest mountain, my heart screams yes, while my brain still struggles to process the feelings of betrayal.

"Part of me already has, but that doesn't change the fact that Gage is trying to marry me off to someone. What does it matter?"

"We can fix that. You won't do anything you don't want to. I won't allow it," Alexa says with so much conviction in her eyes I almost feel hopeful.

But the fact of the matter is, I'm unsafe by myself.

If the bar incident and the kidnapping attempt taught me anything, it's that I can't survive on my own while my father is still breathing.

He won't let one of his pieces go.

"Okay, enough doom and gloom. This calls for more wine and a song change," Jenna says as she rushes for more refreshments.

A weight lifts from my shoulders as I finish telling Alexa and Jenna my story. It still hurts, and I still feel lost, but the feeling is less heavy.

"Your turn," I say with a pat on her thigh.

Alexa goes into minor details about my brother Gage, as I think the rest are too private, and I'm grateful for not having to hear about my brother's sex life. However, from what I've heard, I'm pretty disappointed in him.

He hid his identity from her, much like Vic did to me. But the betrayal is twice as bad since Alexa and Gage have had a relationship since birth. We all grew up together. We formed bonds at a very young age and are family, even if not by blood. She not only thought of him as a best friend but also more, from what I hear in her drunken ramblings and tears.

If he would have told her who he was right away, she would have embraced him immediately. His leaving hurt her just as much as it hurt me. If not more.

The bottom line is that the guys are idiots, and there's no reason for all the secrecy.

By the end of our bottles, we vow to buy an island and ban all men. We will allow only women. Wine will be on tap, unless it's Sunday, then we switch to mimosas, obviously. It's a solid plan, and something I'm truly contemplating.

Jenna has no man to complain about but decides to be mad at Gage since he inadvertently ruined her night.

"You guys don't understand. They sounded hot." Jenna fans herself like she's overheating.

"They could've been complete gargoyles under those masks... just saying," Alexa says, pointing her chopsticks at her.

"One had trippy-ass eyes. They were so light that they were almost white. A guy with eyes like that can't be ugly."

I inhale an audible breath, and Alexa looks over at me. "What?"

"He's definitely not ugly, but he's scary as fuck, if it's who I'm thinking of."

"Girl, tell me more." Jenna's now on her stomach, palms under her chin and legs crossed at the ankles behind her.

"They're part of a motorcycle club Vic was in. They're all best friends."

"You never mentioned that!" Alexa yells

"It wasn't important to the story."

"Bullshit. That makes him sound even hotter. You had a biker daddy."

"First, never say that shit again. The guys were nice, I guess. At least they were to me, and funny as hell, but they're bad news, like, in the criminal activity kind of way. Their moral compass was broken when they were born, and they've been raising hell ever since."

"They sound like a delicious pool of warm water I want to drown in for a little while." Jenna pretends to do butterfly strokes on the bed.

"Bitch, give me the rest of your bottle. You're done for the night."

I giggle, watching Alexa wrestle the bottle away from Jenna.

"So, what do you plan on doing with biker daddy?"

I scrunch my nose. "That name grosses me out."

"You know it doesn't. You miss him."

"Possibly," I say with a shrug.

"Do you want to be with him?"

Yes.

"I'm not sure."

"I have a certified letter for a Rosie Gallo Moretti."

"That's me." The mail courier hands me a manila envelope, then walks off.

My heart skips a beat as I take in Vic's writing scrawled across the front.

Since Halloween night two days ago, I haven't heard a single word from him. For someone so intent on spending that night with me, then begging me for another chance, he sure ghost-ed me fast.

Dear Rosie,

I wanted to apologize for letting you down and for the sadness I've caused. My desire to keep you close clouded my vision. Torn between my own selfish desires and doing the honorable thing, the right thing. You see, people have come and gone in my life, but you remained a constant for years—I couldn't bear the thought of losing you, the memories we created together, and the bond we shared. The lies weighed heavily on me, and I think they always will.

You deserve to know the real me. I think it's only fair to you.

My name is Rush Victor Whilcott. I'll be twenty-two on No-vember 18th. Art has been more of a lifeline than a hobby to me. It was how I escaped and coped with my childhood. I spent my early years hungry and yearning for love and attention. As I grew up, I wasn't sure where I fit in since I had zero family left after my parents died. I was terrified of rejection and losing people once I formed a connection because that's all I ever knew. Loss.

I made a lot of mistakes but found my family through my friendships with the guys. Once I got out of prison, my last remaining relative died, and I was given money and the deed to the forest and lake. Half of me wanted to burn it to the ground out of sheer spite, but when I saw the clearing with the dock, it gave me the same peace riding and your letters gave me.

For a second, I imagined sitting beside you at the end of the dock. Us watching the sunset together. Hand in hand. You with a breathtaking smile on your face and me with a smile on mine while I looked at you.

I'm glad my foolish thought became a reality. I will cherish it always, as I've cherished every letter, every laugh, every hug, and every moment I shouldn't have taken, but took anyway, with you.

Our time together exceeded all expectations, and I am in awe of your remarkable soul.

I made a deal with your brother so you could be free. My hope is that you cross off the rest of your firsts, add more, many more, and most of all, be happy. No one is more deserving than you.

Fly free, princess.

-Rush Victor Whilcott

My tears mingle with his words until they swim, and I can no longer read the writing.

"Lex, I need your keys," I yell down the hall.

"They're on the... Are you okay?"

"No." I hand the letter to her.

She reads it over, her eyebrows raised in shock before her eyes get misty around the corners. "He just offered himself on a platter to Gage for you to be free."

I grab the letter from her and hold it to my chest. "He can't. I can't let that happen, Lex."

"What are you going to do?"

"I need to talk to Gage."

"My keys are in my bag. Do you want me to come?"

I shake my head. I need to do this on my own. "I'll be back."

I race to Gage's, mere miles from Alexa's place, storm into his house without knocking, and find him in his office.

"Is this true?" I say, holding up my letter.

"Is what true?"

"Vic sacrificed himself for me to be free."

284

"Sacrificed himself sounds dramatic, but yes. He works for me now," he says, making my heart clench in my chest.

"Why would he do this for me?"

"You know why."

My chin trembles as a tear escapes my lid.

"Take it back. I want him to be free. You can marry me off to whoever you want."

Gage shakes his head. "What's done is done."

"I can't believe this. How can you do this to him?"

"He did this to him."

Twenty-Eight

Vic

Sitting with my feet dangling above the dark water, I'm consumed by the eerie stillness of the night, intensifying my somber state of mind. The night sky is empty, lacking even a single star, as if they, too, decided to stay hidden tonight.

The decision I made to let Rosie go brings me a conflicting mix of unease and tranquility. Contrary to popular belief, the experience of being selfless does not live up to the hype and is not as fulfilling as people make it out to be.

It fucking hurts, and the pain will most likely never subside.

But I will endure the pain, imagining the breathtaking smile on her face as she reads my final letter. I hope it clips the final string, granting her the freedom to soar with no limitations.

When she ran, I told myself I would do anything to have her back. It was selfish. I was selfish.

Life is a series of choices, and she should have the freedom to make her own.

Rosie is a vibrant force that transcends the words we exchanged. No matter how vivid my dreams and imagination are, they'll never compare to her in person.

I wonder if I'll ever see her again. Maybe down the line at Gage's house, with kids, or worse, another man. The thought makes the hole in my chest ache.

The unmistakable creak of the dock catches my attention, and I freeze while my stomach flips. Even without her voice, I can spot her from a mile away. Why is she here?

"Thought you'd be halfway to California by now," I say as I attempt to keep my voice even.

My heart beats out of my chest as I hear her steps creak across the dock.

"Why? Why would you do this?"

Okay, not what I was expecting.

"Come sit." I tap the spot next to me. "I told you I'd do anything to help you."

"By giving your freedom away for mine?"

"Yes."

"Take it back," she says as her voice cracks.

I grab her small hand and look into her sad eyes. "I can't, and I won't."

A notch forms between her eyebrows, and I hold myself back from running my thumb across it to smooth it out. "What about the guys? Won't you miss them?"

"They were part of the deal, too."

"Why would they do that?"

"We're family. It's what we do," I say with a shrug.

The guys were ecstatic to have a connection to Gage. Rosie's father's actions caused significant financial damage to the club, leaving a substantial void. This agreement to work for Gage signifies greater financial resources, influence, and safety.

"This is insane. I can't let you guys do this. I'm going to find a way to get you all out of this."

I shake my head at her. "Our letters became a lifeline during my most challenging years, granting me the freedom and comfort I desperately needed. Let me give you the thing you want most. Now you can make more firsts, and most importantly, you can be you. You can be free."

"What if I don't want that anymore?" she says with tears in her eyes.

"What do you want?" I ask, confused.

"You." Rosie grabs my shirt, dragging my face close to hers. "I want you. I love you, Vic."

Her words bounce around in my head.

She came back.

She didn't leave me.

She loves me.

"I love you so fucking much."

My lips crash down on hers with more force than necessary, but I can't help myself.

I need her.

All of her.

As I pull her onto my lap, she lets out a surprised gasp, her eyes widening. I gaze up at her figure silhouetted against the night sky. Her bright green eyes, sparkling with excitement, light up her face as a small smile appears on her lips. I can't help but reach out and softly stroke her cheek. Her eyes flutter shut as if my touch is a cure. When really, hers is mine.

"Say it again," I whisper.

"I love you."

The feeling of weightless euphoria fills me like no drug could.

She is my drug.

She is my antidote.

She is my everything.

"Say my name," I say, wanting to hear her call me by my first name.

"I love you, Rush."

Epilogue

Rosie

One Week Later
I raise the wine bottle to my lips with a smile as I look over at the girls. Jenna and Jess became fast friends while Alexa was on her disaster of a date. Half of me thinks she shouldn't push Gage, but the other half hopes she gives him hell every step of the way. Their arranged marriage is still happening, and I can tell it will be the most entertaining event of my life. I'll have popcorn and Sour Patch Kids at the ready.

"We can still run... all of us," Alexa says with a smile.

"I'm in." Jenna shrugs.

"Not a chance," I say with a laugh.

Tonight is my bachelorette party. It's the night before my wedding, and I'm filled with an overwhelming sense of joy and peace.

For tonight, I have an unlimited amount of alcohol, enough comfort food to keep us fed for a month, and my best friends, all in superhero pajamas.

"Okay, now that we're all here," Jenna says as she gives a pointed look at Alexa. "Here's to Rosie. Let's drink to her bagging a man who's fine as hell, and let's hope he knows how to use that tongue."

"I'll drink to that," Jess says before downing her ginger ale. Something shifted within her after the night of the attempted kidnapping, and her demeanor has changed ever since. Sometimes I catch glimpses of a carefree side I've never witnessed before, like tonight, but other times, she seems to meticulously ponder every word and action. It still breaks my heart to think I'm the reason she's different.

"Sometimes you need a censor," Alexa says with a scrunch of her nose.

"Says the girl who looked ten seconds away from fucking in a very public parking lot."

"Ew, Jenna, I don't want the reminder," I say as I take another drink. Hoping it will wash that image from my brain.

Jenna points her finger at me. "You know it's true. The tension was intense. I could feel it from across the parking lot. Alexa's marriage to your brother will be lit!" she exclaims.

"More like an unfortunate house fire, which is why I'm not marrying him."

"Yeah, sure. I guess we'll see how that goes." Jenna laughs.

"Okay, back to the bride. Did your brother tell you anything else?" Jess asks.

"Just not to run. As if I would." I roll my eyes. "And he said to pack warm."

"Bora Bora," Jenna exclaims. "It has to be. I wish I could get fake married just for the honeymoon."

"I bet we can find you someone to get real married to," Jess offers.

"Ugh, pass. I enjoy being a lone wolf, and let's be honest, no one can handle my level of awesomeness."

"Your delusions are getting worse," Alexa tells Jenna.

"Not any worse than yours. Mrs. Gage Gallo Moretti."

"I'm going to kill you!" She looks at Jenna.

I love this. The friendships, the sisterhood. And now I'm marrying my best friend.

"Wait, I thought we were toasting me."

"Right." Alexa grabs my shoulder and looks at the girls as we get into a big huddle. "Here's to Rosie, who defied the odds of the families and got the ending she fought for. I've seen you in many seasons, and this one is by far my favorite. You are strong and so damn beautiful. I know many more seasons are coming, and I can't wait to see how you navigate with the grace and compassion you've always had. I love you."

I look out the window as the car stops at a gate. Towering trees create a majestic frame on both sides. Two stone columns support the big wrought-iron gate with intricate detail on the front. With an audible creak, the giant gate swings open, allowing us to pass through. Pillars adorned with lights illuminate the newly concreted pathway.

We make our way further into the forest before the car parks in front of a stone home that looks newly built as well.

A giant sign hangs across the home's double doors under the wood arch of the entry. "For my beautiful wife, who wanted a house by the lake."

"He built me a house?"

"How romantic," Alexa whispers next to me.

"Is this all I have to do for you to forgive me?" Gage asks Alexa in a hopeful voice.

"You can build me a thousand homes, and it still wouldn't be enough."

"Sounds like a challenge."

My mother rounds the corner of the house. A joyful squeal escapes my lips. As soon as I step out of the car, I wrap my arms around her neck. I haven't seen her since the fateful night I ran. Gage thought it would be for the best, and my mother agreed.

"You look beautiful, my darling baby girl."

"Thank you, Mama," I say, tearing up.

She rubs my back and murmurs, "Don't cry. It's okay."

"I'm sorry I left. You must have been so worried."

"I was, but I don't blame you."

"You don't?"

"No. I'm glad you did."

"Me too," I say honestly.

"Papa?" I ask, needing to know.

"He doesn't know I'm here."

"I'm glad."

"Me too, baby."

Pulling away, she gives me a reassuring smile before grabbing Alexa and Gage and walking around the house.

"You look amazing, sis," Marco says from the door. He looks handsome in his all-black suit.

"You like it?" I do a twirl.

"You look like a princess on her fairy-tale day," he says as he steps closer and hugs me. "I'm proud of you. I don't think I'll ever get the vision of you climbing down the side of the house out of my mind."

"You saw?"

"Who do you think kept our father busy while you ran from the grounds? I had a feeling you'd try to run that night after dinner."

"Thank you," I say.

We all tried our best to stay out of our father's way unless necessary, so for him to seek our father out and distract him for me to run warms my heart.

We part as the music changes. Marco looks around the corner of the house. "As soon as I walk around, wait thirty seconds, then start walking."

"Okay," I tell him as my stomach drops.

My breath catches in my throat as I round the corner. Vic stands at the end of the dock, right in front of a huge floral archway. As I approach, I'm overwhelmed by the sight of thousands of roses, ranunculus, peonies, and hydrangea in different hues of white, creating a breathtaking display that perfectly complements my bouquet.

The black tuxedo clings to Vic's body in all the right places, but it's his face that commands my gaze. Even from afar, I see his huge smile across his handsome face.

White chairs are situated on either side of the dock as I move along the rose-petal pathway. I catch glimpses of our closest family and friends standing, but Vic's presence consumes my sight.

Our hands interlock, and a wave of pure bliss washes over me. Filling every fiber of my being with a profound sense of contentment.

Home.

He is my home.

Vic leans in. "You're beautiful, baby."

As someone clears their throat, our attention shifts to Trey. He stands there, dressed in a suit, with a mischievous smile, ready to officiate our wedding.

"Ready to get married, fuckers?" he whispers to us, and I can't help but feel torn between laughter and tears at the sheer hilarity of the situation. Who the hell let him get his license to officiate this wedding?

"Rush, I've fallen in love with you countless times over the years as your words danced across the pages and worked their way into my heart. I promise to love you endlessly and with every ounce of love that lives within me. My heart will forever choose you today, tomorrow, and for all eternity."

When it's Vic's turn, he pulls out a little paper. As I watch him, my eyes widen in astonishment as he unfolds the paper, its edges frayed and creased just like the picture of me he had.

"Rosie,"—his voice trembles as he clears his throat of emotion while tears rim his eyes—"I want all your firsts, your lasts, and everything in between. You were my endless sunshine in eternal darkness, and I want to feel your warmth for an eternity. In exchange, I will give you all of me. You own me. You always have and always will. I love you. Now, and forever."

A tear runs down my cheek. Vic's eyes soften further.

"You may kiss your bride." Vic leans down, and before I know it, he sweeps me off my feet. I let out a surprised squeak before his lips are on mine. He's giving me the ultimate fairy-tale kiss, stealing the breath from my lungs and leaving me weak in his arms.

THE END

If you want to find out more about Gage and Alexa's love story, book two, **All Your Lies**, comes out this Spring.

Acknowledgements

Thank you to any reader who picked this up on a whim and decided to give my debut novel a chance. It means the world to me.

www.ingramcontent.com/pod-product-compliance
Lightning Source LLC
Chambersburg PA
CBHW020353110726
47899CB00006B/1709